A TRIO IN TROUBLE

Youthful Richard Selwyn was perilously near ruin. Against all good sense and against his sister Camilla's level-headed advice, he had taken as his guide to London the most notorious and unscrupulous rake in all the realm, the pernicious Sir Peregrine Mowbray.

Honest and good-hearted Charles MacNeil was painfully near despair. Though he and the high-born Elizabeth St. John were ideally made to complete each other's happiness, her brother, the Viscount, shattered their dreams with his disdain for Charles's humble origins.

But young and beautiful Miss Camilla Selwyn faced the most difficult dilemma of all. For instead of gaining the upper hand over the infuriatingly superior St. John, she was, to her dismay, on the brink of falling under his spell. . . .

TOWN TANGLE

TOWN TANGLE

by
Margaret Summerville

A SIGNET BOOK

NEW AMERICAN LIBRARY

NAL BOOKS ARE AVAILABLE AT QUANTITY DISCOUNTS
WHEN USED TO PROMOTE PRODUCTS OR SERVICES.
FOR INFORMATION PLEASE WRITE TO PREMIUM MARKETING DIVISION,
NEW AMERICAN LIBRARY, 1633 BROADWAY,
NEW YORK, NEW YORK 10019.

SIGNET TRADEMARK REG. U.S. PAT. OFF. AND FOREIGN COUNTRIES
REGISTERED TRADEMARK—MARCA REGISTRADA
HECHO EN CHICAGO, U.S.A.

SIGNET, SIGNET CLASSIC, MENTOR, PLUME, MERIDIAN and NAL BOOKS
are published by New American Library,
1633 Broadway, New York, New York 10019

First Printing, April, 1986

1 2 3 4 5 6 7 8 9

PRINTED IN THE UNITED STATES OF AMERICA

1

The heavy traveling carriage made its way slowly on the snow-covered road, the horses straining mightily against high winds and bitter cold. The snow whirled about, making visibility extremely poor, but despite this, the vehicle plunged onward. Some short distance ahead, however, the road seemed to vanish. The exhausted animals floundered in knee-deep snow drifts and the carriage lurched to an abrupt halt.

"A thousand curses!" cried Lord St. John as he was nearly thrown from his seat inside the vehicle.

"Oh dear," said his companion, a very dapper gentleman, who strained to maintain his dignity after being jolted forward into the opposite seat.

St. John frowned and muttered an oath as the two gentlemen righted themselves. In his happiest moods, Anthony, second Viscount St. John, was a formidable-looking man, but when he was angry, even the most stout-hearted were known to quail before him. The dapper gentleman, the Honorable Trenton Fitzwalter by name, was one of the few people who could safely ignore St. John's black humor. He smiled at his friend's expression.

"I daresay, Tony," he said, looking quite unconcerned, "seems as if we've run into a bit of ill luck."

"Damn," said the viscount, looking out the carriage window but seeing little except the falling snow. "You stay here, Fitz. I'll see what's wrong."

"Admirable, Tony, for I have no intention of leaving this carriage. Might soil my boots."

This comment elicited a slight smile from St. John, but

he quickly frowned again as he left the shelter of the coach. The snow was coming down fiercely and the blustery wind made it numbingly cold.

"My God," said the viscount. "Hopper! For God's sake, man, where are you?"

"Here, m'lord."

The viscount found his coachman standing by the horses. The man was covered with snow and looked nearly frozen. The coachman's assistant was trying vainly to push snow from around one of the carriage wheels. " 'Tis no good, m'lord," said Hopper, wiping the snow from his face. " 'Tis too deep. We'll not get through. Come, Harry, 'tis no use. We're stuck tight as you please and the horses be tired out and can pull no more. I fear we'll go no further, m'lord."

Lord St. John cursed under his breath and surveyed the scene. The landscape was a mass of white and icy flakes continued to swirl wildly around him. The viscount was nearly up to his boot tops in the snow and he had some difficulty walking. Making his way over to the coachman's assistant, he shook his head at the snow entrapping the carriage wheels. The viscount made no remark, but walked over to Hopper.

St. John patted one of the horses. "Poor devils," he said. "They are nearly spent." He looked at the coachman. "Where the deuce are we, man? Is there shelter nearby?"

Hopper pointed with a snow-encrusted glove. "Aye, m'lord. There is a house up ahead. Back amongst those trees."

The viscount looked off into the distant countryside and could just barely discern a house amid a blur of trees. "Well, Hopper, at least we can thank Providence for that. We must unhitch the horses."

"Aye, m'lord. Harry and I will see to that. Your lordship and Mr. Fitzwalter must go on ahead."

"Very well, but do hurry. The both of you are nearly frozen. Warm yourselves in the carriage. At least you will be out of this damnable wind."

The coachman nodded and St. John hurried back to the carriage and threw open the door.

"Get out, Fitz."

The viscount's friend gazed at him in horror. "Are you daft, Tony? You expect me to go out into that? It's not exactly cozy in here, but it's a damned sight better than out there."

"I fear, Fitz, you have no choice. We're stuck in the snow, but, fortunately, there's a house nearby. We'll have to walk."

Mr. Fitzwalter continued to look appalled, but he drew his cloak around him and stepped gingerly out of the carriage. He instantly let out a cry. "Egad, Tony, it's a foot deep!"

"And it will be two feet deep if we don't hurry." St. John started trudging off through the snow and his reluctant friend felt he had no recourse but to follow him.

As they plodded through the snowdrifts, Lord St. John cursed himself for his rash departure from his country estate Ramsgate. If only he had not quarreled with his stepmother, Amanda, he reflected, he would still be warm and comfortable. But no, he had lost his temper and had gone off in a fury, setting out under a gray and threatening February sky. Yet, the viscount had never imagined the intensity of the storm that had come upon them.

The wind whipped St. John's cloak about him and he glumly continued on through the snow. Suddenly, he heard a cry behind him and looking back, he found Fitzwalter sprawled in a pile of snow. St. John hurried toward him. "Are you all right, Fitz?"

Fitzwalter looked up at him with a comical expression. "Am I all right? Why shouldn't I be? Here I am, tromping about the provinces in a snowstorm, almost breaking my neck on some damned ice, and ruining my new pair of boots in the bargain."

The viscount laughed and put a hand out to help his friend up. "Courage, old man. We're almost there."

Fitzwalter got up and brushed himself off. "That's very comforting, Tony," he said, his teeth chattering. They continued on and as they neared the house, the viscount

was none too cheered by its appearance. It was a large
structure of gray stone and its Tudor architecture proclaimed it to be several centuries old. It looked quite
dreary and rundown and St. John feared for a moment that
it was uninhabited.

Mr. Fitzwalter was usually more critical than his friend
in matters of architecture and, on most occasions, he
would have declared the house "frightful." However, at
the moment, all Fitzwalter cared about was getting inside
to someplace warm.

Finally arriving at the front door, St. John lifted the old
brass door knocker and pounded it loudly against the
peeling wood. They waited for a few moments and then an
impatient St. John again pounded the knocker against the
door. This time it slowly creaked open and an elderly,
stoop-shouldered man peered out at them.

The man regarded the two snow-covered strangers with
a look of bewilderment and, when he made no move to let
them in, St. John brusquely pushed open the door and
walked into the entrance hall. Fitzwalter followed behind
and gave a small sigh of relief to find himself inside. The
servant continued to regard them with a befuddled expression and St. John found himself becoming annoyed. "What
is this place and who is the master?" he demanded in an
imperious tone.

The servant cowered before the viscount, but he man-
aged to speak. " 'Tis Selwyn Manor, sir, and Sir Jarvis
Selwyn, Baronet, be master here."

"Well, tell Sir Jarvis Selwyn, Baronet, that the Viscount St. John and Mr. Fitzwalter wish to see him."

The servant shook his head. "Master be at his household accounts, m'lord, and he don't like to be disturbed."

St. John eyed the servant with such an incredulous
expression that Fitzwalter almost burst into laughter. The
viscount's astonishment was quickly replaced with anger.
"You will go tell your master that we wish to see him or,
by God, I will go find him myself!"

The servant mumbled an "Aye, m'lord," and hastily
retreated.

Fitzwalter regarded his friend with amusement. "Good

heavens, St. John, your wrath is terrible to behold. The poor fellow was positively quaking.''

The viscount frowned. ''I was in no mood to suffer that simpleton,'' he said, shaking some snow off his cloak and looking about the entrance hall. St. John noted the ancient suit of armor that stood vigil at the arched doorway and the pair of medieval axes that were crossed above it. A boar's head, which by the look of it was nearly as ancient as the suit of armor, stared grimly down at him. ''Good God, what a place,'' muttered the viscount.

Mr. Fitzwalter nodded. ''I daresay, it does seem abominable, Tony, but it is undoubtedly preferable to freezing to death.''

They were interrupted by the reappearance of the timorous servant. ''Sir Jarvis will see you, m'lord, sir.'' He took their coats and then had the two gentlemen follow him down a dimly lit hallway. The servant stopped before a door and, with some reluctance, opened it. '' 'Tis Lord St. John, Sir Jarvis, and Mr. Fitzwalter,'' he announced fearfully.

The viscount and Fitzwalter entered the small, dark room. They were both quite surprised to find that the fearsome Sir Jarvis was a slight, balding gentleman with spectacles. He was sitting hunched over a desk in the corner of the room, staring grimly at a book that was propped open in front of him. The baronet seemed so intent on the book's contents that he did not even look up when they entered the room. ''The pirate,'' he grumbled. ''Whoever heard of paying such a price for a leg of mutton?'' When the servant gave a discreet cough, Sir Jarvis looked up in annoyance. ''What is it?'' he barked.

'' 'Tis the gentlemen I spoke of, sir,'' said the servant nervously. ''The Viscount St. John and Mr. Fitzwalter.''

The master of Selwyn Manor eyed the strangers with undisguised irritation. St. John, who was used to people fawning over him, was somewhat taken aback by his host's uncivil behavior. ''I am St. John, Sir Jarvis, and this is my friend Fitzwalter. We hate to intrude upon you, but I fear we have run into some difficulty. Our carriage is stuck in the snow a half mile or so down the road. My men are still there with the horses and I do not doubt that they could use some assistance.''

Sir Jarvis scowled but turned to his servant. ''Jackson! Go get Jud and Tom. Tell them to go help them. And be quick about it, man!''

The servant nodded and retreated with surprising haste for a man of his apparently advanced age.

The viscount looked over at the cantankerous baronet. ''Thank you, Sir Jarvis.''

''Hmph,'' muttered the older gentleman ill-naturedly. ''Damned foolish business. Gadding about in such weather.''

St. John stared at Sir Jarvis as if he could not have heard him correctly. His rank and wealth had always secured the viscount the most deferential treatment and he could scarcely believe that an obviously poverty-stricken, countrified nobody would address him in such an insulting manner.

Fitzwalter saw the angry look on his friend's face and thought it best that he intervene. He did not like their uncivil host any better than the viscount, but he had no desire to find himself back outside in the snow. ''It was dashed silly of us, Sir Jarvis,'' said Fitzwalter with his most ingratiating smile. ''Yes, dashed silly starting out on such a day. But we are grateful to you, sir. And, I say, if one must get stranded, it is certainly a piece of luck to get stranded here.''

The baronet eyed the dandy with some surprise. ''Eh, what's that?''

''Well, Sir Jarvis, I was just saying to my friend St. John here what a magnificent house this is. It evokes such a sense of . . .'' Fitzwalter seemed to grope for the right word. ''History. Such a sense of history, Sir Jarvis.''

St. John frowned at Fitzwalter. The churlish baronet deserved a setdown and, instead, his friend was placating the fellow. The viscount was about to make a cutting remark about Selwyn Manor and its ''sense of history'' when he was distracted by the sound of loud barking and laughter from the hallway. ''Come, Uncle,'' cried a feminine voice, ''you can't hide away with the household accounts all day!'' The door burst open and a large dog bounded into the room, followed by a young woman. She stopped on the threshold and stared at the viscount and Mr. Fitzwalter in surprise.

His lordship was in turn surprised. He had not expected to find an attractive young lady at dreary Selwyn Manor. A connoisseur of female beauty, St. John surveyed the woman with a critical eye. Although her features were slightly off the mark of classical perfection, her nose being a trifle short and her mouth a bit too wide, there was something about her that the viscount found very appealing. Perhaps it was her dark, auburn hair, which was tied in what appeared to be a rather hasty knot on her head. Or maybe it was the lady's merry brown eyes or dimpled smile. And, although realizing she was too short for fashion, St. John thought her figure quite admirable.

The viscount's scrutiny was suddenly interrupted when the lady's canine companion, an Irish wolfhound, ran over and eagerly sniffed at his boots. The young woman gave a stern command and the dog, giving the viscount's boots a rather doleful look, went obediently over to his mistress and lay down at her feet.

The lady glanced over at Sir Jarvis for enlightenment about the strangers and he somewhat grudgingly obliged. "These gentlemen are stranded near here, Camilla. Their carriage is stuck in the snow. The Viscount St. John and Mr. Fitzwalter. My niece, Miss Camilla Selwyn."

At hearing the identities of the gentlemen, Camilla Selwyn regarded them with keen interest. The name St. John was familiar to her as it was to almost everyone in the kingdom. The first Viscount St. John had been a noted war hero, having distinguished himself on numerous occasions during the recent conflict. When he had died gloriously in battle against Napoleon, the whole nation had mourned.

Camilla studied St. John curiously, realizing that he must be the son of the famous general. He was an exceedingly handsome man, she thought, noting his finely chiseled features, blue eyes, and curly black hair. He was very tall and his lean frame was perfectly suited to his impeccable traveling clothes. In Camilla's estimation, the only thing that marred his splendid appearance was his haughty expression which bespoke a proud and perhaps unpleasant disposition.

In contrast, the viscount's companion, Mr. Fitzwalter, wore an expression of complete affability. Although of slight build and certainly less handsome than St. John, Fitzwalter was no less impressive than his friend. His modish attire proclaimed him a dandy of the first stare and Camilla was certain that he must be a leader of fashion.

The amiable Mr. Fitzwalter advanced upon Camilla first. "How very good to meet you, Miss Selwyn. Finding a lovely lady here makes being stranded in a snowstorm far less dreadful." He smiled his most charming smile and Camilla gave him her hand.

"I know you are speaking sheer flummery, Mr. Fitzwalter," said Camilla, returning his smile, "but I appreciate it nevertheless." She looked from him to the viscount. "How very unfortunate for you gentlemen to get caught in the storm. Were you traveling far?"

"We were returning to town, Miss Selwyn," replied the viscount rather stiffly.

"Returning to town on such a day as this?" Sir Jarvis regarded St. John as if he were an idiot. "You must be in a deuced hurry to get there. I cannot understand why. I never go to town myself for, indeed, the last time I went to London, I very much regretted it. That was in 1785 or was it '86? I cannot recall, but I met all manner of rascals there. One I remember particularly. He was—"

"I am sure that London society grieves at your absence, sir," said St. John, cutting off Sir Jarvis rudely. "We are very tired and would greatly appreciate it if you would show us where we might rest."

The baronet regarded him in some astonishment and Fitzwalter hurriedly stepped in. "We do appreciate your kindness in taking us in like this. It is so good of you."

Camilla had been startled by the viscount's incivility and found her joy at having such illustrious company diminished. She had been about to mention his father but no longer had any desire to make conversation. "I shall have Jackson show you to your rooms. I'm sure your ordeal has been most exhausting. I shall have him call you for dinner." Camilla rang for the servant, who appeared instantly and soon led the guests away.

Sir Jarvis watched them go and then shook his head. "What ill luck that such fellows should turn up on my doorstep. Rules of hospitality declare that I must shelter and feed them despite the fact that they are coxcombs, the both of them. And the grand Lord St. John! By my honor, he is the most pompous, ill-mannered fellow! You see, Camilla, what sort of men you would meet in London. Well, nothing can be done but to pray for good weather."

Camilla laughed and even the crusty Sir Jarvis allowed himself to smile.

2

Camilla Selwyn frowned as she tried to decide which dress to wear. She had narrowed her selection to her two best frocks, but as she surveyed them displayed there on the bed, she found herself thinking they were both shabby and decidedly provincial.

Camilla had never before been overly concerned about her clothes, a fortunate circumstance considering her pitifully small clothing allowance. However, the presence of the London gentlemen made her self-conscious. They were dressed so grandly and certainly the ladies of their acquaintance wore only the most fashionable attire. Her dresses were undeniably plain and not in the least stylish. Certainly, Lord St. John and Mr. Fitzwalter would think her a poor country miss indeed.

Camilla shrugged. "But I am a poor country miss," she said aloud, taking up her blue silk gown. It had always been her favorite and it would have to do.

As Camilla began to dress, she thought of the two strangers. How her friends would envy her for having the son of the famous General Lord St. John as a houseguest. A wry smile crossed Camilla's countenance. She did not feel so very fortunate to have the illustrious viscount at Selwyn Manor. It was obvious that he felt very superior to them and was not pleased at the prospect of staying there. At least Mr. Fitzwalter was a much more agreeable gentleman, decided Camilla. Indeed, he seemed quite pleasant and had not a trace of his friend's arrogance.

Camilla sat down at her dressing table and started to fix her hair. To her dismay, her auburn tresses seemed unusually unruly and her efforts to duplicate the fashionable coiffure she had seen in one of the ladies' magazines were woefully unsuccessful. Camilla sighed as she surveyed the results of her work in the mirror. Then deciding she had done her best, she rose and finished dressing.

A short time later, Camilla left her bedchamber and started toward her Aunt Lucinda's room. Because she knew that that lady would be so very excited about the company, Camilla had purposely delayed telling her the news. Arriving at her aunt's door, she knocked lightly upon it. "Aunt Lucinda?"

"Camilla, do come in! Hurry!" Entering the room, Camilla found her aunt, a short middle-aged woman, standing at the window. She was wrapped in a large white shawl and perched atop her head was a lace cap, somewhat askew. "Camilla, what is going on in this household? I saw Jackson in the corridor and he muttered something about gentlemen from London and then he scurried off like a frightened rodent." She eyed her niece. "And you are wearing your blue dress. Something is happening!"

Camilla smiled. "Poor old Jackson. He's not used to company."

"Company? Company here at Selwyn Manor?" Lucinda Selwyn looked quite astonished.

"Yes, Aunt. Two gentlemen from London, the Viscount St. John and a Mr. Fitzwalter. They were traveling to town and got stranded in the storm."

"Good heavens! The Viscount St. John, you say? You cannot mean the war hero? Oh, no, he is dead, is he not? I remember seeing the most tragic lithograph illustrating the unhappy moment. It would be his son, would it not?"

Camilla shrugged. "I do expect so, but I did not determine that for certain."

"Whatever do you mean?"

"It is only that I did not converse with Lord St. John very much. Indeed, he was so very toplofty and barely civil."

"My dearest Camilla, you cannot expect a man of his rank to be overly civil. I must say, I cannot believe he is here. What good fortune for us! But you said there is another gentleman?''

Camilla nodded. "A Mr. Fitzwalter. He seemed to be very nice.''

"Fitzwalter?'' Aunt Lucinda looked thoughtful. "Is he of the Ponsonby Fitzwalters?''

"Really, Aunt, I do not know.''

Lucinda Selwyn regarded her niece in exasperation. "Good heavens, Camilla, I thought you a good conversationalist.''

"Well, you will have plenty of opportunity to discover all about the London guests at dinner.''

"Dinner,'' muttered Aunt Lucinda. "Oh, dear, what will they think of us when they sit down to Cook's dreary fare?''

"Lord St. John will simply confirm his opinion that we are unworthy of his august consideration. I fear he was none too pleased at finding himself at Selwyn Manor. He seemed quite ill-humored.''

"But surely it was only that he was upset at being caught in such dreadful weather. Oh, this is so very exciting, Camilla. But what shall I wear?'' Lucinda's face took on a worried expression. "All of my things are so dowdy. But there is the lavender silk.''

"That would be perfect, Aunt. Come, I shall help you.''

After assisting Lucinda to get ready for dinner, Camilla escorted her aunt out of the room. The two ladies started toward the stairs and just as they reached them, a masculine voice called to them. "Aunt Lucinda! Camilla! Do wait!'' Camilla turned to see her brother Dick. Twenty-year-old Dick Selwyn was only two years younger than his sister, but his impulsive nature and boyish high spirits often made him seem much younger. There was a close resemblance between brother and sister, with Dick sharing Camilla's dark eyes and auburn-colored hair. He also had inherited the Selwyn slight build and often bemoaned his lack of height.

Dick hurried to them. "Cam, Aunt Lucinda! Is it not the dashed best news this whole dreary winter? Guests at Selwyn Manor, and proper Corinthians from what I am told! Do I look presentable?''

"You look very handsome," said Lucinda.

"Well, I know this coat is not quite the thing."

"Really, Dick, you look fine." Camilla tried to speak with conviction, but knew well that her brother would look very shabby alongside the London guests. His evening coat was well worn and too large for his spare frame and his ill-fitting knee breeches and stockings gave him an awkward rusticated look.

"I am so eager to meet them," said Dick. "To finally have company from town! We are like hermits here, never seeing anyone who is in the least interesting."

"It is splendid," agreed Lucinda. "But let us not dawdle here. Let us join our guests."

Dick eagerly took his aunt's arm and started down the stairs. Camilla followed after them, hoping that her brother and aunt would not be too disappointed in the company.

Lord St. John, Fitzwalter, and Sir Jarvis stood in Selwyn Manor's drafty parlor awaiting dinner. Of the three, only Fitzwalter seemed in good spirits. His friend St. John was in a very ill humor and cursed the fates that had deposited him in these uncomfortable surroundings.

Sir Jarvis, too, was most unhappy with Dame Fortune. The baronet had no great fondness for London gentlemen who fribbled away their time and their fortunes and he had immediately judged the viscount and Fitzwalter as men of that stamp. The miserly Sir Jarvis thought it a great pity that he would have to pay for meat to feed them and reflected sourly about his bills from the butcher.

Although Trenton Fitzwalter prided himself in his ability to make conversation, Sir Jarvis thwarted him quite successfully. Each time Fitzwalter made a comment or asked a question, the baronet replied with a single word or disinterested grunt. Undaunted, Fitzwalter pointed toward a painting over the fireplace. "I say, Sir Jarvis, that's an interesting gentleman in that portrait."

The baronet looked up. "My father, Sir Eustace Selwyn."

"Really," said Fitzwalter, raising his quizzing glass to study the painting. "I do note some resemblance."

St. John looked at the portrait and a shadow of a smile

appeared on his face. A thin, bewigged gentleman dressed in clothes of the previous century stared down grimly at his posterity. There was indeed a resemblance between father and son and the viscount had little doubt that Sir Eustace was as much of a curmudgeon as the present baronet.

Fitzwalter began questioning Sir Jarvis about some other artifacts in the room and St. John grew increasingly impatient as he listened to the baronet's grudging replies. The viscount was becoming dangerously bored when Camilla Selwyn entered the room with her aunt and brother.

St. John looked at Camilla and decided that he had not erred in his initial impression of that young lady. He found there was definitely something very attractive about her. The blue silk gown she wore was trimmed with ribbons and lace, and although it appeared several seasons old to the viscount's practiced eye, it suited her figure quite splendidly. He noted that her dark hair was now arranged in a fashionably careless style, her auburn locks intertwined with ribbon, and St. John thought she looked quite charming.

Camilla, aware of the viscount's scrutiny, nodded to him in greeting. "Good evening, my lord."

Before St. John could reply, his friend Fitzwalter approached her with his languid smile. "My dear Miss Selwyn, how lovely you look."

"Thank you, Mr. Fitzwalter," said Camilla, smiling. "I hope you have rested."

"Indeed, I have, ma'am."

While Camilla addressed the gentlemen, both Lucinda and Dick Selwyn were eyeing the guests with great curiosity. Dick noted their stylish attire with envy and was overjoyed at having such obvious tulips of the ton at Selwyn Manor.

Camilla turned from Mr. Fitzwalter to her aunt. "I must introduce you to the rest of the family. This is my aunt, Miss Lucinda Selwyn, and my brother Richard. The Viscount St. John and Mr. Fitzwalter."

St. John merely nodded but Fitzwalter took Lucinda Selwyn's hand and smiled. "I am charmed, ma'am. I see beauty runs in the Selwyn family."

Sir Jarvis grumbled, but Lucinda smiled delightedly. "You are a rascal, sir."

Fitzwalter raised his eyebrows in surprise. "I, a rascal, ma'am?"

Lucinda smiled. "Indeed, you are, young man. A charming rascal, but a rascal nonetheless. You must be of the Ponsonby Fitzwalters. You have the Ponsonby nose."

"How good of you to notice," replied Fitzwalter. He had always considered the Ponsonby nose a curse, although his numerous relations considered it a mark of distinction.

The elder Miss Selwyn nodded. "I was acquainted with Lady Charlotte Fitzwalter many years ago. Such a lovely woman."

"She is my grandmother."

"Your grandmother, Mr. Fitzwalter! Good heavens! I feel as if I am in my dotage."

"Hardly, ma'am. It is obvious that that is a very long way away."

"Not so very long, sir, I fear. I remember your grandmother very well. She was so kind to me during my first Season. Might I hope she is well?"

"She is indeed, Miss Selwyn."

Lucinda looked wistful. "How long ago that was. Nearly five and twenty years have gone by. Oh, I shall not dwell upon it now." She directed her attention to St. John. "How do you do, my lord? It is such an honor to meet you. You must be the son of Arthur St. John!"

Camilla, who was watching the viscount, noted that his cool expression became decidedly frostier at Lucinda's words. "That is correct, ma'am," he said. "I am his son."

Lucinda nodded. "You must be so proud of him. He was such a remarkable man."

Fitzwalter gave his friend a sidelong glance. He knew that St. John was heartily sick of hearing about the exploits of his heroic father. The viscount did look quite grim as Lucinda Selwyn, a nostalgic gleam in her eye, continued.

"Dear me, I shall never forget your father. He was so handsome and so very dashing. He was Colonel St. John

then and I believe there was not a girl in town who did not
have a *tendre* for him. Indeed, it was a crushing blow that
he was already married.'' She smiled sweetly at Sr. John.
''You are so like him. And did you marry young like your
father, or might a lady still set her cap for you?''

St. John's demeanor, which had been frosty, now grew
decidedly frigid. ''I am not married,'' he said.

Camilla, knowing that her aunt was exceedingly tactless
at times, tried to prevent her from commenting further. ''I
think the snow has stopped. It is quite lovely, don't you
think so, Aunt?''

''Snow? I never did care for the stuff. I should be happy
to see it melt.''

''As would I, ma'am,'' said St. John.

Lucinda did not take any notice of the remark, although
Camilla, knowing well the viscount's intent, glanced over
at him in some irritation. ''I don't believe I ever met your
mother, my lord,'' continued Lucinda. ''Let me see, I
cannot recall her maiden name.'' Aunt Lucinda looked
expectantly at the viscount.

To her great surprise, he ignored the remark completely
and turned to Camilla. ''A fine looking dog you had with
you, Miss Selwyn.''

''Yes, Rufus is an excellent dog.'' Camilla looked at St.
John strangely, wondering at his abrupt change of topic.

Dick took this opportunity to enter the conversation.
''Oh, there is not another dog in the county to match
Rufus. He is a smart one, he is.'' Dick Selwyn began to
discourse on Rufus's virtues, oblivious to the bored look
on St. John's face.

Camilla, noting St. John's expression, was glad when
the butler arrived in the room to announce that dinner was
ready. Sir Jarvis Selwyn muttered that it was about time
and unceremoniously led the way to the dining room.

Selwyn Manor's dining room contained an ancient, massive oak table with highbacked chairs. Candles in two
large brass candlesticks on the table provided a flickering
light while a scant fire sputtered in the fireplace. Lucinda
Selwyn pulled her shawl around her and regarded her
brother in exasperation. ''Good heavens, Jarvis, it is so

cold in here that I have gooseflesh. Look at poor Jackson. He is shivering!''

"Hrmph . . ." muttered the baronet. "You are forever complaining about some nonsense, Lucinda. It is warm enough in here."

Lucinda frowned. "We don't all have ice in our veins like you, Brother." She turned to the servant. "Jackson, see that more wood is put on that fire."

"You shall do no such thing, Jackson," growled the baronet. The servant looked helplessly at Camilla, who quickly intervened.

"It is rather chilly in here, Uncle, and the fire appears to be almost out."

Sir Jarvis shrugged. "If you say so, Miss, but I think you are all spoiled."

St. John and Fitzwalter exchanged glances. As the servant fetched another log, they all were seated.

Finding that he was positioned between Sir Jarvis and Lucinda Selwyn at table, the viscount decided that dinner would be a rather trying experience. Fortunately, the baronet said little and seemed content to concentrate on his meal. However, Lucinda seemed quite loquacious. Prudently avoiding the topic of the viscount's mother, she began to talk about her favorite subject, gardening. St. John found himself stifling yawns as Lucinda described the various ills that had beset her rose bushes the previous year and the unhappy fate of the vicar's zinnias. The viscount looked enviously across the table at his friend Fitzwalter, who was seated next to Camilla. As he watched the two of them laugh and talk together, St. John's mood grew even darker.

Camilla found she was enjoying dinner due to the jovial company of Mr. Fitzwalter. He regaled her with stories of life in London and then described in detail the idiosyncrasies of various members of the royal family. Camilla laughed at his droll comments and thought Mr. Fitzwalter a most congenial man.

St. John continued to direct his attention toward Fitzwalter and Camilla. He tried to ignore Lucinda's prattle, but found her incessant talking combined with the unpalatable dinner did little to improve his temper.

St. John, who had one of the finest cooks in London, was appalled by Selwyn Manor's meager fare. His soup was cold, his mutton tough, and his pudding was an unappetizing lump. And then, of course, there was the wine which the viscount, with his discerning palate, could only classify as "swill."

After what seemed like an eternity to St. John, dinner ended and Sir Jarvis announced he was going to bed. The rest of the company went to the parlor where the viscount's attention was immediately monopolized by Dick Selwyn. That young man was eager to hear all about London and was undeterred by St. John's unfriendly manner. "I say, sir," said Dick, eyeing the viscount with admiration, "it is such an honor having you and Mr. Fitzwalter here. This place is such a dreadful bore most of the time, except during hunting season, of course. I'll wager you're never bored in town." Dick did not allow St. John to comment, but continued, "Gad, what a lark I would have! Going to London! The first thing I would do is get some new clothes."

The viscount, who considered the youth a great bumpkin, eyed Dick's provincial outfit and thought that at least the young Selwyn had some sense. Dick nodded vigorously. "That is what I'd do. I'd get some bang-up clothes." He regarded St. John with great interest. "I say, that is a dashed fine neckcloth you're wearing, but it looks devilishly tricky. Do you think you could show me how you tie such a thing?"

St. John raised an eyebrow. "I think you might be better advised to ask my friend Fitzwalter about that. He is quite the arbiter of fashion in town."

Dick looked over at Mr. Fitzwalter, who was talking to Camilla and Lucinda. "Is he? I thought he cut quite a dash. I shall have to get his advice then." Dick Selwyn took his leave of the viscount and hurried over to Fitzwalter.

St. John stood looking glumly at the mantel clock and wondered how much longer he would have to endure the situation. Although it was still quite early, he wanted only to go to bed and hoped the party would soon disband. At least, he reflected, he was finally being left alone.

Unfortunately for St. John, this welcome solitude was of short duration. He looked over to see Lucinda Selwyn approaching. Although the fact that she was accompanied by Camilla somewhat improved matters, St. John knew that he could not endure one more remark on troubles besetting garden flowers.

"Oh, dear," exclaimed Lucinda. "You are being ignored, Lord St. John. We cannot have that, I assure you. We have left Mr. Fitzwalter to my nephew. He is such a charming young man, your Mr. Fitzwalter. But then, all the Ponsonby Fitzwalters are charming. It is a matter of breeding, after all. I knew his grandmother, my lord. Did I mention that?"

"You did indeed, ma'am," replied the viscount sullenly.

"Why, perhaps I did. I also knew his cousin Lady Margaret Fitzwalter. How I should love to see her again. Mr. Fitzwalter said we must all come to town and call upon him. Is that not so very kind of him?" Lucinda directed an expectant look at St. John, but was disappointed when he did not add his own invitation to Fitzwalter's. She continued. "I daresay, I should like nothing better than to see London again, although I fear I shall never get to town."

The viscount did not seem at all upset at this declaration.

"Oh, I do not mind so much myself, I suppose," continued Lucinda, "but I do wish Camilla might go. Is it not abominable, Lord St. John, that my niece has never been to London?"

"That is unfortunate," said the viscount, looking at the young lady.

Camilla reddened slightly and wished desperately that her aunt would not embarrass her further. "I assure you, Aunt, I am quite content here."

St. John eyed her skeptically. "Is that so, Miss Selwyn? You are perfectly content to stay here?"

His tone suggested that such a possibility was quite addlepated, and Camilla bristled. "I am, my lord. I prefer the country."

"But if you have never been to town, Miss Selwyn," said the viscount, "you have not the means for comparison."

"That is what I tell her, Lord St. John," said Lucinda, nodding.

Camilla was growing increasingly irritated. "Perhaps I have not been to London," she said, "but I have often been to York."

"York, Miss Selwyn?" St. John's eyebrows arched in amusement. "With experience of such a metropolis, you will doubtlessly be disappointed by London."

He smiled for the first time, but it was a mocking smile that infuriated her. "Perhaps I would be disappointed in London, Lord St. John. Indeed, after conversing with Mr. Fitzwalter, I was beginning to regret never having had the opportunity to go there. Now, however, I realize that not every gentleman in town is so charming. Some, it seems, are not even civil."

The viscount's eyes widened in surprise at this unexpected setdown. "Miss Selwyn, I did not mean—"

"Excuse me, my lord," said Camilla, cutting him off. "I think it is time for me to retire. Good evening."

She turned and walked away, leaving St. John quite amazed that Miss Camilla Selwyn had the audacity to speak so to him. Lucinda appeared surprised at her niece's behavior and tried to apologize. "I am sure Camilla did not mean offense, my lord," she said.

St. John regarded her coolly. "And I am certain that she did," replied the viscount. "Pray excuse me, ma'am. I think I, too, shall retire."

St. John's departure upset Lucinda, who had, up to that time, thought the dinner a great success. She rejoined her nephew and Fitzwalter, who had watched his friend's exit with interest. Lucinda's good spirits were quickly restored, however, when Mr. Fitzwalter very obligingly stayed on, telling them very amusing stories, and it wasn't until several hours later that the rest of them went to bed.

3

Anthony St. John was quite happy to see the pale light of morning stream into his dreary bedchamber. He had spent a miserable night and had had little sleep.

Rising from the bed, the viscount dressed hastily, reflecting as he did so that the accommodations at Selwyn Manor were quite abominable. The bed was hard and the bedclothes threadbare, affording hardly any protection from the cold. All night long the wind had howled, rattling the windowpanes and causing the ragged draperies to flutter with the drafts.

St. John left his uncomfortable room and walked down the corridor to Fitzwalter's door. He tapped lightly upon it. "Fitz, are you up?"

The door was opened quickly. "Tony, of course I am up. Good God, you cannot know how I have suffered in this horrible room."

"I can know indeed, Fitz," replied the viscount, smiling slightly as he entered his friend's room.

"Look at this, Tony. Is it not frightful?"

"The room?"

"Not the room," replied Fitzwalter a trifle impatiently, "my neckcloth. I was attempting a waterfall, but my fingers were so stiff with the cold, the result is ghastly. I must try again." He started to untie the offending strip of white linen from around his neck. "Really, Tony, it is a terrible pity that we were in such a hurry leaving Ramsgate that Semple and Briggs could not have accompanied us. I am not accustomed to being without a valet and my appearance will suffer for it. Why, I look perfectly dreadful."

St. John eyed his friend critically and frowned. "By God, Fitz, I believe it was a mistake leaving Semple behind."

Fitzwalter paled and turned to study himself in the mirror with a worried expression.

The viscount burst into laughter. "I am only quizzing you, Fitz! You look as handsome as ever."

"Tony! You must not joke about such things!" Fitzwalter continued to eye his reflection in the mirror for a time and then took up a fresh neckcloth. "I don't know if I can manage this. No one ties a waterfall like Semple. The man is a true artist."

The viscount directed a somewhat exasperated look at his friend. "I cannot know why you care one fig for your appearance in such surroundings as these. Surely, it does not signify what these provincial nobodies think."

"My dear Tony, one either takes care about one's appearance or one does not." Fitzwalter attempted once again to tie his cravat, and then threw up his hands in frustration. "Damn, it is hopeless!"

"Oh, let me do it." St. John took up the ends of white linen and very quickly tied his friend's neckcloth. "There. Perhaps it is not up to Semple's standards, but it will have to do. I promise you it will pass inxpection here."

Fitzwalter turned once again to the mirror to examine the viscount's handiwork. He was noticeably relieved. "I am eternally in your debt. Indeed, that is not bad by half, Tony. Of course, it is not precisely a waterfall . . ."

"I caution you, Fitz, do not criticize my artistic endeavors or I shall take it very ill indeed. Now, do put on your coat and let us go downstairs. At least there might be a fire somewhere."

"The way old Selwyn guards his firewood? You are an optimist, Tony." Fitzwalter grinned as he put on his coat and then the two friends started for the door.

Standing in the dining room, Camilla Selwyn scrutinized the sideboard and frowned. The breakfast food laid out there looked quite splendid compared with the usual fare at Selwyn Manor, but Camilla knew very well that the guests were accustomed to far more magnificent repasts. She wondered why she cared. Certainly, Lord St. John did not deserve her consideration. Camilla frowned at the thought of the viscount. Still, she reflected, there was Mr. Fitzwalter.

"Camilla, good morning, my dear."

"Oh, Aunt Lucinda." Camilla smiled and kissed her aunt upon the cheek. "Did you sleep well?"

"I must confess I did not sleep well at all. I was far too excited. In truth, I kept thinking of our guests. Oh, my dear, it is so exciting having such gentlemen about. You should not have left so hastily, Camilla. Mr. Fitzwalter was so amusing. The stories he told! But don't worry, I shall relate them to you at first opportunity. A pity Lord St. John was not more agreeable."

Camilla nodded. "I think him quite insufferable."

"Indeed, that was apparent. I do wish you had not lost your temper last night."

"I did not lose my temper, Aunt Lucinda. It is only that I do not think I should tolerate such rude mockery from a man simply because he is a viscount."

Lucinda mulled this over. "Perhaps you are right. You so often are. But still, my dear, one must make allowances for men like St. John. Do be civil to him this morning."

"I shall certainly be as civil to him as he is to me," said Camilla.

"That is good," said Lucinda, a trifle uncertainly. "You know, my dear, I had hoped his lordship would take a fancy to you."

"Aunt Lucinda! What a cork-brained notion!"

"Why? Good heavens, you are an attractive girl and St. John is undoubtedly one of the most eligible bachelors in the country. I am sure his fortune is enormous."

"Surely, you must realize that the viscount thinks me beneath his consideration. And, in any case, I have no interest in him. Indeed, I pity any woman marrying a man of his haughtiness and conceit."

Lucinda regarded her niece with disapproval. "Well, there is Mr. Fitzwalter. He is so very charming and you do like him."

"Of course, I like him. Indeed, Aunt, I only hope the roads continue to be impassable and he will be forced to stay here one more day. That would surely give him enough time to make an offer for my hand."

"Do you think so?" Aunt Lucinda looked hopeful and Camilla burst into laughter.

"Oh, Aunt, I am only gammoning you. I pray you, cease talking about such absurd things. Tell me what you think of breakfast."

Lucinda did not look at all amused, but she good-naturedly glanced over at the sideboard, noting the array of food. "At least my brother is presenting his guests with a respectable breakfast."

Camilla smiled. "I fear I saw to the breakfast. Uncle knows nothing about it. I daresay, he will be sorely vexed to see that so much has been prepared ."

"Well, I do think he owes his guests a trifle more hospitality than last night's dinner. Only my brother would serve such food to illustrious personages as Lord St. John and Mr. Fitzwalter. He does not care in the least if we both should die of humiliation. But I am glad you have seen to breakfast. And should he make any comment about it whatsoever, he will hear from me."

Lucinda had hardly finished her remark when Sir Jarvis Selwyn stepped into the dining room. He did not appear to be in a good humor and he frowned deeply as he neared Camilla and Lucinda. "What's this? What do I smell?"

"It is just breakfast," said Lucinda.

"Breakfast?" Sir Jarvis approached the sideboard and lifted the lid of one of the covered dishes. "Mutton chops for breakfast? This is great extravagance!"

"But, Uncle, we do have guests."

Lucinda nodded vigorously. "And most distinguished guests."

"Distinguished?" Sir Jarvis regarded his sister with a disgusted look. "Is that what you call them, sister? They are fops and wastrels, both of them. I know their kind and do not think them fit company for my niece. Aye, fops and wastrels, and the sooner they quit Selwyn Manor, the happier I'll be."

"And the happier they'll be," said Lucinda sharply. "Really, Jarvis, you are the most vexatious man."

Before Sir Jarvis could make a suitable reply, they were joined by St. John and Fitzwalter. Ignoring his host's red face and angry expression as well as Lucinda Selwyn's frown, Fitzwalter smiled. "Good morning to you, sir, and to you ladies."

"Good morning, gentlemen," said Lucinda, smiling broadly at them both. "You have arrived just at the proper time. Let us all sit down. I am certain you are quite hungry."

St. John looked at Camilla, who met his gaze boldly. "Good morning, Miss Selwyn."

"Good morning, Lord St. John," replied Camilla coolly. She then turned and went to her place at the table.

"So the chit is still peeved with me," thought his lordship, strangely bothered by Camilla's attitude. Women were always throwing themselves at him, while this country miss seemed to have no interest in him whatsoever. St. John frowned and sat down in his chair.

When they were all seated, the butler began to serve breakfast. Fitzwalter was happy to see the quality of the food had evidently improved and was quite cheerful. "And where is Mr. Selwyn?" he inquired.

"Dick?" said Lucinda. "I expect my nephew will be here shortly."

"If he does not sleep the day away as he usually does," added Sir Jarvis sourly.

St. John looked at his host and wondered how anyone could endure his company for very long. He glanced over at Camilla Selwyn, noting that she looked very pretty in her simple morning dress of pale green muslin with long sleeves and high collar.

"Oh, here is Dick now," said Lucinda, gesturing toward the door. All eyes turned to Dick Selwyn. It was obvious that the young man had taken great care with his appearance that morning, but the effect was most infelicitous. He wore a striped coat that was ill-fitting and obviously the work of an inferior tailor, as well as a pair of very tight yellow pantaloons. His shiny Hessian boots were decorated with garish orange tassels and his formerly straight hair now sported a few lifeless curls resulting from the curling papers he had laboriously used the night before.

It required all of St. John's discipline to refrain from bursting into derisive laughter. Fitzwalter eyed the young man with undisguised dismay, an expression shared by Camilla Selwyn, who suspected her brother had lost his senses.

"By my faith," cried Sir Jarvis, "what is this, sir? What are you about?"

Dick reddened. "What do you mean, Uncle?"

"You know very well what I mean. Those ridiculous clothes."

"Jarvis," cried Lucinda, jumping to her nephew's defense. "Dick looks quite nice in his new clothes."

"Nice? He looks like a player in some cheap theatrical troop. Well, don't stand there gaping at me. Sit down, young coxcomb."

Dick Selwyn directed an angry look at his uncle and then shamefacedly sat down at the breakfast table. Trenton Fitzwalter, who deplored young Selwyn's appearance, nevertheless felt sorry for him. "Such coats are quite the thing in town, Mr. Selwyn," said Fitzwalter, taking care not to look over at the viscount.

"Are they?" Sir Jarvis looked quite astonished.

"Indeed so," said Fitzwalter with such an air of authority that no one could think of contradicting him.

"Fashion," growled the baronet. "Only the most corkbrained idiots take any note of it."

Camilla hastened to change the subject. "The weather is so much better today. Already some of the snow is melting."

"That is good news," said Sir Jarvis. "Perhaps you gentlemen will be able to be on your way this afternoon."

Camilla looked over at the visitors, rather embarrassed at her uncle's eagerness to be rid of the company. The viscount did not seem to notice the remark and Mr. Fitzwalter smiled at her, obviously amused.

"How I should like living in town," said Dick, finally

emboldened to speak. "I mean to say that the country is so dull."

"A dull fellow finds every place dull," muttered Sir Jarvis.

"Town is a wonderful place to be during the Season," said Lucinda. "I had two Seasons when I was a girl and it was the most exciting time of my life. Of course, that was five and twenty years ago and, yet, I suspect that things have not changed so much. How I wish I might go to London once again." She looked over at Camilla. "And how I regret that you have missed all the fun and excitement, my dear."

"Stuff and nonsense," said Sir Jarvis. "Camilla is fortunate to have escaped such trumpery. A London Season! Bah, she is better here than in London contending with all the fools and knaves who are running about." At the words "fools and knaves" the baronet directed his gaze toward St. John and Fitzwalter with obvious intent.

"Well, I think it a pity that neither of us has had the opportunity to go to London," said Dick resentfully.

"And so do I," said Lucinda.

The baronet frowned at his sister. "There are many country fellows who do nothing but disgrace themselves in London."

"And you think I would be one of them," said Dick hotly.

"I do indeed," said Sir Jarvis. "You are exactly the sort of empty-headed young jackanapes to do so. No, my lad, as long as you are under my authority, you will stay here at Selwyn Manor."

"Have you forgotten, Uncle, that I shall be one and twenty in less than one month's time? Then I shall do as I please."

"I forget nothing and when you reach your majority, you may go to the very devil for all I care."

Dick glared at Sir Jarvis and then looked over at Fitzwalter and St. John. "I shall receive my inheritance then. Twenty-eight thousand pounds."

"And money in such hands as yours, Dick Selwyn, will not last for long," said Sir Jarvis.

"Not like it lasts in yours, Uncle. By God, you still possess every ha'penny you ever had!"

"Dick!" cried Camilla, quite alarmed. "I pray you, calm down!"

Dick stood up. "I will not calm down! And I shall no longer bear my uncle's insults. Thank God it is not long until I am my own man." Then, after glaring once again at his uncle, Dick Selwyn rose and stormed out of the room.

There was a period of awkward silence, broken finally by Sir Jarvis. "I must apologize for my nephew. He forgets himself." The baronet then returned to his food. St. John exchanged a glance with Fitzwalter and then, following their host's example, they began to eat their breakfast.

Camilla looked down at her plate, dreadfully embarrassed. She was certain that the London gentlemen must think her family quite dreadful. Indeed, what could they think with Dick and her uncle shouting at the table like ruffians? What tales St. John and Fitzwalter would tell when they returned to town about the comically barbaric Selwyns!

"It is not too much longer until we can expect the daffodils," said Lucinda suddenly. Camilla directed a bewildered look at her aunt. "Yes, the daffodils," continued Lucinda. "I must tell you gentlemen all about them."

Camilla suppressed a sigh as her aunt launched into an ecstatic monologue about the joys of spring flowers. Some time later, Lucinda allowed Mr. Fitzwalter to express his opinion whether he preferred hyacinths to tulips. Happy to finally have an opportunity to speak, Fitzwalter discoursed at length on this topic.

Glancing over at the viscount, Camilla noted that he looked very bored. Doubtlessly, he was wishing he were as far away from Selwyn Manor as possible. Indeed, reflected Camilla glumly, at that moment, she would have liked to flee Selwyn Manor herself. Certainly, the conflict between her brother and uncle was becoming more and more intolerable.

Her mind wandering, Camilla thought back to the early days when she and Dick had first come to Selwyn Manor.

She had been eleven years old and Dick nine when their father died, leaving them orphans with their uncle as guardian.

Looking over at her uncle, Camilla remembered their arrival at Selwyn Manor. Sir Jarvis had seemed so gruff and rather formidable and they had both been glad that Aunt Lucinda was there, too, to welcome them. Yet, it had not taken Camilla long to breach Uncle Jarvis's seemingly cold exterior and soon she and the baronet were devoted to each other.

Dick, however, took far longer to develop any affection for Sir Jarvis. Their difference in temperaments made them clash from the beginning, Dick being a high-spirited lad prone to mischief and his uncle a strict, humorless man. Although Camilla knew that Sir Jarvis was, in his own way, fond of his nephew, they had never got along. Dick chafed constantly under the baronet's stern discipline and as he neared manhood, matters grew worse.

The fact that his uncle gave him such a paltry allowance was especially galling. Dick had almost no money to spend, despite the substantial inheritance left to him by his maternal grandfather. Knowing that he would very soon have this money, Dick grew bolder and he quarreled incessantly with his uncle.

"My dear, what do you think of Mr. Fitzwalter's idea?"

Camilla looked at her aunt in some confusion. "Mr. Fitzwalter's idea? Oh, I am sure it is splendid."

"Then I shall plant violets near the old fountain. How clever of you to suggest it, Mr. Fitzwalter. Oh, how I wish you gentlemen could be here in the spring. How I should love to show you all my flowers!"

St. John's expression clearly showed a lack of enthusiasm at the idea. He looked at Lucinda Selwyn, deciding she was the most insufferable woman he had ever met. No, he corrected himself. His stepmother, Amanda, was definitely more insufferable, but certainly this Selwyn woman came second.

At that moment, they were interrupted by the appearance of the butler, Jackson. "Excuse me, Sir Jarvis. Lord

St. John's man wishes to speak with him. He be waiting in the library.''

''What? Can't you see we are at breakfast, man?''

''Oh, I am finished, sir,'' said St. John eagerly. He rose quickly and tossed his napkin down on the table. ''Pray excuse me.'' He nodded to the ladies and left the room, and his hasty departure only confirmed Camilla's opinion that the viscount was very anxious to leave their company.

St. John followed Jackson from the dining room and into the library where the coachman, Hopper, was patiently waiting.

''Good morning, m'lord.''

The viscount nodded in reply. ''How are the horses, Hopper?''

''Right enough, m'lord. Well rested and eager to go again.''

''As I am. Have you any idea when we might leave this place?''

''That is why I have come, m'lord. I saw a man a short while ago who had just come from the village. He said there was almost no snow south of there and the road was well passable. 'Tis only two miles to the village and Harry and me thought we'd have no trouble getting there.''

''Thank God. Then we will go as soon as you can be ready.''

The coachman bowed slightly and left the viscount standing there in the library. St. John had no desire to rejoin the company, and was happy to be away from the talkative Lucinda and his unpleasant host. Even the attractive Miss Camilla Selwyn was insufficient reason to return to the dining room.

He frowned as he thought of that young lady. It was obvious from her attitude that morning that she disliked him heartily. Well, he told himself, what did the opinion of one country miss matter? St. John turned his attention to the contents of the Selwyns' library and tried to forget Miss Camilla's fine dark eyes with their disapproving glances.

He began to study the titles of the books on one of the shelves, and was surprised to see that Selwyn Manor's library boasted a very respectable collection. Seeing a glass case on the opposite side of the room, St. John walked over to it. On display beneath the glass was a medieval manuscript. Beside it was a neatly-lettered placard describing the book as the oldest one in the library. It was, the card said, in the possession of the first master of Selwyn Manor, a Sir Thomas, who died in the year 1490. The viscount stared at the book for a long time, reflecting on its great antiquity and the fact that it had remained in the Selwyn family for more than three hundred years.

An ironic smile crossed St. John's face. Although the Selwyn family may be impoverished and provincial, he thought, it could be proud of its position as an old landed family.

St. John turned away from the manuscript and walked to the window to look out at the snow-covered ground. How he envied the Selwyns their ancient lineage and decaying family manor house. He, Viscount St. John, had neither. Indeed, although St. John's rank was illustrious and his wealth enormous, his title was of recent vintage.

His father, Arthur St. John, had been a remarkable man, rising from obscure origins to renown by talent and force of will. The first viscount had had only the most tenuous connections to the nobility and gentry. Indeed, an alarming number of his antecedents had been ignominiously middle class.

Arthur St. John's first wife had been an heiress, the daughter of an extremely wealthy man who had made his fortune in the textile business. Moving as he did in the first circles of London society, Anthony St. John was constantly aware of the shortcomings of his ancestry. His late mother's relations were a great embarrassment to him, and he tried hard to disassociate himself from them.

However, his stepmother, Amanda, was there to constantly remind him of his low birth and inferior breeding. She was a member of the Mountifort family and through her veins flowed the bluest blood in the realm. The Mountifort family had not been enthusiastic when Amanda had married the widowed Arthur St. John. Since the newly created Viscount St. John had been a very dashing fellow and a war hero, the Mountifort family had finally accepted him. However, they clearly thought their daughter had married beneath her.

St. John turned away from the window and returned once more to the book collection. Then, trying to put all thoughts of his stepmother and her Mountifort relations from his mind, he picked up a book and started paging through it.

"Tony, there you are!"

"Fitz, so you have escaped from the Selwyns. How did you manage it?"

"My dear Tony, you are so awfully hard on our hosts. I find them quite pleasant and as they have heard none of my stories before, I need not worry that I am repeating myself."

"Fitz, you have never worried about that in the past."

"Tony!" cried Fitzwalter in mock indignation.

The viscount grinned at his friend. "Well, Fitz, I hate to deprive you of such an attentive audience, but Hopper has just told me that the roads are passable enough. We are leaving as soon as possible."

Fitzwalter did not look at all happy at this information. "I must say I was beginning to enjoy my stay here. Of course, it will be good to return to town. I have not seen my tailor in the longest time." He glanced around the library. "I daresay, this is not what I would have expected from Sir Jarvis. It appears to be an admirable collection. Oh, look!" Fitzwalter gestured toward the display case. "How very quaint. A medieval manuscript. I do love such things." He hurried over to it, followed by his friend.

While the gentlemen were perusing the antique book, Camilla Selwyn was making her way to the library. As she neared the doorway, she heard St. John's voice and his words made her stop short. "Now, Fitz, tell me why you find the Selwyns so charming."

"They are charming."

"You mean amusing."

"I mean amusing and charming."

Camilla listened guiltily at the doorway, but was so

interested in the conversation that she waited to hear the rest of it.

"Fitz, of the family, only Miss Camilla Selwyn is in any way presentable."

"My dear Tony, she is far more than merely presentable. I find her enchanting. And I do like her aunt so very much."

"Good God, Fitz! That woman? How I abhor such females, talking incessantly and always about their glorious youthful memories. She talks of her London Season as if she had been the most sought-after girl in town. I'm sure she is most imaginative. Indeed, Fitz, I think you are oddly charitable where these Selwyns are concerned. I imagine you will even find good to say about that fellow Dick."

"Indeed, yes."

"The fellow is a bumpkin!"

"He is but a trifle unpolished. But I do like him. He has a charming naiveté I find refreshing."

"Charming naiveté? So that is what it is. I took it for stupidity."

Both of the gentlemen burst into laughter and Camilla burned with indignation. How dare St. John say such things? She entered the room, her face red and her eyes blazing dangerously. "Gentlemen!"

The viscount and Fitzwalter turned in surprise. "Oh, Miss Selwyn," said Fitzwalter.

Ignoring him, she faced St. John. "I heard your remarks, Lord St. John. I am astonished that even you would say such things."

"And I am astonished that a lady would listen to a private conversation not intended for her ears."

"Obviously not intended for my ears!"

"Miss Selwyn, I assure you—"

Camilla cut off his words. "No, do not try to make excuses. I know how trying it has been for you to endure our company. At least you may be heartened at the prospect of amusing your friends in London with tales of your stay at Selwyn Manor."

Not allowing the viscount to reply, Camilla turned abruptly and left the library.

"Oh dear," said Fitzwalter, very much upset. "We really must do something, Tony."

"We must pack and leave as soon as possible," St. John replied irritably. Then he turned and walked briskly from the room, followed by a reluctant Fitzwalter.

4

Camilla Selwyn sat in her sitting room, attempting to work on her embroidery. The wolfhound Rufus dozed at her feet as Camilla halfheartedly added a few stitches to the canvas. Looking down at her work, she sighed, and then, pushing the frame aside, she rose from her chair and walked to the window.

Spring was arriving, proclaimed by Lucinda's daffodils. It was a time Camilla dearly loved and yet this year she felt no joy in the changing season. There was too much strife at Selwyn Manor, too much bickering between her brother and uncle.

In the month that had passed since the visitors had left Selwyn Manor, Sir Jarvis and Dick had quarreled incessantly. Having had a glimpse of life in London, her brother was even more restless and eager to be out from under his uncle's authority. That he had had to wait even a few weeks had seemed intolerable to him.

Thus, life in the household had been very unpleasant, the atmosphere charged with tension. What made it even worse for Camilla was that she could not forget St. John's words about her family. In spite of telling herself numerous times that she did not care one fig for society's opinion, the idea that a man like St. John viewed her and her family with such scorn was undeniably upsetting.

Camilla had prudently kept the viscount's words to herself, not wanting to hurt her aunt and brother. She did, however, try to quell Dick's enthusiasm when he spoke of going to town and calling upon Fitzwalter and St. John. No matter what she said to discourage him, her brother was certain he would receive a very warm reception upon arriving in London.

"Camilla! You must come with me!" Lucinda Selwyn rushed breathlessly into the room, causing Rufus to raise his shaggy head and view her with alarm.

"Whatever is the matter?"

"It is your uncle and Dick. I fear they will come to blows!"

"Oh, dear, not again!"

Lucinda nodded. "If only my nephew would be more patient! It is his birthday in but two days and then he will have his independence. But do hurry, Camilla, you are the only one who can make them see reason."

Although not convinced of her abilities to avert a battle, Camilla dutifully followed her aunt down the stairs to the drawing room. She could hear Dick's voice long before she entered. "You cannot bear the fact that in two days' time I shall be my own man! I shall be able to do whatever I want and shall no longer have to live here like a pauper!"

Camilla and Lucinda entered the room to see Sir Jarvis shake his fist at his nephew. "You insolent puppy! This is the gratitude I get for taking you into my home! So you will be your own man, will you? And I am sure you will lose no time in flying off to town."

"That's right, Uncle. I'm going to London and now that I shall have my own money, I can live the way I want. And there is nothing you can do to stop me!"

"You young jackanapes!" cried the baronet. "Go then! Go to London! Become a fop and a wastrel like the rest of them!"

Camilla hurriedly stepped in between them. "Uncle! Dick! I pray you cease!"

"I shall indeed cease. I shall not waste my breath any further on this thankless cub," said Sir Jarvis testily.

"Nor shall I," said Dick. "I have no need of ever speaking with him again." He brandished a piece of paper he was holding in his hand. "This makes me a free man!"

"What is it, Dick?" said Lucinda.

"It is from Charles MacNeil in answer to my letter. He looked down at the missive. "This is what he says. 'Certainly you are welcome to come to London to make the arrangements concerning your inheritance. Indeed, it would simplify matters for me not having to travel to Selwyn Manor. As your solicitor, I shall endeavor to advise you as to the prudent management of your income and capital.''

"Charles might as well save his effort," muttered Sir Jarvis. "You'll take no prudent advice, I'll be bound."

"Please, Uncle," said Camilla. She turned to her brother. "I do hope you will listen to Charles. You may rely on him for good counsel. He is such a clever man."

Dick frowned, not liking to hear the solicitor praised. Charles MacNeil was the son of Sir Jarvis's former butler and he had grown up with the Selwyns. Although Dick was fond of Charles, he had been plagued in his youth by his uncle's constantly comparing the two. An industrious, ambitious young man, MacNeil had all the qualities to endear him to the baronet. Dick had always resented that his uncle had seemed to prefer his servant's son to his own nephew.

Charles was doing very well for himself in London. Sir Jarvis had assisted him through university, but it was MacNeil's own determination and talent that had enabled him to rise quickly in his profession. Now working for a prestigious legal firm, Charles had risen far above his station.

"Do not think I am not capable of looking after myself," said Dick.

Lucinda nodded vigorously. "Indeed, you are well able to do so, Dick. You will manage admirably on your own."

Dick smiled thankfully at his aunt. "As soon as I have established myself in town, you and Camilla must come and join me."

"Oh, Dick, that would be wonderful!" cried Lucinda. "How I have longed to return to London!"

Dick turned to his sister. "You will come, won't you, Cam?"

Camilla hesitated. "I don't know, Dick."

"Don't expect your sister to join you in your folly," grumbled the baronet.

"Jarvis!" cried Lucinda. "If you would but think of Camilla, you would urge her to go to town. Good heavens, she is nearly three and twenty and has never had a Season. How will she ever find a husband? She has no prospects here."

"She is better off without a husband than marrying one of those idle fellows in town."

"You say that only because you want the poor girl to waste her life away staying here with you. Well, I am going to London and I shall do everything in my power to encourage Camilla to do the same."

Sir Jarvis glared at his sister, but made no reply. He turned angrily away and stormed out of the room.

"Good riddance," said Lucinda. "My brother is the most insufferable man!" She looked over at her niece. "You must come to London, my dear. You must have your chance rather than be closeted away here."

"Aunt Lucinda is right," said Dick. "Surely, you can't be so bird-witted to prefer staying in this dreary place. Say you will come. It will be such fun! You will see!"

"I must think it over, Dick. Who will look after Uncle if we abandon him?"

"You have looked after him enough, my dear," said Lucinda. "He shall do very well without you. You must not put aside this opportunity."

Camilla said once again that she would think on the matter, and taking this remark as a probable affirmative answer, her aunt grew very cheerful. Lucinda then began to talk excitedly of all the things they would see and do in London.

Camilla only half-listened, so intent was she on her decision. Unlike her brother, Camilla was not so anxious to depart from Selwyn Manor. She loved living in the country and although Sir Jarvis's household was rather spartan, Camilla considered it her home. She had never had much desire to go to London and certainly did not wish to enter the glittering social world there.

Camilla knitted her brows in concentration. If she did not go to London, her brother Dick was all too apt to get into trouble. Perhaps if she were there, she could somehow keep him out of it. Although she loved him dearly, Camilla knew that her brother was not the most sensible of men. She had little doubt that Dick's impulsive nature could land him in quite a muddle in town.

"Excuse me," said Camilla, interrupting Lucinda. "I must see Uncle." She then hurried off before they could say anything more to her.

As expected, Camilla found Sir Jarvis in the library. He was sitting in his favorite chair with a book, his reading spectacles perched on his nose. The expression on his lean face was grim.

"Uncle?"

"Oh, it's you, Camilla."

She walked over to him and sat down in a chair next to his. "I wanted to talk with you, Uncle Jarvis. You see, I've decided to go to London with Dick."

The baronet's face fell, but he quickly recovered and said in his usual gruff voice, "Well, go, then. I fancy you are eager to be rid of me, too."

"Of course not, Uncle." She reached out and took his hand. "I do not wish to go and I shall miss you very much. But I fear that if Dick is left on his own, he may get into some type of mischief in town."

Sir Jarvis grunted. "I'd say that is a dashed inevitability."

Camilla smiled. "Then you see that I must go and keep an eye on him."

The baronet seemed to ponder this and then nodded. "Perhaps that would be a good idea, Camilla. I know my sister will be of no help. Indeed, she will only encourage his foolish ways. She has always coddled the cub."

Camilla paused. "Uncle Jarvis, you mustn't be too upset with Dick. He is young, after all, and has a somewhat excitable nature. He feels too constrained here and needs to be out in the world."

Sir Jarvis took off his spectacles and looked at his niece. "Perhaps I have been hard on him, but I know how the world can take advantage of a naive country lad. I don't like the idea of your brother idling about in London, acquiring all manner of bad habits, drinking and gaming away his fortune.

"Yes, perhaps it would be best if you joined him in town. You are a sensible girl, Camilla, and if anyone can keep my thick-skulled nephew from tomfoolery, it is you."

Camilla smiled and Sir Jarvis continued, "I suppose your aunt is right. About you, I mean to say. I have been unreasonable keeping you here. A fine girl like you should go out in society and find a young man. A decent fellow, mind you, not one of those deuced fops."

"Really, Uncle Jarvis, I am not looking for a husband. I am quite on the shelf."

"Stuff and nonsense. 'Twill be a lucky fellow who gets you, my girl."

Camilla laughed and rose from her chair. She then leaned down and kissed her uncle on his cheek. "You must be certain to take care of yourself when I am gone. And please, don't shout at poor old Jackson."

Sir Jarvis smiled. "Oh, very well, you bossy female."

Camilla laughed again and then departed, leaving the baronet to stare glumly after her.

5

As the post chaise made its way through the bustling streets of London, Camilla Selwyn was filled with misgivings. She was unaccustomed to the city and was somewhat dismayed by the noise and congestion she was finding there. Camilla realized that she should have been excited by her first glimpse of the great metropolis, but instead, she was filled with a longing for the green hills surrounding Selwyn Manor.

Camilla glanced over at her aunt, who was gazing out the window with delighted eyes. The only other inhabitant of the carriage was the wolfhound Rufus, who was asleep on the floor. Lucinda turned away from the window and shifted in her seat, dislodging her foot from beneath the wolfhound's chin. "I daresay it is so wonderful to be so near our journey's end." She looked down at the dog. "You know I am fond of Rufus, but he is an exceedingly large dog and there is scarcely room to put one's feet."

Hearing his name, Rufus looked up and regarded Lucinda quizzically. "Well, you know I could not bear to leave him behind," said Camilla, patting the dog's brindled head.

Lucinda smiled indulgently at her niece and then turned her attention once again to the window. "Oh, how I have missed the city. I know you will love it."

Lucinda did not seem to expect a reply, and Camilla remained silent as she continued to stare out the carriage window. It had been more than two weeks since her brother Dick had left Selwyn Manor. He had hurried off, taking few of his belongings and instructing them to await

word from him before coming to town. Camilla had not
been enthused at the plan, distrusting her brother's abilities
to make their living arrangements, but he had insisted on
leaving at once. Dick had sent a letter not long afterward
filled with glowing accounts of the city. He had leased a
"bang-up" townhouse and was most anxious that Camilla
and Aunt Lucinda join him immediately.

And so Camilla and her aunt had hastily packed and
engaged a post chaise for the journey. Camilla had thought
a post chaise something of an extravagance, but Lucinda
had chided her, saying she must cease acting like a pauper.

"Camilla?"

Camilla looked over at her aunt. "Yes, Aunt?"

"Why, you looked so very pensive. Do tell me what
you are thinking. Indeed, I thought you would appear far
happier at coming to London."

"It is only that I worry about Dick. He has never been
on his own before, nor has he had more than a few
shillings to spend. Now that he has a substantial income—"

"My dear girl, you worry needlessly. Certainly Dick is
very young and inexperienced. But he is not a cabbage
head!"

Camilla did not look altogether convinced of this statement, but thought it best to refrain from commenting. She
changed the subject. "Will we arrive soon?"

Lucinda nodded. "It should not be so very far." They
passed a spacious park and then came into a residential
area. There were rows of neat brick houses with wrought-
iron fences and Camilla saw well-dressed ladies and gentlemen walking in front of them.

"This looks like a very respectable neighborhood,"
commented Camilla.

"My dear girl, it may be respectable enough, but I
assure you that no member of the ton would live here. I do
hope Dick found us a residence in a more fashionable area.
I am unfamiliar with the address of the place, but surely he
was well advised as to where we should reside."

"Certainly a house such as one of these would be more
than adequate," said Camilla.

Aunt Lucinda frowned. "I can see that it is not going to

be easy to rid you of my brother's influence. Oh, look, now we are coming to a much more suitable area. I do believe I recollect this street. Why, yes, there is the residence of the Earl of Chesbrook. I went to a lovely party there.''

Camilla surveyed the house belonging to the Earl of Chesbrook with interest. ''It is very grand, is it not?''

''Oh, yes, but then there are others far grander.'' As if to confirm Lucinda's remark, the post chaise turned at the next intersection and they found themselves on a street lined with elegant townhouses even more imposing than those they had just seen. To Camilla's considerable surprise, the carriage pulled to a stop in front of one of the houses.

''We must have arrived,'' said Lucinda happily. ''Oh, how clever of Dick to have found such a fine place.''

''There must be a mistake,'' said Camilla, studying the house from the window. It was a stately edifice built in the graceful Georgian style and it made the house of the Earl of Chesbrook look quite insignificant by comparison.

The driver opened the door of the carriage. ''Are you sure this is the correct place?'' asked Camilla.

''Indeed, it is, miss,'' replied the man. ''This is the number.''

The man assisted Camilla and then Lucinda from the vehicle and they proceeded to the door. ''Truly, Aunt, this house is above our means.''

''Nonsense. Dick could not have arranged for it if that were so.''

Aunt Lucinda took up the shiny brass door knocker and let it fall soundly against the door. In a moment it was opened by a distinguished looking man attired in the garb of a butler.

''The Misses Selwyn?'' he said. ''The master is expecting you. Do come in, ladies.'' He ushered them inside. ''I shall inform Mr. Selwyn that you have arrived. Do follow me.'' The butler led them from the entry hall into a splendidly furnished parlor and then bowed and left.

''Oh, Camilla, what a beautiful house!'' Aunt Lucinda walked about the room, excitedly scrutinizing the furniture and paintings that decorated it. "However did Dick do all this so quickly?"

The younger Miss Selwyn stood in the center of the room, a look of bewilderment on her face. She had never seen such a place. It was elegantly appointed in the modern style with chairs and tables reflecting the classical and oriental influences of the current vogue.

The walls were painted a pale mauve and on them were hung some impressive French and Italian paintings. "Are you not amazed at what charming taste your brother has?" said Lucinda.

"Indeed I am," said Camilla, studying one of the paintings, a sprightly rococo work featuring half-clad ladies in a bucolic landscape.

At that moment Dick Selwyn appeared at the door. "Cam! Aunt Lucinda! I am so glad to see you both!"

Camilla turned to face her brother and was struck speechless at his appearance. She regarded him with a stunned expression, thinking that had she not heard his voice, she would not have recognized him. He was dressed in a coat of bright blue superfine, a vividly striped waistcoat, and pantaloons of a startling yellow color. From his waistcoat dangled numerous fobs and seals that jingled noisily when he moved. The points of his shirt collar were so high that it made turning his head an impossible task and the white linen cravat about his neck was tied in an enormous and intricate bow. Dick's hair had been elaborately styled into fashionable Corinthian curls and upon his cheeks, Camilla noted, were spots of rouge.

Lucinda hurried to her nephew and embraced him heartily. "Oh, Dick, how very handsome you look!"

"Do you think so?" Dick grinned at the compliment. "I found the most bang-up tailor. And I have a valet. He is quite a good fellow. He came with the house."

"Came with the house?" Camilla had not moved from where she was standing and continued to stare at her brother.

"Aye," said Dick. "It is a bang-up house, just as I said. I bought all the furnishings and for a good price, although that don't signify in the least now that I am a gentleman of means. Come, let us all sit down and I shall tell you all about it.''

Lucinda and Dick sat down on an elegant sofa and Camilla sat in an armchair across from them. She continued to regard her brother with disbelief. At first opportunity, Dick pulled a gold snuffbox from his pocket and noisily took a pinch of snuff. ''This, too, came with the house,'' he said, handing the tiny gold box to his sister. ''I am told the Prince Regent himself has none finer.''

Camilla turned the gold box over in her hand, noting its delicate filigree work. ''You said your valet came with the house?''

Dick nodded. ''This was the home of the Honorable Herbert Randall, better known as Buck Randall.''

Dick's expression implied that his sister and aunt should have heard of this gentleman, and when they regarded him blankly, he smiled patronizingly at them. ''Not being from town, you would not know of him, but Buck Randall was what one would call a tulip. He was known to everyone and was a most intimate acquaintance of His Royal Highness.'' Dick looked over at Camilla and was a little disappointed that his sister seemed unimpressed.

''And how did you happen to obtain the house of this 'tulip'?'' asked Camilla.

''Well, as luck would have it, it became available on the very day I arrived in town. Of course, there was a bit of a farrago with solicitors and Randall's creditors.''

''His creditors?''

Dick nodded. ''Poor fellow. Seems he lost all his blunt months ago at the gaming tables. Dashed odd, for they say he always had the devil's own luck. But he was very much in debt and flew off to France. I was deuced lucky to take the house. There were other gentlemen very much interested.''

''And what did Charles think of your taking a house such as this?'' inquired Camilla.

''Charles? What has he to do with it?'' Dick changed the subject. ''Oh, I have Buck Randall's valet. He is a Frenchman, but then, that is not his fault, I suppose.''

''Indeed not,'' said Aunt Lucinda charitably. ''And he

appears to know his duty well. Oh, Dick, you look so well and happy.''

"Happy? I am indeed. Why, never before have I been my own man. And I have made some very promising acquaintances. Sir Peregrine Mowbray is one. He is cousin to the Marquess of Claridge. Oh, and I have called upon both Mr. Fitzwalter and Lord St. John.''

Camilla looked horrified. "You didn't!''

"I did indeed. Unfortunately, neither of them was home. I left my card, of course, and expect to receive calls from them very soon.''

"I knew you would do well if given the opportunity, my boy,'' said Lucinda, regarding her nephew fondly. "Not many lads new to town would have found such a splendid house.''

"But, Dick,'' said Camilla, "is this not too grand a house for us? It is so large and doubtless was very expensive.''

"'Pon my honor, Cam, we can well afford this and much more. The two of you will be the best-dressed ladies in town.''

"You always were a thoughtful young man,'' said Lucinda. "I do need new clothes as does your sister.''

Dick nodded and directed a critical gaze at his Camilla. "It won't do you going about in town looking like that, Cam.''

Camilla looked insulted. "This is my best traveling outfit.''

"That is what I mean. My word, if you would but see the ladies here in town, you would certainly not step outside the door dressed like that. Oh, don't fly into the boughs! You must take more note of fashion now that we are established in town. Pierre has said—''

"And who is Pierre?'' asked Camilla, quite disgruntled at her brother's words.

"He is my valet. I call him Pierre because I cannot, for the life of me, manage his other name. Pierre is far simpler. But Pierre has told me the names of all the best dressmakers.''

"And is he such an authority?''

"Why, of course, Cam," replied her brother. "Indeed, his sister is employed by Madame LeClerc. All the ladies of the first circles have their gowns made there. I have already arranged for the two of you to see her tomorrow."

"Really, Dick," protested Camilla. "We have only just arrived. I cannot think about new dresses."

"Poppycock," said Lucinda. "If we are to be out in society, we cannot appear like impoverished country ladies. Dick is so very considerate to have arranged things."

"And you must not worry about money. Buy what you will."

"Dick." Camilla regarded him disapprovingly. "You are not being sensible. Do you know the cost of dresses ordered from such establishments as this Madame Le-Clerc's?"

"Do not mention costs to me, Cam. I warn you, I am heartily sick of hearing about money. For all the years we lived with Uncle Jarvis, all he ever talked about was the cost of this and the cost of that. I will not have you taking his place. You will have new clothes and damned expensive ones at that!"

Camilla raised her eyebrows at her brother's words. She was unaccustomed to him speaking in such a manner and wondered at the transformation a few weeks in London had wrought. He was, indeed, very much his own man, it seemed, and was very much determined to exercise authority over her.

Suddenly feeling very weary, Camilla restrained her temper. "Very well, Dick Selwyn, but if we will soon be joining this Buck Randall, it will be your doing."

Dick laughed. "You need not fear any such thing as that. Now, you ladies must go and rest. You must be tired after the long journey from Selwyn Manor."

They all rose from their chairs and Dick started to escort the ladies to their rooms. They were met at the door by the butler. "Your pardon, sir, but Sir Peregrine Mowbray is here. He said he has the conveyance."

Dick Selwyn seemed quite excited by this news. "Show him in immediately, Baxter." The butler vanished and Dick turned to Camilla and Lucinda. "You must meet Sir

Peregrine. And wait until you see what he has brought me.''

"But, Dick, I thought I was not well-dressed enough to meet your new friends," said Camilla. "Perhaps it would be best if we met him at another time."

Dick appeared to consider this suggestion, but before he could make a reply, Sir Peregrine Mowbray entered the room. "Selwyn, I have them for you," he said. Then, noting the ladies, he stopped. "Oh, I am sorry. I did not know you were occupied."

"Mowbray, I told you my sister and aunt were coming. They have just arrived. Miss Lucinda Selwyn and Miss Camilla Selwyn, may I present Sir Peregrine Mowbray?"

"Charmed and delighted." The newcomer took first Lucinda's and then Camilla's hands and bowed over them.

"How very nice to meet you, sir," said Lucinda. "Why, Dick had just mentioned you. I was so happy to see him making friends so quickly."

"Indeed, he has, ma'am," returned Sir Peregrine.

Lucinda then asked some additional questions, allowing Camilla ample opportunity to scrutinize Dick's new acquaintance. He was a big man with broad shoulders and muscular frame, who was fashionably dressed in a well-fitting coat, pantaloons, and gleaming boots. Camilla thought him handsome in a rough sort of way with his square chin and rugged features. He had dark brown hair and a receding hairline that he attempted to conceal by careful combing. Camilla guessed he was some ten years older than her brother.

Sir Peregrine looked at Camilla, eyeing her with such keen interest that Camilla was somewhat disconcerted.

"You have brought them, Mowbray?" asked Dick eagerly.

"I have indeed."

"Whatever have you brought, Sir Peregrine?" said Lucinda.

"Well, ma'am, your nephew is a clever fellow and has persuaded me to part with a great prize, perfectly matched grays and a fine high-perch phaeton."

"You must see them," said Dick. "Come, let us all go

and see them.'' Before the ladies could say a word, Dick grasped Lucinda by the arm and started to the door. ''Aunt Lucinda, you have never seen anything more beautiful.''

''Nor have I, Miss Selwyn,'' said Sir Peregrine, directing a significant glance at Camilla. ''Would you do me the honor of accompanying me, Miss Camilla?''

Camilla reluctantly took Mowbray's proffered arm. There was something about Sir Peregrine that Camilla did not like, although she could not, at that moment, have explained what that might be. She said nothing as she walked with him from the room and out of the house.

''Oh, Dick! They are beautiful!'' exclaimed Lucinda. ''Camilla, have you ever seen such horses?''

''Indeed, I have not.'' Camilla tried hard to hide her feelings, but she was actually quite appalled to see the splendid horses and equipage waiting there before the house. Dick's new vehicle was an open carriage with what Camilla thought was a ridiculously high driver's seat in front. Hitched to the phaeton were four spirited, dappled-gray horses. Camilla was well acquainted with all manner of horses and considered herself a good judge of the animals. Her expert eye immediately discerned that these grays were exceedingly fine specimens.

''Bang-up bits of blood and bone, don't you think?'' said Dick proudly. ''I cannot wait to take the ribbons.''

''You will drive them, Dick?'' said Camilla.

''Of course. Really, Cam, what a goose-capped question.''

Camilla was about to retort that she knew very well her brother had not the skill to handle horses such as this, but she said nothing.

''You'll have to allow your sister to drive now and then, Selwyn,'' said Sir Peregrine, smiling at Camilla. ''And your aunt, too. It is quite the fashion for ladies to drive a four-in-hand.''

''I fear I have no wish to do so, Sir Peregrine,'' said Camilla coolly.

''Oh, if only I might,'' enthused Lucinda. ''But I am far too timorous for that. But I daresay, I shall be most eager to ride in such a magnificent carriage. You must take us out as soon as possible.''

"Then, come, Aunt," cried Dick. "Do get in. We shall take her out."

"Oh, I don't think so," said Camilla. "We have just arrived . . ."

"Don't be a spoilsport, Cam. It will only be for a very short ride."

"Oh, yes, it would be great fun!" Aunt Lucinda eagerly climbed into the phaeton, assisted by Dick, who then jumped up into the high-perch seat and took up the reins. "Come, Camilla, do get in, and you too, Mowbray."

Sir Peregrine smiled over at Camilla. "Shall I help you up beside your brother, Miss Selwyn?"

"I think it better if I ride with my aunt."

The big man helped her up and then started to get in after her. "Don't you think, Sir Peregrine, that you might wish to ride up with my brother? You might wish to instruct him on the finer points of driving this vehicle."

Dick, who had heard the remark, appeared offended. "Camilla, I need no instructions."

Mowbray seemed a little disappointed at not being able to ride with Camilla, but nodded. "No, Selwyn, better I ride with you. I've a few things tell you about these horses."

It was with some relief that Camilla watched Sir Peregrine climb up beside her brother. Dick took up his whip and they started off.

"I feel like a very grand lady," said Lucinda. "Oh, I wish Jarvis might see us. How he would disapprove!"

Camilla nodded absently, thinking that she did not approve very much of such a regal carriage. She did not doubt that Dick had paid dearly for such magnificence. A slight frown crossed Camilla's face. It appeared that her fears about her brother were well founded and that Dick was already doing his best to squander his fortune. Camilla sighed and knew very well that she would not enjoy the ride.

6

Lord St. John idly flipped through the pages of a newspaper and impatiently tossed it aside. Then, rising from his chair, he walked over to look out the window. The sun was shining brightly and the flowering trees in front of the fashionable row of London townhouses proclaimed the beauty of the season. While many people would have been cheered by such a sight after the long winter, the viscount found it strangely depressing.

St. John paced across the room and stopped in front of the fireplace. Seeing a card on the mantel, he picked it up. A slight smile came to his face as he read the words engraved in flourishing letters, "Richard Selwyn, Esq." The card had been left at his home some days ago and he had almost been tempted to return the call. Having been so bored in town, the viscount had thought it might be diverting to see the young Mr. Selwyn again.

However, he had soon put such thoughts aside, knowing it unwise to encourage Dick. Indeed, it would hardly do being seen about town with such an unpolished fellow.

And in addition to that, there was the likelihood of seeing Miss Camilla Selwyn again. Reflecting upon her, St. John frowned. It was surprising how many times he had thought of that lady since leaving Selwyn Manor. Remembering how angry she had been at their last meeting, he had often regretted his uncharitable remarks about her family.

The viscount's musings were cut short by the appearance of his butler. "Mr. Fitzwalter is here to see you, m'lord."

"Do show him in, Weeks." A moment later, the Honorable Trenton Fitzwalter stepped through the doorway, appearing in his usual sartorial splendor. He was dressed in a well-tailored coat of dove gray and his snowy white neckcloth was tied in a simple yet elegant fashion. The ivory-colored pantaloons he wore fit his trim frame to perfection and his highly polished Hessian boots showed the diligent work of his valet.

Noting his friend's thoughtful expression and the card in his hand, Fitzwalter smiled. "A communication from one of your many lady loves, Tony?"

"Hardly, Fitz." The viscount handed Dick's calling card to Fitzwalter. Glancing down at the card, Fitzwalter burst into laughter.

"I cannot believe you still have our friend's card. Don't tell me you are reconsidering calling upon him?"

"I have no intention of seeing the fellow, but I am surprised you have not visited him, Fitz."

"Oh, I do intend to do so at first opportunity. I would very much like to see how he is using his inheritance."

"I do not doubt that he is squandering it like a drunken sailor."

"How like Sir Jarvis you sound, Tony!"

"Egad, don't insult me."

"I should never presume to do so. Indeed, the comparison with Sir Jarvis Selwyn was meant to be a compliment. I thought he had many admirable qualities."

"I should be most interested to hear you name one."

"I distinctly remember that our former host held his fork quite correctly at dinner." Both gentlemen burst into laughter and then Fitzwalter continued, "Well, my dear Tony, it is such a lovely spring day. The sun is brilliant, the sky azure, the trees budding out in green all over town, the larks melodiously singing . . ."

St. John groaned. "Good God, Fitz, you're not getting poetical again, are you?"

His friend smiled. "It is difficult not to, Tony, when one has a poetical soul such as mine. We should be out about town on such a day as this. We could take a ride in your new phaeton."

"I would very much like to, Fitz, but I fear I am expecting company. My stepmother and Lizzy have arrived in town and will be calling shortly. Stay and see them."

"My dear Tony, as much as I would so love to see your charming sister, I cringe at the prospect of seeing the fearsome Amanda. I hope you will excuse me."

"Very well, Fitz, but I note your cowardice. You had best go, because they may be here at any time."

"Thank you for the warning. But what about this evening? We could go to the theater. There is a new production of *Hamlet* at Drury Lane and the most enchanting creature is playing the fair Ophelia. Unfortunately, that so-called actor Humphrey Hamilton is playing Polonius. I've seen him in three other plays and he is simply abominable. I daresay, the true tragedy of tonight's play will be that fellow's acting." He paused. "Of course, on the other hand, it might be diverting to see a sword thrust through the fellow.

"But if tragedy does not suit you, we might go to Covent Garden instead. I am told that a rather amusing farce just opened there. Prinny reportedly laughed so hard during it that he split out a seam in his breeches. I fear it was rather embarrassing for HRH. They had to rush his tailor to the theater to . . . make the necessary repairs."

St. John laughed and Fitzwalter smiled. "Well, what do you say? The theater and then a late dinner and perhaps afterward a few games of cards at White's?"

"It sounds like an admirable plan, but I fear I am otherwise engaged."

"A romantic tête-à-tête I presume?"

"Certainly not. I am dining here with Amanda and Lizzy."

Fitzwalter looked disappointed. "Perhaps tomorrow then."

"That would be fine."

"Then I shall be off, Tony." He smiled. "Do give my love to Lizzy and my . . . kindest regards to Lady St. John."

The viscount smiled in return and his friend departed.

                            *   *   *

Lady Amanda St. John leaned back against the leather
seat of the carriage and frowned. How tiresome it was to
have to visit her stepson and how she wished she had not
made plans to dine with him. Of course, Lady St. John
knew her daughter Elizabeth was looking forward to it.
She directed a glance at that young lady, who was sitting
across from her and gazing out the carriage window. Indeed, since arriving in London a few days ago, this was
the first time her daughter seemed enthusiastic. But then
the girl was so devoted to her half-brother, reflected Lady
St. John irritably.

Continuing to watch Elizabeth, her ladyship wondered
how mother and daughter could be so different. A pretty
girl of eighteen with dark hair and blue eyes like her
brother, Elizabeth St. John was an independent spirit who
continually thwarted her mother's plans for her. She did
not enjoy society and was not eager for her second London
Season.

In contrast, Amanda St. John adored society, wanting
always to be in the thick of things. As a girl she had been
one of the most sought-after young ladies in town, with so
many suitors that it had been difficult to keep track of
them. She was also a great beauty, tall and statuesque with
a proud bearing. At the age of eight and thirty, her blond
hair and magnificent green eyes could still dazzle all manner of gentlemen.

It worried Lady St. John that her daughter had had such
little success her first Season. Whereas Lady St. John had
reveled in being surrounded by young men at parties and
balls, Elizabeth had seemed completely disinterested, dis-
couraging all but the most diligent of suitors.

"Look, Mama! It is Fitzwalter," said Lizzy, seeing that
gentleman walking down the street. "I shall call to him."

"You will do no such thing, Elizabeth. A lady does not
call out of carriage windows."

Lizzy turned to her mother with a disappointed look. "I
would like to see him."

"But I would not." Lady St. John looked out the
window and saw Fitzwalter sauntering away. "I have

never liked him and have never known what anyone sees in him.''

Lizzy made no reply, knowing very well that her mother's dislike of Fitzwalter stemmed from his being her brother's dearest friend. It was a constant source of unhappiness to her that her mother and her brother did not get along. Indeed, they quarreled incessantly and Lizzy often felt herself in the middle.

Lizzy thought of the last time she had seen her brother. He and her mother had exchanged bitter words and Tony had left Ramsgate in a rage. Although a subsequent letter from him had somewhat mollified Amanda, Lizzy had no illusions that their relationship would be more amicable.

''I know how much you look forward to seeing Anthony, but it is a pity we cannot spend this afternoon at Madame LeClerc's. You must have the final alterations on your gown for Lady Claverham's ball. There is so little time.''

''Oh, Mama, we can see Madame LeClerc at any time. Indeed, I do not know why this dress matters so much.''

Lady St. John looked horrified. ''I daresay, at this moment I can think of few things more important.''

Lizzy was about to disagree but she caught herself and remained silent. She did not want to provoke her mother and turned her attention back to the window.

It was not long before the carriage came to halt in front of the viscount's residence. A liveried servant hurried to assist Lady St. John and Lizzy down from the vehicle. They were met at the door by the butler, who quickly ushered them into the drawing room where St. John awaited them.

''Tony!'' Lizzy let out a delighted cry and hurried to throw her arms about her brother in an exuberant embrace. St. John returned her embrace and then stepped back and smiled affectionately down at her.

''Hello, Infant.'' Glancing over at his stepmother, all the warmth left his voice as he added, ''Amanda.''

''Anthony.'' Lady St. John eyed her stepson critically, but was disappointed when she could find no fault with his appearance. As usual, he was dressed in the height of fashion and his dark hair was neatly arranged in the Corinthian style.

Determined to be on his best behavior, St. John bade the ladies to be seated and then addressed his stepmother in a more civil tone. "I hope your journey back to town was not too tiring, Amanda."

Lady St. John shook her head. "The journey was quite unpleasant. The roads are in abominable condition and that mutton-headed driver of mine hit every bump."

"Oh, Mama," said Lizzy, "it was not so bad as that. The weather was very good and the scenery quite lovely."

Lady St. John regarded her daughter with a look of annoyance and continued, "Truly, I detest such journeys, but I am glad to be back in town at last. Life in the country is so tedious."

Neither St. John nor Lizzy replied to this remark and to break the ensuing silence, the viscount walked over to a desk and returned with a small gilt-edged book. "I have something for you, Lizzy."

"Oh, Tony, thank you," said Lizzy, taking the book eagerly from his hands. She looked at the cover and smiled. "It is a book of Mr. Wordsworth's poems."

St. John smiled. "I know he is a particular favorite of yours."

Lizzy lovingly turned the pages and then hugged her brother again. "It is a wonderful present." She handed the book to her mother. "Isn't it beautiful, Mama?"

Lady St. John barely glanced at the book and gave it back to her daughter. "You know I cannot abide poetry, Elizabeth. And I abhor poets."

"You didn't always abhor poets, Amanda," said the viscount with a slight smile. "I remember you once seemed quite fond of Byron. The unfortunate baron was forever showing up at your dinner parties."

Lady St. John shrugged. "Of course, he was at my dinner parties. Byron was all the rage then and one had to invite him. But I never cared for the man. And I don't think he is a fit subject for your sister's ears."

"Oh, Mama," said Lizzy in exasperation.

"And furthermore, Anthony, I don't think you should encourage your sister in her bad habits."

St. John lifted an eyebrow. "Bad habits?"

"This book reading! Good heavens, the girl always has her nose in a book. She will ruin her eyes and besides, gentlemen do not approve of bookish girls. Really, I would hope you would encourage your sister to care more about important matters. Why, just moments ago she acted as if her gown for Lady Claverham's ball was a matter of no consequence whatsoever."

The viscount directed a look of mock dismay at Lizzy. "I cannot believe it."

Lizzy laughed and Amanda frowned. "I know it is useless talking to the two of you, but mark my words, a girl who thinks so little of such things can scarcely be a success."

"Yes, I do not doubt it, for it is the empty-headed females who always seem to do the best in society," replied St. John.

Certain that the remark was intended for her, Lady St. John frowned. Lizzy hastened to change the subject. "I saw Fitzwalter walking down the street just before we arrived at your house. I do hope he will call on us. I so enjoyed his visit at Ramsgate." Realizing suddenly that this was a sore subject, Lizzy grew silent. To her relief, her mother switched to a more innocuous topic.

As Amanda St. John began to talk of Lady Claverham's ball, the first significant social event of the Season, her stepson tried to hide his boredom. He exchanged a glance with Lizzy and then, looking back at Amanda, he reflected it was going to be a very long evening.

7

"Camilla, my dear, good morning," Lucinda Selwyn greeted her niece cheerfully as Camilla entered the dining room.

"Good morning, Aunt," said Camilla, seating herself at the table beside Lucinda. "Did you sleep well?"

"I slept better than I have done for months, my dear. And to awaken to find oneself in a lovely room in such a splendid house in town is simply glorious. I must say, the prospect of a breakfast that might equal last night's dinner is most appealing. How different from Selwyn Manor fare."

Camilla nodded. "But I fear if we should eat so well every day, I shall grow exceedingly stout."

"Nonsense, my dear." At that moment the butler entered the room. "Do start serving breakfast, Baxter," said Lucinda.

The servant nodded and retreated.

"Isn't Dick joining us, Aunt Lucinda?"

"No. He has gone out already."

"Gone at this hour?" Camilla was rather surprised. Dick was not an early riser by nature, and she had expected him to keep town hours once on his own.

"He went to see his bootmaker," said Lucinda. "I do not fancy he will be gone long." Lucinda smiled. "He is doing so well, don't you think? Why, scarcely a fortnight in London and already he has become so very well acquainted with a gentleman like Sir Peregrine Mowbray."

Camilla decided it would be better to refrain from commenting on Sir Peregrine since Lucinda was so obviously charmed by the man. She changed the subject. "After breakfast, I would like to walk in the park. Do say you will come."

"That is a very good idea. One is most assuredly likely to be seen in the park, and we Selwyns must make it known that we are here. But we really do not have any-thing to wear."

"Aunt, I do not care at all about being seen. Indeed, I thought it would be good to take advantage of the weather and allow Rufus a bit of exercise."

"Rufus? You cannot think to take him? Oh, of course, you do." Lucinda frowned. "I do wish he was not so very large. If only he were a tiny spaniel or perhaps a pug, it would be very well to take him about town. Why, on our way here yesterday, I saw a lady with the dearest little white dog. It had a lovely violet ribbon about its neck that matched its mistress's pelisse. The effect was utterly charming."

"I do not think a ribbon about Rufus's neck would do at all," said Camilla with a smile.

"You are right, of course. Very well, we shall take your Rufus to the park directly after breakfast."

As it happened, it was not for some time that the two ladies and the wolfhound set out for the park. The early morning meal had been so very filling that Lucinda had declared a long wait was necessary before any form of exertion. Then, after finally declaring sufficient time had elapsed for proper digestion, Lucinda rustled about for some time bemoaning her lack of any acceptable attire.

Unlike her aunt, Camilla had no difficulty dressing for the park. Already attired in a pale green muslin dress, she slipped on a dark green spencer. Her friends had always admired the tiny jacket, thinking it quite stylish. However, Camilla did not doubt that, by London standards, it was probably not quite the thing. She placed her wide-brimmed leghorn hat atop her head and tied the ribbons beneath her chin. Then, calling for the wolfhound, she joined Lucinda in her room.

After assuring her aunt that she looked fine, Camilla attached a sturdy leather lead to the dog's collar. They then left the house, and as they walked along, Lucinda chatted gaily.

Camilla only partially listened to her aunt, so intent was she on the London scenery. Looking at the fashionable townhouses they were passing, Camilla reflected that it was exciting to be in town. Despite the fact that she preferred the country, Camilla had to admit that the city did make a welcome change.

It did not take long before they entered the park and Camilla smiled at the trees and vibrantly green grass. It was beautiful and there were few people about, a fact quickly noted by Lucinda, who was relieved that their unfashionable attire would go unnoticed.

They strolled for a good distance, pausing now and again to admire a flowering tree or neatly manicured hedge. They had walked for a time when Aunt Lucinda gratefully pointed toward a park bench. "Could we not rest for a few moments, my dear?"

"Yes, of course," said Camilla, and the two ladies sat down. Rufus directed a questioning look at his mistress, who commanded him to sit. The big hound did as he was told, and sat there, his nose twitching excitedly.

Camilla's aunt began to relate some of the adventures she had had when last in London some twenty-five years ago. Just as Lucinda was starting to describe her very first party, Rufus uttered a bark, jumped up, and darted off. Camilla, who did not have a very tight hold on the leash, found it quickly snatched from her grasp. She jumped to her feet as the big dog bounded off. "Rufus!" she shouted. "Rufus! Come back here!" Heedless of his mistress's commands, the wolfhound continued on. Camilla frowned as she espied a rabbit, the object of Rufus's pursuit. The terrified creature ran wildly as the dog strove to overtake his prey.

"Oh, dear," said Lucinda. "But he will come back. Do not fear."

Knowing the wolfhound could run for miles and worried that he might not find his way in such unfamiliar territory, Camilla shook her head. "Wait here, Aunt. I shall go after him." She then raced off.

Lucinda shook her head, thinking it most unseemly for her niece to be running across the park. She sighed and then thanked Providence that the park was so deserted that no one would observe Camilla's unladylike behavior.

Some distance away, a gentleman drove a stylish phaeton pulled by two magnificent black horses through the park. The Viscount St. John was accustomed to driving there at that time, and he seemed preoccupied with his thoughts as he held his spirited blacks to a decorous trot. The sound of a dog's bark made St. John look up and, seeing the enormous hound dart across the path ahead, he pulled the horses to an abrupt stop. Watching the wolfhound, the viscount was reminded of the large brindled creature he had seen at Selwyn Manor.

Moments later, Camilla Selwyn came into view. She was dashing across the grass with the long strides of a practiced runner, her straw hat flopping behind her. The viscount's eyebrows arched in surprise. "Good God!" he said aloud. "Camilla Selwyn!" A slight smile crossed St. John's face as he continued to watch Camilla's progress.

The dog raced after his quarry, skirting the banks of one of the picturesque ponds that dotted the park and vanishing from sight among the trees on the opposite side. Camilla reached the pond and stopped. "Rufus," she cried breathlessly. "Come back!" She stood at the edge of the water, leaning precariously forward to scan the trees for sight of the dog.

St. John turned to his groom, who was riding behind him. "Take the ribbons, Harry," he said. When the servant had done so, the viscount jumped down from the vehicle.

Camilla continued to look for Rufus, who suddenly appeared, barking furiously. "Rufus, come here!" Camilla waved her hand at the dog, who continued to bark and then run back and forth among the trees. She was so intent upon the noisy dog that she did not hear St. John coming up behind her.

"Miss Selwyn!" The viscount's voice startled Camilla, who, whirling around quickly, lost her balance and tumbled backward into the pond. She landed in the shallow water with a loud splash.

"Good God!" cried the viscount, rushing toward her.

"Lord St. John!" Camilla found herself staring up at him with a mixture of astonishment and horror.

"Take my hand," he said, planting his feet firmly and leaning down to her.

As St. John took her hand and helped her up onto the bank, Camilla knew that, without question, it was the most embarrassing moment of her life. There she was, dripping wet and muddy, standing in front of the immaculately dressed and deplorably handsome Viscount St. John.

"I am sorry," he said, taking her arm.

She pulled away and regarded him angrily. "It is your fault!"

Before the viscount could reply, there was another splash and both of them turned around to see Rufus. The big dog had jumped into the pond and was swimming rapidly toward them. "Rufus!" cried Camilla. "What are you doing!"

Reaching the other side, the wolfhound scrambled up out of the water. The dog shook himself furiously, flinging water all over both the viscount and Camilla. Then, to make his infamous conduct even worse, Rufus jumped up on the viscount, placing his enormous and exceedingly muddy front paws on St. John's shoulders. "Down, Rufus!" cried Camilla, rushing to grasp his collar and pull him down. "Oh, dear!" Holding her excited dog, Camilla looked at the viscount and noted the two muddy pawprints on his coat.

St. John glanced down at the unfortunate results of the wolfhound's affectionate greeting and then looked at Camilla. Expecting him to be angry, she was surprised when he smiled. "I deserved that," he said. "And worse yet. I am sorry. I should not have startled you."

"Indeed, you should not have done so," Camilla hastened to reply, but then she smiled. "I must look frightful."

"Well, Miss Selwyn," said St. John, eyeing her bedraggled appearance, "certainly, young ladies of society have been known to dampen their gowns, but it appears you have carried the fashion to the extreme.''

Camilla burst into laughter and St. John joined her. Happy that the humans seemed in far better moods, Rufus barked. Camilla turned to him. ''You must answer to me, my friend. If you had come when called, this would not have happened.''

The wolfhound cocked his head and regarded her quizzically, and they both laughed again. ''Put on my coat, Miss Selwyn, or you will catch a chill.'' Taking off the garment, St. John put it around her shoulders. She looked up at him and, for a brief moment, their eyes met, causing Camilla to experience a most unsettling sensation.

''That is kind of you, Lord St. John,'' she said, pulling the coat around her.

''I must get you home. My phaeton is nearby.''

They walked back to the carriage, Rufus trailing happily after them. The groom hopped down from the vehicle and opened the door. Camilla noted that the man was staring at her with considerable interest. This, she concluded, was not surprising, since he had doubtlessly witnessed all that had happened.

St. John handed her up into the phaeton and glanced over at the dog. ''And what shall we do with you, Rufus?'' said the viscount. ''Oh, very well, get in.''

''Are you sure?'' said Camilla. Rufus did not wait for the viscount's reply, but jumped up into the carriage and onto the seat opposite his mistress. ''We are ruining your upholstery, my lord.''

St. John shrugged as if this were a matter of no consequence and then got into the carriage. Pushing Rufus over, he made room for himself on the seat.

''My aunt Lucinda is waiting for me. She was sitting on a bench.''

''We will find her.'' The viscount turned to the groom. ''All right, Harry, let's go.''

The phaeton started off and Rufus looked well pleased at finding himself with such an advantageous view of the park. ''Miss Selwyn . . .'' St. John paused awkwardly. ''It has bothered me very much that I so offended you at

Selwyn Manor. I have thought of it many times since that day."

Camilla regarded him closely, surprised at his words. Indeed, she had been certain that he had not given her or Selwyn Manor one thought since leaving there. He continued, "I was very rude. I cannot expect you to accept my apology, but I offer it."

Suspecting the viscount was not one accustomed to making apologies, Camilla was favorably impressed by his apparent sincerity. "I do accept it." She smiled. "After all, you did help me out of the pond."

"After causing you to fall in."

Camilla nodded. "I suppose that does make the rescue less noble."

He laughed. "Perhaps we might start again, Miss Selwyn."

"I would like that."

"Camilla!" Lucinda's shrill voice interrupted them.

"Harry, stop." The phaeton pulled to a halt and Camilla waved to her aunt, who regarded her in alarm.

"Camilla, what has happened!" Lucinda recognized the viscount and regarded him in considerable surprise. "Lord St. John?"

"Miss Selwyn. I fear your niece has had a slight mishap. I shall escort you ladies home." He got out of the carriage and assisted Lucinda into it.

She sat down beside her niece. "You are soaking wet, Camilla!"

Looking a trifle sheepish, Camilla started to explain.

Dick Selwyn sat on the drawing room sofa, his legs sprawled out in front of him to better admire his new boots. The black Hessians shone brilliantly and Dick regarded them with a well-satisfied look. The sound of voices at the door made Dick spring to his feet. Camilla and his aunt were home! He started toward the entry hall, anxious to exhibit his new boots.

Lucinda, Camilla, and St. John met him at the entrance to the drawing room. The wolfhound followed closely behind them. "Oh, Dick," cried Lucinda. "Your poor sister had a misadventure in the park!"

"A misadventure? Good lord, Cam, you are all wet!"

"Excuse me," said Camilla, directing a smile at her brother's horrified expression. "I must change." She then hurried off.

"Good day, Selwyn," said the viscount.

"Lord St. John." Dick grinned happily at his guest and, although thinking his lordship a trifle tardy in returning his call, he was happy to see him. Dick did think it very odd, however, to see St. John standing there in his shirtsleeves.

"Oh, your sister has my coat," said the viscount, noting Dick's look.

"What happened to Camilla? She is not hurt?"

"Certainly not," said Lucinda. "She only fell in the pond."

"Fell in the pond?" Dick looked shocked.

"It is all the fault of that dog," said Lucinda. "You and your sister must make the animal mind better, I daresay. It was very fortunate that Lord St. John happened by to assist Camilla." Lucinda frowned at Rufus, who looked guiltily at her.

"That was good of you, my lord, helping my sister, although falling into ponds ain't typical of Cam, it seems to me."

"It was most unfortunate," said Lucinda, who, in truth, thought the incident most fortuitous in reacquainting the viscount with her niece. Lucinda had not failed to note the lack of animosity displayed by Camilla toward St. John and, indeed, there was something in the way his lordship looked at her niece that made Lucinda hopeful.

"Sit down, Lord St. John," said Dick, graciously ushering his guest to the sofa. "Come, Aunt Lucinda, do sit down." Rufus followed until a look from Dick stopped him. "Off with you," he said. "You've got into enough mischief, my lad. Go to the kitchen and have Cook find you a bone."

At the word "bone," Rufus wagged his tail and obligingly ran off. Dick waited for his aunt and the viscount to be seated and then sat down grandly in an armchair across from St. John. "It is good to see you again, sir."

"I trust you are enjoying your stay in town."

"I am very much, sir. I am having the best of times. I know Camilla and Aunt Lucinda will enjoy it, too, but they are just arrived from Selwyn Manor. Why, they came here only yesterday."

"It is so wonderful to be back in London," said Lucinda, but before she could begin any reminiscences, St. John hurried to speak.

"Is this not the former house of Buck Randall?"

"It is, indeed," said Dick proudly. "I expect you knew the gentleman."

"We were slightly acquainted," said St. John, looking about the drawing room and wondering how Dick Selwyn could afford such a place. The viscount knew that the young man's inheritance, although substantial, was hardly the sort of fortune needed to support such a grand way of life.

"I wish I had known Buck Randall," said Dick wistfully. "By all accounts he was a nonesuch." Dick pulled his gold snuffbox from his pocket. "This was his, you know. Care for a pinch?"

St. John declined politely and Dick continued, "Mowbray was a very good friend of Randall's."

"Mowbray?" St. John's dark eyebrows raised questioningly.

"Sir Peregrine Mowbray. He is a very good friend of mine. I believe you know him."

"I do," said his lordship. Since he detested Peregrine Mowbray more than any other man in the kingdom, the viscount made no further comment. At that moment, Camilla reappeared. She had changed her wet clothes and was now attired in the blue dress St. John remembered her wearing at Selwyn Manor. The viscount rose to his feet. "Miss Selwyn."

"I have your coat, my lord. One of the maids sponged it a bit and thinks it will be fine after it is dry."

St. John took the coat and put it on. "Yes, no harm

done whatsoever. I doubt the same can be said for your dress."

"Oh, don't worry about that," said Dick. "Cam is getting all new things. I will no longer have my sister going about like an impoverished governess."

St. John frowned at him. "Your sister would never be taken for that, I assure you, Selwyn," he said disapprovingly.

Camilla glanced over at him, flattered by the remark, and Dick hurried to reply, "Oh, I know that, of course."

"Indeed," said Lucinda, entering the conversation. "But Dick is right. I fear, Lord St. John, that both my niece and I have so few clothes. My brother kept a tight guard on his pursestrings, which hardly surprises you, my lord, I'm sure. A lady cannot go about town ill-dressed. That is why Camilla and I must hasten to have so many things made. But, my dear sir," Lucinda directed an incredulous look at St. John, "my niece is completely indifferent to such things. I must virtually force her to go to Madame LeClerc's."

"Aunt Lucinda, I pray you do not bore his lordship with these matters," said Camilla, hoping to divert her aunt from any further remarks about her meager wardrobe and unnatural indifference to fashion.

The viscount was, however, not in the least bored. It interested him that Miss Selwyn did not seem to care for new dresses. It was all very well for his sister to express such sentiments, for Lizzy was never without dozens of new things, all in the latest mode. Miss Selwyn, on the other hand, had been forced to make do with a few simple frocks. One would have expected her to be very quick to take advantage of her brother's fortune. Certainly, the majority of females of St. John's acquaintance were all too eager to spend all that they could at a fashionable modiste's.

Although it later surprised him, the viscount stayed unusually long at the Selwyns', enduring Aunt Lucinda's prattle and Dick's silly remarks. He had been strangely reluctant to depart, and once having taken his leave of the Selwyns, he allowed Harry to drive him home. During the ride back, St. John folded his arms in front of him and found himself reflecting about Camilla Selwyn. A smile appeared on his face at the picture of her emerging from the pond, embarrassed and angry. He remembered how her wet dress had clung to her excellent figure and then how she had finally smiled at him.

The viscount continued to ponder this for the rest of the way back to his townhouse. The groom, quite interested in his master's reflective state, thought of the young lady and smiled knowingly.

8

"Oh, Tony! It is beautiful!" exclaimed Lizzy St. John as she caught sight of the shiny black phaeton standing at the curb. "And what splendid horses." Lizzy held her brother's arm as they approached the vehicle.

The four spirited blacks harnessed to the carriage appeared impatient to be off. "I thought you would enjoy a ride," said the viscount.

Lizzy smiled at St. John. "Indeed, I would!" She directed a mischievous look at him. "I do hope you are going to allow me to take the ribbons."

"I value my life more dearly than that, Infant."

Lizzy laughed and her brother helped her up into the driver's seat. He then sprang up beside her and took the reins. After glancing back to see that the groom was ready to be off, the viscount whipped his horses and maneuvered the carriage out into the street. Soon they were traveling along at a spirited trot.

"Oh, this is such fun," said Lizzy. "And so much more diverting than going to the linen drapers, which is what Mama wanted me to do. Of course, Mama thinks going to the linen drapers is quite exciting." Lizzy sighed. "I fear I am a great disappointment to her."

"Nonsense."

"But I am. I know she wishes I were more like her."

"I thank God you are not," said St. John. "You are fine just the way you are, miss."

Lizzy smiled fondly at her brother and then turned to view the passing scenery. They continued on, chatting pleasantly and thoroughly enjoying the good weather. Driv-

ing through a residential neighborhood, St. John realized
he was nearing the street where the Selwyns lived.

"I don't think I have ever been on this street before,"
said Lizzy. "It is quite lovely here."

"The Selwyns live nearby. I told you about them."

"The Selwyns? You mean the family you stayed with
during the snowstorm?"

"Yes."

"Oh, I would so like to meet them. They sounded very
interesting. Why don't we call upon them?"

Thinking of Camilla, the viscount thought this idea most
agreeable but he feigned indifference. "If you wish to."

"Yes. Very much."

St. John turned his horses at the next intersection and
arrived shortly at the Selwyns' fashionable townhouse.
They were admitted by the butler, who was pleased to see
St. John return. He bowed obsequiously. "I shall inform
Miss Camilla you are here, my lord."

The servant had no sooner left the entry hall when there
was a thunderous bark and the wolfhound Rufus bounded
into view. Tail wagging furiously, he rushed up to the
viscount, who seemed quite glad to see him. "Rufus, old
fellow," he said, patting the enormous dog on the head.

"Oh, I am sorry." Camilla Selwyn smiled apologetically as she hastily appeared in the entry hall. "Rufus can
be such a nuisance."

St. John looked at Camilla and thought she looked
especially lovely. She was wearing a simple frock of pale
yellow muslin and her auburn curls were arranged in a
charming French style. As he gazed at her, the viscount
found himself thinking she had the most delightful smile
he had ever seen.

"Miss Selwyn." St. John nodded his head in polite
greeting.

"Lord St. John. It is so good of you to come. My Aunt
Lucinda and Dick are out and will be so disappointed to
hear that they have missed you." Camilla smiled at Lizzy
and looked to St. John for an introduction.

"Miss Selwyn, may I present my sister, Elizabeth St.
John? Lizzy, this is Miss Selwyn."

Camilla extended her hand to Lizzy. "I am so happy to meet you, Miss St. John."

"And I you," returned Lizzy.

Rufus barked and Lizzy laughed. "I am glad to meet you, too. Your name is Rufus, is it not?"

"It is indeed," said Camilla. "Oh, dear, how ramshackle of me to have you standing here in the entry hall. Do come in. I hope you can stay for tea."

Camilla led her visitors into the drawing room and they all sat down. Rufus promptly positioned himself in front of the viscount and sat there staring at him with adoring brown eyes. Camilla smiled. "Rufus is very fond of your brother, Miss St. John. Indeed, I have never seen him take so to anyone."

"Dogs love Tony," said Lizzy. "If only he had such an effect on humans."

"I caution you, Infant. You had best take care."

Camilla laughed and then rang for the servant to bring tea.

"My brother has told me, Miss Selwyn, how he and Mr. Fitzwalter were stranded in the snow and how your family gave them shelter. It was certainly fortunate that your house was so near."

"Indeed," said Camilla with a meaningful smile. "I know his lordship thought himself extremely lucky." St. John's eyes glimmered with amusement and Camilla continued, "Well, perhaps it is best not to speak of snowstorms on such a day as this."

Lizzy nodded. "You are right. We must enjoy the spring." She looked around the room. "Your house is lovely and so very modern."

"It is that," said Camilla. "Oh, I had nothing to do with the furnishings. My brother Dick may take credit for that, but in truth, it is a certain Mr. Buck Randall who is responsible."

"Buck Randall?" Lizzy's eyes grew wide. "Did he live here?"

"He did indeed," replied Camilla.

"That is very exciting." Lizzy turned to her brother. "You knew Mr. Randall, did you not, Tony?"

St. John nodded. "We were acquainted."

"But he was too wicked to be your friend, is that not true, Tony?"

The viscount smiled at his sister's words. "Mr. Randall was not precisely wicked. He was reckless and rather foolhardy. He had the misfortune to be addicted to gaming, and, although for many years he won a considerable fortune, luck finally deserted him."

"Poor man," said Lizzy.

They were interrupted by the butler. "A gentleman is here to see you, Miss Camilla."

Camilla regarded him in some surprise. "Another caller, Baxter?"

The butler nodded. "The gentleman requested that I give you this message, 'The dutiful knight wishes to see the princess.' " Baxter's expression showed that he found these words cryptic and rather annoying.

Camilla, however, appeared overjoyed. "Oh, do show him in immediately, Baxter." As the butler disappeared, Camilla turned to her guests. "It is a very dear friend. I have not seen him for several years."

St. John watched the doorway with keen interest. A gentleman appeared. He was a tall, handsome young man with red hair, who bore an expression of complete affability. He grinned broadly at Camilla.

"Princess Cam!"

"My dear Sir Charles!" Camilla hurried to greet her guest, who extended both his hands to her. "How I have missed you!"

"And I you!" he said, taking her hands in his and bending down to bestow a kiss upon her cheek. They then exchanged such affectionate looks that St. John frowned and wondered who this unwelcome gentleman might be.

"Perhaps I have come at a bad time," said the tall, red-haired man, glancing over at the viscount and Lizzy.

"You could never come at a bad time. Come, Charles, I must introduce you. Miss Elizabeth St. John and the Viscount St. John, may I present Charles MacNeil?"

St. John rose stiffly to his feet and extended his hand. "Sir Charles."

To his surprise, the other man laughed. "Oh, I am plain Mr. MacNeil, Lord St. John. I was only a knight in my childhood fancies."

"You see, my lord," explained Camilla, "Charles and I were children together and poor Charles was my true knight whose duty it was to rescue me from dragons and assorted villainy."

Charles MacNeil grinned. "But I think it was Camilla who did the rescuing most of the time. I was always getting into scrapes and the good princess would have to intercede with my father."

"We were very silly, I'm afraid. Now, of course, Charles is such a sober fellow. He is a solicitor, you see." She smiled at him again. "How good it is to see you looking so well and so prosperous. Do sit down. We were going to have tea."

"I cannot stay for long, I fear," said Charles, lowering himself into an armchair near Lizzy. "I have an appointment with a client."

"It must be so very interesting having a profession, Mr. MacNeil," said Lizzy.

MacNeil smiled at her. "It is at times, although many find the law dreary business indeed."

"I do not think it at all dreary. Why, I have only just read *Principles of Scottish Law* by Professor Cameron. I found it quite fascinating."

"Did you, Miss St. John? Good heavens, it appears you are a remarkable young lady. And do you think the Scottish legal system has any advantages?"

Lizzy found herself a bit surprised at MacNeil's reaction and his seemingly sincere interest in her opinion. "There are several things I might mention," said Lizzy, beginning a lengthy discourse. Finally realizing that she had not allowed anyone else to speak, Lizzy stopped. "Oh, dear, I am talking too much. I daresay, I am boring my brother and I am not allowing Miss Selwyn to speak to Mr. MacNeil. I know you must have many things to talk about."

Camilla smiled. "I certainly don't have anything to say that would interest Charles more."

St. John, while astonished at his sister's knowledge of the topic, was frightfully bored. He took the opportunity to change the subject. "You knew Miss Selwyn as a child, Mr. MacNeil?"

"Indeed I did, Lord St. John."

"Then your estate was near Miss Selwyn's home?"

MacNeil grinned at the question. "Estate? No, indeed, my lord. You see, my father was employed by Miss Selwyn's uncle, Sir Jarvis Selwyn, as butler."

The viscount looked startled for a moment. "I see," he said, adopting an expression of cool haughtiness.

"He was an excellent butler, I assure you, Lord St. John," said MacNeil, noting the viscount's reaction and suppressing a smile.

"Your father must be very proud of you," said Lizzy. "You have done so well for yourself."

"We are all very proud of Charles," said Camilla.

St. John found himself irritated by the ladies' admiration for MacNeil. He was irked by the man's audacity. Here he was the son of a servant acting the part of a gentleman.

Camilla looked from Charles to St. John and, noting the viscount's expression, she frowned. It was obvious that his lordship did not approve of Charles.

MacNeil rose from his chair and announced his intention to leave. "I really must go, Camilla. I shall come to tea another time. It was an honor to meet a lady of your perception, Miss St. John." He bowed slightly to the viscount. "Lord St. John."

"MacNeil," said the viscount coldly.

When he had gone, Lizzy turned to Camilla. "Mr. MacNeil is such a charming gentleman."

St. John raised his eyebrows. "One might say that if, indeed, one considered the son of a servant a gentleman."

The comment cast a pall on the conversation, but a distraction arrived as the servants entered with the refreshments. Camilla ignored the viscount's remark and poured the tea. "And have you been long interested in the law, Miss St. John?"

Lizzy nodded as she accepted her cup of tea. "Mama

thinks I am a frightful bluestocking, but I must confess a great interest in law and politics.''

St. John, who had hitherto been proud of his sister's unconventional accomplishments, found himself suddenly wishing that Lizzy limited her interests to embroidery and watercolor painting.

"How very clever of you, Miss St. John," said Camilla. "I confess most of my reading is confined to novels." She smiled. "I remember that as a girl, Charles thought me very silly reading the sort of things I did. Not that he did not read novels, too, but he read most everything in Uncle Jarvis's library as well. I remember that at a very young age, he debated with the vicar over all manner of subjects.''

Lizzy seemed clearly impressed by this information, but her brother only frowned. It seemed that this Charles MacNeil had had ideas above his station at a very early age. Indeed, thought St. John, MacNeil probably harbored unsuitably republican sentiments.

"I am very glad to have made Mr. MacNeil's acquaintance," said Lizzy. She turned to her brother. "And I do think him a nice gentleman, Tony. Perhaps he was not born a gentleman, but he certainly has become one.''

"One does not 'become' a gentleman, Lizzy," said the viscount sternly. "One is either born a gentleman or one is not a gentleman.''

Camilla was finding St. John quite insufferable and was reminded of her original opinion of him at Selwyn Manor. Perhaps it was rather a good deal to expect a nobleman to accept a man like Charles, but certainly St. John should have acted with far better grace. "I think if you had the opportunity to know Mr. MacNeil better, Lord St. John, you would better appreciate him. I only wish he might have stayed to tea.''

"And I assure you, Miss Selwyn, I have no wish to take tea with a man who is better suited to serving it.''

Camilla's brown eyes opened wide in astonishment. She set her tea down and rose from her chair. "Then I am so very glad that Charles did not stay. I would not have wished to subject you to such *lese majesty*, my lord.''

St. John rose to his feet. "I think we should take our leave of Miss Selwyn, Lizzy."

Lizzy looked apologetically at Camilla and then got up from her chair. St. John nodded curtly to Camilla and then led his sister from the room.

Once outside, he grimly helped Lizzy into the phaeton and, after ordering the groom to drive, he got in beside her. "Pouting is very unattractive, Lizzy," muttered the viscount as they started off.

"I am not pouting, Tony." She looked over at him. "It is just that you were quite horrid to Miss Selwyn. I did not think you capable of such rudeness."

"I just do not believe Miss Selwyn should have behaved so familiarly with an inferior."

"Oh, Tony," said Lizzy disgustedly, "you are so medieval. You are bad as Mama!"

"That will be enough, miss," said St. John testily, and they rode the rest of the way in silence.

9

Trenton Fitzwalter entered the Viscount St. John's house. He smiled languidly at the butler who admitted him and was promptly escorted to his lordship's sitting room. There he found the viscount sitting at an untidy writing desk, sifting through papers.

"My dear Tony, don't you have someone to do that sort of thing for you?"

"To do what, Fitz?"

"Whatever you are doing. It looks dashed tedious, old friend."

"That it is," muttered the viscount, not looking up. He studied one of the papers with a frown.

Fitzwalter regarded his friend quizzically. "Is something the matter, Tony?"

St. John glanced up and tossed the paper down disgustedly on the desk. "I've just received a letter concerning some property I purchased in Devonshire. It appears my solicitor has a few things to answer to me about."

"Indeed? Well, you mustn't worry yourself with such matters now, Tony. The weather is far too fine to be trapped inside. Let us leave this place at once."

"And where do you propose we go?"

"Why, I thought we might call upon young Selwyn."

"I have no intention of doing so," returned the viscount irritably.

"Come now, Tony, do be reasonable. After all, the Selwyns did rescue us from that storm, did they not? Surely, the least we can do is return Dick Selwyn's call."

The viscount frowned. "I have already visited the Selwyns and I have no desire to do so again."

Fitzwalter regarded his friend in astonishment. "You have already visited them?"

"Yes." At his friend's questioning look, he continued in explanation, "I met Miss Camilla Selwyn in the park a couple of days ago."

Fitzwalter raised an eyebrow. "You met Miss Selwyn in the park?"

"It was merely by chance, Fitz. And then, when I happened to mention the Selwyns to Lizzy yesterday, she insisted that we call upon them."

"And you didn't ask me to come with you?" Fitzwalter appeared hurt. "And what is worse is that you didn't even tell me about all of this last night, although we dined together and you had ample opportunity to do so."

"There was little worth mentioning."

"My dear Tony, I daresay, there must be a good deal worth mentioning for you to be in such an ill humor. Whatever happened?"

"Nothing happened. Oh, very well. Shortly after Lizzy and I arrived, Miss Selwyn had another visitor. A man named MacNeil."

"An old beau?" asked Fitzwalter.

St. John scowled. "An old childhood friend. Lizzy and I were very civil to him and then he had the temerity to admit the nature of his relationship to Miss Selwyn."

Fitzwalter eyed his friend with keen interest. "Do go on."

"He was the son of her uncle's butler!"

"And that is all? Truly, Tony, you disappoint me. I thought you were about to tell me something quite shocking."

"By my honor, Fitz, is it not shocking enough that a common fellow appears at a lady's door, greeting her like a long lost brother, I might add, and then very casually and without a trace of embarrassment announces that he is the son of a servant."

"He sounds like an audacious fellow, I'll be bound," said Fitzwalter with a smile.

"So you think this very funny?"

"My dear Tony, I cannot know what has so distressed you."

"I was accompanied by Lizzy, who seemed to find nothing wrong with talking to the man as if he were a proper gentleman."

"Good heavens, man. It is not as if he asked for her hand in marriage!" When St. John did not smile, Fitzwalter tried to suppress his amusement. "Well, I am heartily sorry that this bold fellow MacNeil so upset you. I had my heart set on seeing the Selwyns."

"There is nothing to prevent you from doing so. Just do not expect me to accompany you."

Fitzwalter regarded the viscount thoughtfully for a moment. "Then perhaps I shall go. You are in such a devilish mood, my dear friend, that I fear you would not be good company." Fitzwalter grinned. "Then excuse me, Tony. You will be dining at the club tomorrow?"

St. John nodded.

"Then I shall see you there." Fitzwalter turned and walked out, leaving the viscount to stare gloomily after him.

"Miss Selwyn, how very good to see you again."

Camilla smiled at Trenton Fitzwalter as he entered the parlor. "How nice of you to call, Mr. Fitzwalter." The wolfhound Rufus, who had been sleeping on the floor, looked up. Seeing Fitzwalter, the big animal put his head back down and went promptly to sleep again.

"I am glad that my arrival usually is met with more interest," remarked Fitzwalter. "I daresay, if I were St. John, the noble hound would be more enthused." Looking over to see Camilla's response at the mention of the viscount's name, Fitzwalter noted that a slight frown appeared on Camilla's fair countenance.

"Please do sit down," said Camilla and Fitzwalter obediently seated himself in an elegant chair. Camilla sat down on the sofa across from him. "My aunt Lucinda and Dick will be dreadfully disappointed that they missed you. I fear I do not expect either of them back very soon."

"That is unfortunate. I did wish to see them. But you must all come and call upon me soon."

"We would be most happy to do so."

"Good." Fitzwalter paused and took a pinch of snuff from his elegant enameled snuffbox. "So, tell me, Miss Selwyn, what do you think of London?"

"I have been here hardly long enough to have formed an opinion."

Fitzwalter smiled. "But you must have formed an opinion of London society?"

Camilla shook her head. "I have not had the opportunity, Mr. Fitzwalter. We know so few people here."

"Why, my dear Miss Selwyn, you know me and I daresay that is sufficient."

Camilla laughed. "I'm sure you're right."

Fitzwalter grinned and returned his snuffbox to his pocket. "I must see that you and your family receive some invitations immediately."

"That would be very kind, sir. My aunt was just lamenting how we were being ignored. Poor Aunt Lucinda thought we would be besieged by visitors upon our arrival."

"But you have not been totally devoid of callers. I am told you received my friend St. John and his sister Lizzy yesterday."

"Yes, that is true." Camilla frowned and hesitated. Finally she spoke. "Mr. Fitzwalter, I fear that Lord St. John was quite vexed with me."

"Vexed with you, ma'am? That hardly seems possible."

"I know that Lord St. John is a very good friend of yours, Mr. Fitzwalter, but sometimes he can be rather . . . trying. I do hope you won't be offended at my saying that."

"My dear lady, as St. John's friend, I am in a very good position to know that he is certainly trying at times." Fitzwalter smiled. "He told me about your Mr. MacNeil."

"Oh." Camilla shook her head. "I know that Charles—Mr. MacNeil—is not the sort of person with whom his lordship usually associates, but he is a good man. Surely, you would not have been so averse to speaking civilly with him."

"Certainly not," replied Fitzwalter, "though as Mr. MacNeil is undoubtedly a man of intelligence and discernment, he may have been averse to speaking civilly to me."

Camilla laughed. "I do wish you had been there."

"And so do I. But do not worry about St. John. He will come to his senses."

"I am not so sure. Why, he appeared quite upset to see Miss St. John speak pleasantly with Mr. MacNeil."

"Tony is very protective of his sister and I fear he was not at all pleased to discover that your Mr. MacNeil's background was not . . . illustrious." Fitzwalter stroked his chin thoughtfully. "There is something I must explain to you. Tony St. John sets great store on rank and fortune. His mother, you see, was the daughter of a tradesman."

Camilla looked astonished. "Lord St. John's mother?"

"Indeed. Oh, she was very rich, the only child of Nicholas Chandler."

"Nicholas Chandler? The man known as the textile king?"

"The very same. He was a man of little polish, but great natural cleverness. Myself, having an ancestry filled with dull Fitzwalters and even duller Ponsonbys, would welcome such a progenitor. However, Tony always considered his mother's family an embarrassment.

"But I hope you will not judge him too harshly, Miss Selwyn. From his early years, St. John has had his ignoble ancestry thrown in his face at every turn. Why, that gorgon, his stepmother, never fails to remind him of it. It has caused him to be very sensitive to such things. You may think him a dreadful snob, but I do hope you will understand."

Camilla pondered Fitzwalter's words in silence. So the grand and very proud viscount was ashamed of his ancestry? It seemed very odd that a man like St. John, the son of a war hero, who had wealth, rank, and position, would be so bothered by the fact that his grandfather had no noble blood. "Whatever his lordship's reasons, I cannot accept his rudeness concerning Mr. MacNeil."

"Tony is often rude. I think it has become a habit." Fitzwalter smiled and changed the subject. "Do tell me about your family, Miss Selwyn. I know your aunt must be very glad to be back in London.''

Camilla smiled. "Oh, yes, she is quite thrilled."

"And what of your brother Dick? As I recall, he was most eager to come to town. Has the great city lived up to his expectations?"

"It most certainly has. My brother is like a small boy left alone in a confectioner's shop. He cannot believe his good fortune."

Fitzwalter laughed. "I am glad he is enjoying himself."

"Oh yes, he is enjoying himself. He has fallen in with some new friends in town and is always flying off to go somewhere or another. This afternoon he went to a horse race with Sir Peregrine Mowbray."

Fitzwalter frowned. "Mowbray?"

Camilla did not fail to note the change in Fitzwalter's expression. "Do you know him?"

Fitzwalter hesitated. "Yes, and I fear I must warn you, Miss Selwyn, that Sir Peregrine Mowbray is a person who is best avoided."

Camilla regarded him with a concerned look. "Yes, I thought that the moment I met him."

"You have admirable judgment, Miss Selwyn. Mowbray is a detestable fellow. I do not wish to alarm you, but there have been other times that Mowbray has befriended young gentlemen of good fortune new to town. Such unfortunate gentlemen usually find themselves a good deal poorer in a short time. You see, Mowbray is a very clever fellow. He encourages his newfound friends to game away whatever they have, and, as he is a gamester of considerable skill, he is most times the beneficiary of his friend's ill luck."

"You mean that he schemes to take money away from young gentlemen?"

"That is precisely what I mean."

"Such conduct is infamous," said Camilla.

Fitzwalter nodded. "Mowbray is well known to me. We were at Eton together. He was one of the elder boys and a dreadful bully. He made my life completely miserable, having picked me out as his chief victim. That is how I met Anthony St. John."

Camilla regarded him with interest and he continued, "Tony was my senior by two years and far too august a personage to take notice of me. Although younger than Mowbray, he was well able to handle the fellow. Indeed, I think Tony was the only one who had no fear of the blackguard, and Mowbray hated him.

"Anyway, one day I incurred Mowbray's wrath and he set upon me furiously, beating me with a stick while his numerous hangers-on cheered. One of the other lads ran for Tony, who came at once." Fitzwalter grinned and there was a nostalgic gleam in his eye. "No famed pugilist could have taken Mowbray neater. Tony felled him with one blow, never even mussing his hair in the process, and Mowbray blubbered like a baby. It was a very great moment and I thought Anthony St. John even more a hero than his father. We have been friends ever since." Fitzwalter directed a meaningful look at Camilla. "He is a generous and noble fellow, despite how he may have appeared to you and MacNeil."

Before Camilla could reply, Fitzwalter rose hastily to his feet. "I must be off. Now, I insist you and your aunt and brother call upon me at first opportunity. Good day, Miss Selwyn."

When Fitzwalter had left, Camilla returned to the drawing room and sat down in a chair near her sleeping wolfhound. There she pondered Fitzwalter's words, thinking first of her brother and his unfortunate friendship with Mowbray, and then of St. John.

10

The following morning Anthony St. John scowled as he looked over the papers on his desk, and then glanced up as the butler entered the room. "Mr. Williamson to see you, my lord."

The viscount frowned at hearing the name of his solicitor. "I shall see him here, Weeks. Show him in."

A tall, distinguished man appeared and bowed politely to the viscount. "Good day to you, my lord."

His lordship acknowledged the greeting with a curt nod. "I wished to see you, Williamson, regarding your handling of my affairs."

Williamson regarded him with a worried expression. "Is something wrong, my lord?" St. John thrust a paper at the man, who took it and scanned it quickly. "I do not understand, my lord."

"You understand very well. Do not give me that calf look, sir, and tell me you know nothing of this. I recall you personally advising me to purchase this property. My man in Devonshire has informed me that the land is worth far less than what I paid for it."

"He is mistaken, my lord," replied the solicitor. "That was a very wise purchase and will turn a tidy profit for your lordship. If I may be so bold, my lord, my firm has long represented you, and if I may be a trifle immodest, we have done very well. Your esteemed father always had complete confidence in us."

"Well, I am not my esteemed father," said St. John coldly. "So my man is mistaken, is he? Is he also mistaken in telling me this property I so wisely purchased was in reality owned by a certain individual who, by coincidence, is married to your sister?''

Williamson drew himself up to his full height and looked boldly at the viscount. "If you are implying any impropriety, my lord, I must—"

"I am not implying, Williamson," said St. John, rising to his feet. "I am beyond that, I assure you. Do you take me for a simpleton, sir? I accuse you of feathering your nest at my expense, and, by God, I shall spare no effort to prove it. Now get out of my sight!''

Williamson quailed under St. John's glowering look and retreated hastily.

After he had gone, the viscount frowned and returned to his desk. "Solicitors," he muttered aloud. They were rascals, every one of them. Now he must find another solicitor and, doubtlessly, he would be a rogue as well.

St. John's thoughts turned quickly to another troublesome solicitor, Charles MacNeil. He shook his head, remembering the fellow's damnable familiarity with Camilla Selwyn.

St. John thought of Camilla and how her brown eyes sparkled when she smiled. He frowned again, knowing that she now considered him a preposterous snob. Even Fitzwalter seemed to share her opinion. The viscount looked thoughtful. Perhaps he had been overly proud.

St. John sat in rather dismal reflection for some time and then took up his quill pen and began to write a brief note. Completing the note, he rang for the butler, who arrived as he was blotting the words. "Weeks, this note must be delivered at once.''

"Very good, my lord." The servant bowed and left St. John, who continued to sit pensively at his desk for some time afterward.

Charles MacNeil escorted his client to the door and then returned to his desk. It had been a hectic morning and he had many more appointments scheduled. Charles had just begun to leaf through some papers when his clerk peered into the room. "A note for you, sir.''

"A note?''

"Aye, sir," returned the clerk, handing it to MacNeil. " 'Tis from Lord St. John."

"St. John?" MacNeil looked somewhat puzzled and opened the communication with great interest. It said, "Come at once. St. John."

The clerk, a lanky young man with pale blond hair, eyed MacNeil expectantly. To his great disappointment, that gentleman only folded the note and placed it in his pocket. "Is Sir Lawrence in, Rigby?"

"Aye, sir."

"Good." Charles hurried off, leaving his clerk dying of curiosity. MacNeil found his mentor, Sir Lawrence Neville, studying a page in a ponderous legal tome. "Excuse me, Sir Lawrence."

"Charles? Come in, lad." The older man smiled affectionately at MacNeil, whom he had come to regard as a son.

"I received a note, sir. It is from the Viscount St. John. He asks me to come at once to see him."

"Most curious, Charles. Do you know this gentleman?"

"I met him once just two days ago." Charles extracted the note and looked down at it. "It is very curt, with the tone of a royal summons." He smiled at Sir Lawrence. "From the look of St. John, he is well accustomed to giving commands. It would do him good if I ignored it."

"Would that be wise?"

"I doubt it. Indeed, with your permission, sir, I shall go immediately."

"Of course, of course. Lord St. John is a very important man. You must see what he wants of you. I shall be most interested to hear the result of your meeting with him."

Charles nodded, and after bidding farewell to his employer, he made his way to the viscount's townhouse. St. John's butler admitted him and quickly led him to the library. After informing Charles that his lordship would be there shortly, the servant retreated, leaving the solicitor to look about the room. As he admired its tasteful decor, Charles wondered what purpose St. John might have in sending for him.

A few minutes passed and then the viscount entered.

"MacNeil. Thank you for coming so promptly." He sat down in a chair and looked up at the solicitor. Charles, noting that the viscount did not ask him to be seated, stood there regarding his lordship with interest.

"You are probably wondering why I have asked you to come."

"I was, my lord."

"Miss Camilla Selwyn has spoken highly of you."

"That is very good of Miss Selwyn."

"I hope she is not mistaken in her estimation of your abilities."

"My lord?"

"I should like you and Sir Lawrence Neville to handle all my legal and financial affairs. I have dismissed my former solicitors."

Charles's face registered his surprise.

"I trust you will find such an arrangement acceptable," continued St. John.

"Indeed, I shall, my lord. Why, I should be the greatest muttonhead if I did not." Charles grinned, but seeing the viscount's tight-lipped expression, he quickly looked serious. "Sir Lawrence will be very pleased. We shall endeavor to do all that is possible to warrant your trust, my lord."

"I shall expect you in the morning at ten o'clock. There are a number of things I wish you to see to immediately. Good day to you, MacNeil."

Thus dismissed, Charles made a polite bow and left St. John. As the butler escorted him out, Charles could scarcely believe his good fortune. He was bringing his firm a new client who was not only one of the richest men in the kingdom, but a peer as well. It was rather perplexing, thought MacNeil as he stepped out the viscount's door. He had been quite certain the haughty lord had disliked him. When Charles had been introduced to St. John at Camilla's house, the viscount had been very remote, and, after learning that he was the son of the Selwyn's former butler, his lordship had been positively glacial. Charles shook his head and smiled, deciding that the ways of great nobles were most inscrutable.

As he started down the walk toward the street, a well-sprung vehicle pulled up at the curb. "Mr. MacNeil!"

Charles looked up to see a young lady waving to him from the carriage window. "Miss St. John!" He smiled broadly and lifted his tall beaver hat in greeting.

A liveried footman assisted Lizzy from the carriage as Charles approached. Lizzy was followed by an older woman, whom Charles judged to be a maid by her prim gray clothes.

"Oh, how good to see you again, Mr. MacNeil."

Realizing it must appear odd for him to be at her brother's house, Charles hastened to explain. "Lord St. John has asked Sir Lawrence Neville and me to represent him."

"Oh, how marvelous! You are to be my brother's solicitor!"

Charles nodded. "I am so very pleased. I shall do all I can to serve him well."

"Oh, I know you will, Mr. MacNeil." Lizzy would have liked to linger there on the walk talking to her brother's new solicitor, but her maid cleared her throat noisily. The servant was under strict orders from Amanda St. John to keep a close watch on the young lady. The dutiful woman thought it most unsuitable for Lizzy to stand there in public view talking to her brother's solicitor.

"It was very nice to see you," said Lizzy rather reluctantly. "Good day, Mr. MacNeil."

"Good day, Miss St. John." Charles lifted his hat again and the two women continued on to the viscount's door. Charles started on his way, but soon found himself glancing back at the very personable Miss St. John.

11

Camilla Selwyn sat at the writing table in the drawing room studying a pile of bills that had recently arrived. Her aunt Lucinda was seated on the sofa, intently scrutinizing a fashion magazine. After a time, Lucinda looked up. "Camilla, I have found the perfect ball gown for you."

Camilla did not look up from the bills. "We have not been invited to a ball, Aunt," she said.

"Yes, but you said Mr. Fitzwalter was going to see that we receive invitations. I do not doubt that very shortly we will be invited to a ball. Therefore, we must be prepared. We must see Madame LeClerc immediately about our ball gowns." Lucinda continued to discuss the merits of the dress illustrated in the magazine and, glancing over and noting that her niece did not seem to be attending, she frowned. "Camilla," she said sternly, "I should be glad if you listened to me when I spoke."

"Oh, I am sorry." Camilla looked apologetically at her aunt. "It is just that these bills are most distressing."

"Bills," muttered Lucinda. "I daresay it is most impudent of such persons to deliver bills so soon. Dick has scarcely been in town more than a fortnight and already we receive bills! It is quite ridiculous. But I do not wish to talk of such trivial matters.

"How I wish I had been home when Mr. Fitzwalter called yesterday. He is such a charming man. With his patronage we shall have no trouble succeeding in society. I must say, before Mr. Fitzwalter made his visit, I was beginning to grow worried at our lack of callers. Of course,

Lord St. John has been here twice and I know he will call again.''

"I have told you, Aunt, that you must not expect him. His lordship left here extremely vexed with me.''

"So you said, but surely you exaggerate. Indeed, perhaps we should call upon him ourselves.''

"Aunt!'' cried Camilla. "Certainly not!''

"Oh, very well. At least we may call upon Mr. Fitzwalter. You did tell me he invited us.''

"Yes, of course. We shall return his call very soon.''

Lucinda appeared encouraged, but seeing that her niece had once again turned her attention to the boring stack of bills, she rose from the sofa. "Do excuse me, my dear. I think I shall take a short rest.''

After her aunt had gone, Camilla continued to look over the communications from Dick's creditors. As she did so, her frown grew deeper. Certainly, he had spent more during his short stay in town than he had in the past several years at Selwyn Manor. Camilla knitted her brows in concentration. If Dick continued in this manner, he would squander his inheritance in a very short time.

Rising from the writing table, Camilla paced across the room. There must be some way to prevent him from doing so, she thought. After standing for a moment considering the matter, Camilla had an idea. "Charles,'' she said aloud. He was handling Dick's financial affairs. In all likelihood, Charles MacNeil could do something to stop Dick's lavish spending. Camilla nodded, deciding to see Charles immediately. Thus resolved, she left the drawing room and went to her room to fetch her bonnet.

The law clerk Rigby bade Camilla be seated and went off to tell Mr. MacNeil that he had a feminine visitor. Charles's store was rising rapidly in Rigby's eyes that day. Just that morning he had received a letter from the Viscount St. John and now a pretty young lady, who was so obviously quality, was there to see him.

Rigby smiled to himself. He had always liked and respected Mr. MacNeil, thinking him by far the cleverest and most able of all Sir Lawrence Neville's assistants. He

was also a good-natured gentleman who was never cross
like most of the others. And now the firm was buzzing
with the news that MacNeil had obtained Lord St. John,
one of the richest men in England, as a client. It was
certainly a feather in his cap, reflected Rigby.

The law clerk found MacNeil in Sir Neville's library,
intently scrutinizing a legal volume. "Mr. MacNeil, there
is a young lady to see you, sir. Her name is Miss Selwyn."

Rather surprised that Camilla had come to the law office, MacNeil closed his book. "I shall see her at once.
Show her in here, Rigby."

"Aye, sir." Rigby scurried off.

Moments later, Camilla appeared. "So this is where you
solicitors hide away." She glanced around at the book-
shelves crammed with heavy volumes. "I fear these books
look far less interesting than those at the lending library,
Charles."

He grinned. "Indeed not. They are fascinating, every
one of them. But to what do I owe the honor of your visit,
Princess?"

"I need your professional advice, Sir Charles."

"My advice? I shall give it gladly. Do sit down."
Charles motioned toward a heavy leather armchair and
Camilla was seated. Sitting down in the chair beside her,
Charles regarded her seriously. "Is there a problem?"

Camilla nodded. "It is Dick."

"I thought as much. You are worried about his spending?"

"How did you know?"

"I told him I considered it an unwise extravagance to
take the Randall house. He ignored me. Indeed, he made it
very clear that he would spend his money as he pleased."

"He has bought a carriage and horses and has tailors
and bootmakers working night and day. I fear that there
will be nothing left if he continues this way. Can you not
do something, Charles?"

The solicitor shook his head. "I am sorry, Camilla,
there is nothing I can do. The money is Dick's and he may
use it as he will. I only wish your grandfather had made
more provision for you."

Camilla sighed. "Uncle Jarvis said that Dick would

muddle away his fortune coming to town. I fear he is right.''

"Dick may still come to his senses," said Charles. "He is a colt feeling his oats for the first time. Once he has bought his new clothes and played the Corinthian for a time, he may be more sensible.''

"Charles, you have known my brother too long to believe that.''

The solicitor smiled. "When the opportunity arises, I shall endeavor to advise Dick to be more cautious. Whether he will listen to me is doubtful, however.''

"I would appreciate the attempt, Charles." She looked about the law library again. "I shall tell Uncle Jarvis how well you are doing when I write him. He will be so happy to hear how you have prospered.''

Charles grinned. "Fortune does seem to be with me, thanks to you, it seems.''

"To me?''

"It must have been your recommendation that made Lord St. John hire me as his solicitor. I had not thought I impressed him overmuch upon meeting him at your house.''

Camilla regarded him in surprise. "Lord St. John hired you as his solicitor?''

"Just this morning. I was quite astonished, I assure you. Sir Lawrence was absolutely delighted. A client like St. John does much to enhance the prestige of the firm.''

"I find this quite remarkable," said Camilla. "I am very glad for you, Charles.''

"Of course, he is a rather daunting personage. He summoned me to his house this morning and I felt as though I was in the presence of an absolute monarch. I wondered if I was expected to kneel.''

Camilla burst into laughter. "He is rather grand.''

"Grand? The Prince Regent might take lessons from him. However did you meet him?''

"It was quite by accident. You see, he was stranded in a snowstorm and took refuge at Selwyn Manor. I fear he was not the most congenial of houseguests.''

Charles laughed. "I can well imagine. But it was good of his lordship to call upon you in town.''

"I fear my reacquaintance with Lord St. John was also accidental," replied Camilla with a smile. "We met in the park. He provided me with assistance when I fell into the pond."

"You did what?" Charles regarded her incredulously.

She laughed. "I fell into the pond. Rufus had got away and I was chasing him and then I came to the pond. I did not hear St. John approach and when he spoke to me, I was so startled that I lost my balance and fell into the pond."

"Oh, lord, I wish I had seen it."

"Charles MacNeil! How could you want to witness my humiliation? It was quite mortifying."

"Well, I think it is very funny and it seems to have worked out well enough. You have a distinguished society caller and I have a lucrative, albeit, perhaps difficult, client."

Camilla smiled. "Well, Charles, I shall take no more of your time. I know you are a very busy man. You must call upon us again soon. Aunt Lucinda was quite upset that she missed your visit. She so wants to see you." Camilla then took her leave and departed from the law office. As she returned home, she wondered at St. John's behavior. How odd that he had hired Charles after making it so obvious that he disapproved of him. She looked thoughtful and decided that St. John was a most perplexing man.

12

Lord St. John and Fitzwalter sat in the dining room of White's, eyeing the dinner the waiter had placed before them. "I do believe we have the same abominable boiled fowl with the same abominable oyster sauce every time we dine here," said Fitzwalter. "We should have dined at Watier's."

"I think it is not bad by half," said the viscount, taking a bite of the boiled chicken.

"My dear Tony." Fitzwalter shook his head. "I had thought you a man of discernment."

St. John smiled. "The wine is good. Even you will not be able to fault it, Fitz."

"Of course, the wine is good. Indeed, it is always good and I always drink so much of it that my brain is too befuddled to win at hazard." Fitzwalter took a sip of wine and then put down his glass. "Well, I shall not drink one more drop."

St. John's eyebrows registered surprise. "Are you ill, Fitz?"

"Certainly not. It is only that I intend to remain as sober as a Methodist tonight. I plan to win a very respectable sum, and to do so I must have a clear head."

"My dear Fitz, you have never insisted on a clear head in the past."

"Well, I thought I might try it. One must be willing to attempt new things, after all."

St. John smiled at his friend and continued eating.

Fitzwalter looked unhappily at his plate and then put down his fork. "I must say, I enjoyed my visit with Miss

Selwyn yesterday afternoon. I wish you had come with me. We had a most stimulating conversation.''

Feigning indifference, the viscount took another bite of chicken. ''Unfortunately,'' continued Fitzwalter, ''Aunt Lucinda and young Dick were out. But Miss Selwyn is the most charming, unaffected young lady. I fancy she will be a great success in society.'' Noting that St. John was frowning slightly, Fitzwalter remarked, ''I hope you have got over your fit of pique, Tony. I know Miss Selwyn has forgiven you.''

The viscount regarded him with annoyance. ''You mean I was the subject of your conversation?''

''My dear Tony, you are often the subject of my conversation. Everyone wants to hear all about you.''

''I'm warning you, Fitz . . .''

Fitzwalter grinned at the viscount. ''Very well, I shall never say another word about you. Come, haven't you had enough of that dreadful dinner? I am most eager to try my luck.''

''Very well,'' replied the viscount, and the two friends got up and made their way to the gaming rooms.

Just as they started toward the hazard table, Fitzwalter stopped short. ''Tony! By my faith, there is Dick Selwyn! He is with that scoundrel Mowbray. Miss Selwyn told me her brother had formed a friendship with that blackguard.''

St. John looked across the room and immediately spotted the object of Fitzwalter's attention. Sitting at the hazard table was Dick Selwyn. He was dressed in flamboyant clothes and looked utterly ridiculous. It appeared to St. John that Dick Selwyn was also very drunk, for he was talking loudly and making a fool of himself.

''It appears our friend Dick is enjoying himself,'' said the viscount.

''As is Mowbray, I'll warrant. Whatever money the cub has, I do not doubt that Mowbray will see him shed of it within a fortnight.'' Fitzwalter frowned. ''We must do something, Tony.''

''Do something?''

Fitzwalter nodded. ''Although young Selwyn has a knack for wearing the most offensive garments I have ever seen, we cannot allow Mowbray the pleasure of ruining yet another unsuspecting country fellow. Look at him gloating.''

The viscount eyed Mowbray, noting that the obnoxious baronet seemed very pleased with things. Doubtlessly, he was winning handily, taking as much of Dick Selwyn's fortune as he could.

''You are right, Fitz. Let us greet our old friend.''

The two gentlemen walked over to where Dick and Mowbray were seated. ''By God!'' exclaimed St. John suddenly. ''Why, it is Selwyn! What deuced good luck finding you here!''

Dick Selwyn looked up and regarded the viscount with a dazed expression. ''Lord St. John?''

''Selwyn, old friend,'' cried Fitzwalter, taking St. John's cue. ''How marvelous to see you again.'' He snatched Dick's hand and shook it vigorously. A rather confused Dick Selwyn rose shakily to his feet.

''Mr. Fitzwalter?''

''Of course it is Fitzwalter. I was so disappointed yesterday when you weren't at home when I called.''

''Oh, Camilla told me you had come,'' began Dick.

''Really, gentlemen!'' cried a gray-haired man sitting next to Mowbray. ''We are engaged in a game here.''

''My dear Woodbury, you must excuse me. I have not seen my very good friend Mr. Selwyn for so very long.'' Fitzwalter patted Dick enthusiastically on the back. ''You must join us, Selwyn.''

Sir Peregrine Mowbray was watching Fitzwalter and St. John with obvious disapproval. He rose to his considerable height and glowered down at Fitzwalter. ''What poppy-cock is this, Fitzwalter? What are you about?''

''Whatever do you mean, Mowbray? Selwyn here is my very dear friend. Has he not told you how his family aided St. John and me during that frightful snowstorm? Come along, Selwyn. Bid these gentlemen farewell.''

''Just a moment, Fitzwalter. We are only just beginning.'' Mowbray directed a belligerent gaze at Fitzwalter, who tried hard to suppress the fear the massive baronet still engendered within him.

''And you will continue without Selwyn, Mowbray,''

said St. John, directing an icy look at him. Sir Peregrine appeared for a moment as if he was about to reply, but then turned away and sat down once again at the table. Fitzwalter lost no time in clasping Dick Selwyn firmly about the shoulders and leading him off.

As the three of them retreated across the gaming room, the gray-haired gentleman shook his head. "Damned odd, Fitzwalter and St. John taking that young cub up. I took Selwyn for an insignificant puppy."

"Then that would make three insignificant puppies," said Mowbray, bursting into laughter at what he thought was a fine example of his wit. The other gentleman laughed, too, and returned to their dice.

Camilla was awakened by the wolfhound's bark and looked through the darkened room to see Rufus standing eagerly at the door. "Rufus? Is something wrong?" The sound of voices caused Camilla to rise from her bed. After putting on her dressing gown, she went to the door and listened to a loud masculine voice she now recognized as her brother's.

Camilla frowned. Dick was returning home after another evening on the town and was probably going to wake up the entire household. He was almost certainly drunk and likely to be troublesome with the servants.

Hesitating for a moment, Camilla sighed and then opened her bedroom door. The wolfhound bounded down the corridor and Camilla followed. Angry at her brother, Camilla told herself to hold her temper. Arguing with Dick at such an hour would accomplish nothing. No, she would see him to bed and wait until morning to speak to him.

There was a light in the drawing room and Rufus let out a delighted bark and dashed inside. "Dick," said Camilla as she entered the drawing room, "it is late. Do come—" Camilla halted in midsentence, realizing for the first time that her brother was not alone. There with him were the Viscount St. John and Mr. Fitzwalter.

"Miss Selwyn." Fitzwalter smiled warmly at her. "We are bringing Dick home."

"Aye, Cam," cried Dick, throwing his arm around

Fitzwalter's shoulders. "Ain't it the best of luck? I found Fitzwalter and St. John at White's. They were so glad to see me."

Camilla reddened with embarrassment. She looked over at St. John and noted he was rubbing the wolfhound behind the ears, much to Rufus's delight. "Lord St. John."

"Miss Selwyn," said the viscount, his eyes meeting hers for a moment.

"I was telling Fitzwalter and St. John how much fun I've had since coming to town," said Dick thickly.

"Thank you for bringing my brother home, gentlemen," said Camilla. "I shall get one of the servants to help you, Dick."

"Help me?" Dick Selwyn grinned. "You don't think I'm drunk, do you, Cam?" He took a step toward her and stumbled, but was caught by Fitzwalter.

"Come on, my friend," said Fitzwalter. "I'll help you up to your room."

"There is no need," said Camilla. "I shall fetch a servant."

As if in answer to her wishes, an elderly servant appeared at the door. "Is everything all right, miss?"

"Yes, Martin. Do help Mr. Selwyn to bed."

Martin nodded and hurried over to Dick, who leaned heavily upon him. As it appeared that the elderly servant was about to collapse under Dick's considerable weight, Fitzwalter rushed to help. He and Martin then made their way out of the room, leaving Camilla standing there with St. John.

The viscount found himself staring at Camilla Selwyn and thinking that she looked very lovely standing there in her dressing gown, her auburn hair in charming disarray.

"It was very good of you to assist my brother, my lord."

St. John shrugged. "I was happy to do it."

Camilla paused. "Lord St. John, the last time we spoke we did not part amicably. I was upset with you about Mr. MacNeil. I know how much you disapproved of him. But today I spoke to Charles and learned you had hired him as your solicitor."

"I believe you think he is quite competent."

"He is, of course. I know you will be pleased with his work, but I would not have expected . . . indeed, I was quite amazed that you had hired him. Truly, it was most generous of you."

St. John smiled slightly. "I acted in a most ill-mannered fashion that day. I hope you will accept my apology."

"I do indeed, my lord," said Camilla softly. Their eyes met again with disquieting effect.

At that moment Fitzwalter appeared. "Dick is under his valet's care. You remember the fellow, Tony? Pierre something or other. He was Buck Randall's man. Poor Buck. You must send him some money, Tony. I would send him some myself, but I am a bit short of blunt at the moment." Fitzwalter grinned at Camilla and St. John, and realized from their expressions that he had interrupted them.

"Thank you, Mr. Fitzwalter," said Camilla.

"I am glad to be of service."

"I think we had better leave Miss Selwyn to her rest, Fitz. It is very late."

"It is late. We must be off," said Fitzwalter. "Good night, Miss Selwyn."

Fitzwalter and St. John then took their leave. Camilla sat down on the drawing room sofa and absently stroked Rufus, who was sitting beside her. It was not for some time that she returned to bed.

Before breakfast, Camilla wrote a dutiful letter to her uncle Jarvis. She thought it best to say little about Dick, and, instead, concentrated on trivial matters relating to life in town. As she sealed the letter, Camilla thought about Selwyn Manor and the countryside she loved so well.

Although she was a trifle homesick, Camilla realized that life in London had an undeniable attraction. She smiled, realizing that the attraction was the enigmatic viscount. She thought of St. John, remembering their meeting the night before.

"Camilla, my dear, there you are." Lucinda Selwyn entered the drawing room, interrupting her reflections.

"Good morning, Aunt. I have just finished a letter to Uncle Jarvis. I shall have Baxter post it at once."

Lucinda shook her head. "I cannot know what you think to write to my brother. I doubt he is interested in hearing about us."

"I am sure he would not want to hear about Dick," replied Camilla. "Oh, Aunt, I am worried about him."

"Worried about Dick? Whatever for?"

Camilla gave her aunt an exasperated look. "Aunt, you know very well. Last night he came home in a most embarrassing state of inebriation."

"You worry needlessly, my dear. All gentlemen drink a bit more than what is good for them. In Dick it is but youthful high spirits."

"I cannot excuse it so easily. Last night he quite disgraced himself. Lord St. John and Mr. Fitzwalter had to bring him home."

"St. John and Fitzwalter here last night? This is marvelous! Dick will go far with such friends."

Before Camilla could reply, her brother appeared in the doorway. "Good morning, Aunt Lucinda, Cam," he said cheerfully.

"Good morning, Nephew," said Lucinda. "You look very well." She glanced over at Camilla with a look that suggested her niece's worries were quite nonsensical.

"I feel very well, Aunt," returned Dick. "And I am deuced hungry."

"I am amazed you were able to get out of bed at all," said Camilla coolly. "And that you are hungry is remarkable, considering the state you were in when Lord St. John and Mr. Fitzwalter brought you home."

Dick ignored his sister's look of disapproval and grinned at his aunt. "Did you hear, Aunt? Last night I met those two gentlemen and they were so very glad to see me. And I remember back at Selwyn Manor, Camilla said they would want nothing to do with me." Dick smiled condescendingly at his sister for having such an absurd notion. "They were so happy to see me they insisted I go with them from White's. Jolly good company they were, too."

"Oh, Dick, weren't you ashamed for them to see you like that? You were drunk."

"Drunk? I was not. A bit tipsy perhaps, but far from drunk. And do you think St. John and Fitzwalter have never seen a fellow in his cups? They're gentlemen about town themselves and not averse to having a bit of fun, unlike a certain female relation of mine." He directed a meaningful glance at Camilla. "Don't think they had nothing to drink."

"Lord St. John and Mr. Fitzwalter were not in the sorry state you were in," said Camilla.

"That is only because they hold their liquor so well. I've need of more practice."

"You are certainly getting that." Camilla frowned at her brother and Aunt Lucinda hurried in to smooth over the situation.

"Come, come, my dears, I cannot bear to see the two of you quarreling. You are too hard on your brother, Camilla. I am sure you are exaggerating. Certainly, men like St. John and Fitzwalter would not have been so friendly with Dick if they found his behavior objectionable."

Dick nodded vigorously.

"Then you approve of Dick's spending his nights in notorious gaming establishments, Aunt Lucinda?"

"White's is hardly that," said Dick.

"Indeed not," said Lucinda. "It is very genteel. Only the cream of society are members. Why, that is why Dick met St. John and Fitzwalter there. Only men of their stamp are in attendance. You must make the most of your acquaintance with them, Nephew."

"I shall," said Dick. "Why, everyone speaks of them. Do you know that Fitzwalter's word is law in matters of fashion? The Prince Regent seeks his advice all the time. And St. John, why, he is known to be the best whip in town. And he is a crack gamester, too, as well as popular with the ladies." Dick grinned. "I'm told that Mrs. Darlington was one of his conquests."

"Mrs. Darlington?" said Camilla, trying to sound disinterested.

Dick looked surprised. "I thought everyone knew of

her. She is a famous actress and the most beautiful woman in all of London. St. John is a very lucky fellow.''

Camilla frowned, finding herself very much upset by the remark.

''Well, I think we should go to breakfast,'' said Lucinda. ''Come along, my dears.'' And the three of them departed for the dining room.

13

Lady Amanda St. John reclined wearily on the chaise lounge in her elegant drawing room. It had been a most trying afternoon, reflected her ladyship. She had just returned from the dressmaker's, where she had found her daughter's ball gown in a most unsatisfactory state. The modiste had trimmed the skirt with the wrong type of lace, and had had the audacity to balk at changing it.

What had made matters worse was Lizzy's expressing her opinion, in the presence of the dressmaker, that the improper lace would do very nicely. Perhaps it was not unattractive, conceded Amanda, but it was not what she had selected, and Lizzy would definitely not wear it to the Claverhams' ball.

Lady St. John shook her head, thinking of her daughter. Always headstrong, Lizzy was growing more outspoken. It was, reflected her ladyship, the fault of Lizzy's half brother. Amanda frowned as she thought of St. John. He encouraged her daughter's independent and unacceptable behavior, making Lizzy increasingly difficult to control. Lady St. John thought it most unfortunate that Lizzy and her half brother saw so much of each other.

"Mama, I do hope you are not still cross with me?" Lizzy St. John entered the room.

"And have I not reason, Elizabeth? How could you side with that obstinate woman?"

"I am sorry, Mama, but I did think the dress looked nicer the way Madame LeClerc had made it."

"That does not signify in the least. It was not the way I ordered it. Good heavens, the effrontery of that woman, trying to cover her mistake by claiming it was an improvement. I daresay, we shall take our business elsewhere in the future."

Lizzy thought it prudent to change the subject. "At least your dress was perfect. You looked so beautiful in it."

Somewhat mollified, Amanda smiled. "I must say, it was quite nice. I thought the seed pearls on the bodice most becoming. I shall be very glad to wear it to the ball. I can scarcely believe it is but a week away. I hope you are looking forward to it."

"Oh, Mama, you know I don't like balls."

"My dear Elizabeth, it is unnatural for a young girl not to like balls. And Lady Claverham's ball is always one of the very best."

Lizzy was spared the necessity of a reply by the appearance of their butler. "Your pardon, m'lady. Lord St. John is here."

Amanda frowned at her daughter's expression of delight. "Show him in," she said coolly, rising from her recumbent position on the chaise lounge.

When the viscount came in, Lizzy greeted him with an embrace. "Oh, Tony, I am so glad you're here."

"Good afternoon, Amanda," said St. John, looking over at his stepmother, and knowing very well she did not share Lizzy's opinion.

"Anthony, do sit down," said Lady St. John.

Lizzy led her brother to the sofa where they both sat down. "I was hoping you would come," said Lizzy. "Do tell me about Mr. MacNeil. You said yesterday that he was starting his work this morning."

St. John frowned slightly at his sister's interest, and before he could reply, Amanda cut in. "Who are you talking about? Who is this Mr. MacNeil? Is he the son of Baron MacNeil, the Countess of Haverhurst's Scottish cousin?"

"Hardly," said the viscount. "He is my new solicitor."

"Your solicitor?"

"He is a very nice gentleman, Mama."

Noting her daughter's unusual enthusiasm, she regarded St. John with interest. "Then which MacNeil is he?"

"His family is . . ." he paused, and looked over at Lizzy, "undistinguished. I must admit he is a capable fellow. After but a morning's work, he had a better grasp of my affairs than I do myself."

"I thought him most intelligent and well spoken," said Lizzy.

"And where did you meet this man, Elizabeth?" said Amanda, eyeing her daughter with suspicion.

"At the home of Miss Selwyn. I did tell you how Tony and I visited Miss Selwyn."

"I do not know if I approve of your calling upon people I do not know, Elizabeth. This Miss Selwyn is totally unknown, and that she entertains solicitors of undistinguished family is hardly in her favor."

"But I do like her. Indeed, I liked her immediately and felt that we should become very good friends."

"Her uncle is Sir Jarvis Selwyn," said the viscount. "Theirs is a very old family."

"They are provincial nobodies. I think it most unfortunate that you happened upon this family, Anthony. I do not doubt that they will try to take advantage of the connection, and I don't know why you encourage them." She directed a shrewd look at him. "I fancy the girl is very pretty."

St. John regarded his stepmother with irritation. "She is indeed pretty and entirely respectable. Do not fear that she is not fit company for Lizzy."

Lizzy looked knowingly at her brother. His hiring of MacNeil had made her suspect he had a *tendre* for Miss Selwyn and now his defense of her seemed to confirm it.

"Well, I do not wish to talk any more about her or this solicitor acquaintance of hers," said Amanda. "Before you arrived, we were speaking of the ball."

"What ball?" said the viscount, looking faintly bored.

"What ball indeed!" cried Amanda. "Why, Lady Claverham's ball, of course."

"Do not tell me that dreary event is coming again."

Lizzy laughed and Amanda glared at her stepson. "You know very well it is, Anthony. You are escorting us."

"Oh, yes. How could I have forgotten?"

"My dress is quite lovely, Tony," said Lizzy, "but Mama's is splendid. She will far outshadow everyone."

"Except my own daughter," said Amanda. "I must say that your sister will turn many heads, Anthony."

"Oh, Mama," said Lizzy.

"I daresay your mother is right, Infant," said the viscount.

"And the most distinguished young gentlemen in the land will be there. Only the most select company attend Lady Claverham's ball. For example, I fear that neither your respectable Miss Selwyn nor any of her family will appear there. Why, many would go to great lengths to obtain an invitation, but Lady Claverham is never swayed by pleas for admittance. Her standards are stringent, as well they should be."

St. John frowned, but said nothing. Instead, he resolved to obtain an invitation for the Selwyns at once.

"I do hope, Elizabeth," continued her ladyship, "that you will not discourage the gentlemen at the ball. Especially eligible young men like Lord Cushing or Lord Iverson. So many young ladies have set their caps for them."

"Then why should I add mine, Mama?"

Lady St. John frowned. "Lizzy, you will never find a husband with such an attitude. Why must you constantly reject such promising suitors?"

"Because I think them the greatest bores."

Amanda threw up her hands in exasperation and looked at St. John. "I don't know what I shall do with the girl."

"Come, Amanda, it is hardly so serious."

"Hardly so serious? If this attitude persists, Elizabeth will soon find herself on the shelf."

"Nonsense, Amanda," replied the viscount. "She is only eighteen."

"And I married your father at seventeen."

"I recall that very well, madam," said St. John, frowning.

"And I know well it was not an event to your liking," retorted Lady St. John.

The viscount checked himself. He had no desire to argue with his stepmother. "I must be going," he said. "I fear I have another appointment."

"But you have only just arrived," protested Lizzy.

"Do not pester your brother, Elizabeth," said Amanda. "He has many obligations. Good day, Anthony."

The viscount kissed Lizzy on the cheek and rose from the sofa. Then, after nodding curtly to Amanda, he departed. Once outside, he climbed into his carriage and instructed his driver to go to Lady Claverham's.

14

When Camilla returned to the house after a long walk with her wolfhound Rufus, she found her aunt in the drawing room. Lucinda was sitting at the desk, busily writing. "Aunt, I am back."

"Camilla, my dear." Lucinda glanced at the mantel clock. "Why, you have been gone more than an hour."

"It hardly seemed that long. The park was so lovely. I so enjoyed it."

"Well, I don't know if it is altogether a good idea, your walking about town unescorted."

"I am hardly unescorted. Rufus is with me."

The wolfhound, who was standing beside his mistress, barked.

"It is not the same thing at all," said Lucinda. Camilla was glad when her aunt did not pursue the matter. Instead, Lucinda began to talk excitedly. "While you were gone, we received two invitations. I cannot believe our sudden good fortune. One is for dinner with Sir Phillip and Lady Buckthorne. I met her once long ago, or so she writes me. I cannot quite recall the meeting, but then I met so many people my two Seasons in town. The other is from Mrs. Ashton-Smythe, a cousin of Mr. Fitzwalter." Lucinda smiled. "That dear man. We must thank him for arranging these invitations."

"Yes, it is good of him."

Lucinda nodded. "When one is new to town, a friend like Mr. Fitzwalter is so very useful."

The butler entered the room. "A letter has arrived,

ma'am," he said, approaching Lucinda and extending a silver salver to her.

Lucinda took the letter and eagerly broke the seal. "Whatever could this be? Oh, good heavens!"

"What is it?" Camilla looked alarmed. "Is something wrong?"

"No, indeed. Oh, my dear girl, this is simply marvelous! It is an invitation to the Claverhams' ball!"

"The Claverhams' ball?"

"Why, the Claverhams have given a ball for years. Even when I was last in town, the Claverhams' ball was the most talked about event of the early Season. Only the most elite members of society were invited, and I must say with regret, that I was not included. When I was a girl, I would have given anything to have gone! Oh, Camilla, it is a most wondrous thing being included. And look, a note from Lady Claverham apologizing for the tardiness of the invitation."

"But when is the ball?"

"On Thursday."

"Thursday? That is less than a week away. I don't see how we could have dresses prepared in so short a time."

"My dear, Camilla," said Lucinda, "there is nothing to worry about. Madame LeClerc has already started on ball gowns for both of us. I know you thought it too extravagant to have them made, but I suspected that we would get invited to a ball soon enough and ordered the dresses. How lucky that I did so. Mine is to be fashioned from the most striking pink satin. I left yours completely up to Madame's discretion."

Camilla regarded her aunt with surprise. "She is making me a dress I know nothing about?"

"Precisely. We have an appointment tomorrow for the first fitting. Everything will work out splendidly. Oh, Dick will be so excited. Indeed, I must go and tell him the good news immediately!" Grasping the invitation tightly, Lucinda hurried from the room.

Camilla sighed and sat down on the sofa. It seemed that Mr. Fitzwalter had done an admirable job obtaining invitations for them. Of course, the idea of entering society by attending an exclusive ball was a trifle daunting. After all, they knew so few people in town.

She thought suddenly of St. John and wondered if he would be in attendance. Deciding it was quite likely, Camilla began to view the ball in a different light. She wondered about the dress being made for her. Although at other times such things did not concern her overmuch, Camilla found herself a bit worried. What if the ball gown did not suit her? It was certainly a risky thing to leave such a matter entirely to someone else, even the renowned Madame LeClerc. Camilla frowned and wondered if she could bear to wait until the following day's fitting. Then, trying to put such thoughts of her ball dress aside, Camilla rose and, with Rufus at her heels, went up to her room.

As Camilla Selwyn gazed at her reflection in her dressing room mirror, she could not help but smile. The ball gown created by Madame LeClerc was simply stunning. Fashioned of apricot-colored silk and fancifully ornamented with satin bows of the same color, the dress showed Camilla's admirable figure to best advantage.

Looking from the dress to her hair, Camilla was well pleased. Mr. Carelli, the hairdresser, had arranged her auburn tresses in the latest mode, with short tight curls framing her face and the longer hair in back pulled up in a knot atop her head. The flattering hairstyle was adorned with a single apricot ribbon and the effect was utterly charming.

"Camilla!" Aunt Lucinda hurried into her niece's dressing room. "Oh dear, I was all prepared to wear my grandmother's ruby tonight, and now I do not know if it is quite the thing for the ball. What do you think?"

Camilla eyed her aunt with some misgivings, thinking the gown she was wearing most unsuitable. It was a startling shade of pink, and its low-cut bodice revealed a most indecorous expanse of Lucinda's ample bosom. The skirt and sleeves of the gown were embroidered with bold silver and black peacocks. Perched atop her aunt's head was a tall turban of matching pink satin, that wobbled precariously when she moved her head.

Camilla considered Lucinda's attire rather outlandish, and indeed, upon seeing the dress for the first time at the fitting, had ventured the opinion that it was a trifle daring. Lucinda, however, had dismissed Camilla's comments as sheer nonsense.

"I think your pearls might be better," suggested Camilla.

"My pearls? Yes, perhaps you are right. I shall fetch them. We are so very late, my dear. I hope your brother is ready. You go on downstairs, and I shall join you in a moment."

"Very well, Aunt." Camilla took up her gloves and fan and made her way down to the drawing room. There she found Dick sitting calmly on the sofa.

"Cam," he said, rising to his feet, "don't you look like a fairy princess? There will not be a lady at the ball who can approach you."

"You are kind, sir," said Camilla with a smile. Glancing at her brother's attire, Camilla feared that she could not return his compliments. Dick was dressed in a coat and knee breeches of violet satin and a bright yellow waistcoat. His shirt points were high and rigid, and his cravat was tied in an extraordinarily complex manner. It puffed out from beneath his chin like a monstrous white flower. Dick's hair curled wildly in an approximation of the Corinthian style, testifying to young Mr. Selwyn's perseverance in wearing his hair in tight curling papers all day and all night. Although the result of Dick's painstaking toilette was not altogether successful, he appeared very well pleased with himself.

"Oh, there is Aunt Lucinda now," said Camilla, nodding toward the doorway as Lucinda entered the drawing room.

Dick jumped to his feet and with a flourishing gesture put his quizzing glass to his eye. " 'Pon my honor, Aunt, that is a deuced splendid dress. You look quite striking!"

"Oh, my dear boy, that is sheer flummery," cried Lucinda, very much pleased. "And you do look handsome."

Dick acknowledged the compliment with a grin. "Won't we Selwyns amaze the company?"

"I do not doubt it," said Camilla with a slight smile.

Dick then escorted the ladies out to the carriage, and in a short time they found themselves entering the magnificent ballroom of Claverham House. As the herald announced them, Camilla experienced a thrill of excitement to find herself there among the cream of London society. She tried to adopt an expression of fashionable ennui as she surveyed the great throng of grandly dressed ladies and gentlemen.

They progressed through the crowd and Camilla looked about, trying to find a familiar face, and, in particular, the familiar face of Anthony St. John. "What a bang-up affair," said Dick as he escorted his aunt and sister into the midst of the crush of people.

"Oh, it is so wonderful," said Lucinda excitedly. "But I do wish we knew more of the company. I daresay, I do not see a single soul whom I recognize."

"Why, there is Fitzwalter! Over there." Dick nodded in one direction and Camilla espied Fitzwalter standing among a group of ladies and gentlemen. "Let us go and bid him hello."

"Dick, I do not know if we should presume so much on Mr. Fitzwalter's acquaintance."

Dick regarded his sister as if she were a silly schoolgirl. "Good heavens, Cam. One gets nowhere in society if one does not presume upon acquaintances. And Fitzwalter did get us the invitations. He will be very pleased to see us. Ah, he is looking this way."

Dick waved at Fitzwalter, who eyed him for a second before appearing to recognize young Mr. Selwyn. Fitzwalter then spoke a few words to the ladies and gentlemen surrounding him, and then he headed in their direction.

"You see, Cam, he is coming to greet us. He is a good fellow."

Camilla nodded and smiled as Fitzwalter approached.

"Dear ladies! Selwyn! How marvelous to see you here!"

Dick eyed Fitzwalter with interest, noting his well-fitting coat of black superfine. He found the leader of fashion's evening dress disappointingly plain, but charitably put such thoughts aside. "Good to see you, Fitzwalter," said Dick. "Is St. John here, too?"

"I have not seen him yet, but I know he is to be here."

"That is good," said Lucinda. "I shall be very glad to see another familiar face. I fear we know so few people."

"That will change very shortly," said Fitzwalter with a charming smile.

"Oh, I see Mowbray. Look, there he is!" Dick smiled broadly and Camilla glanced across the ballroom to see Sir Peregrine Mowbray talking to an elderly gentleman. "We must go directly over and see him," said Dick.

"Oh, yes," said Aunt Lucinda. "He is such a nice young man. I would so like to see him. Do you know Sir Peregrine, Mr. Fitzwalter?"

Fitzwalter glanced over at Camilla, who smiled knowingly at him. "I do, ma'am," he said.

"Then why don't we all go and greet him?"

"Aunt Lucinda, I think Mr. Fitzwalter would rather not. Indeed, I would rather not," said Camilla.

Lucinda looked disappointed and Fitzwalter hastened to reply, "Do not allow me to prevent you from speaking to Sir Peregrine, ma'am. Your niece and I will stay here and chat until you return."

"If you think that would be all right?" said Lucinda, looking over at her niece.

"I think it a splendid idea," said Camilla.

Dick, who was very eager to see Mowbray and a trifle irked at his sister for wishing to avoid him, nodded. "Come, Aunt." Lucinda took her nephew's arm and they walked off.

"Mowbray," muttered Fitzwalter. "How can anyone tolerate the fellow? It appears he has charmed your aunt."

"He has indeed. She thinks him a paragon."

Fitzwalter shook his head. "Poor lady."

Camilla smiled. "Well, let us not speak of him, Mr. Fitzwalter. I must thank you so very much for seeing that we received an invitation to the ball. My aunt was so very thrilled."

Fitzwalter regarded her in surprise. "I fear I cannot take

credit for doing so. Indeed, obtaining an invitation to the Claverhams' ball is beyond my abilities. Lady Claverham and I never got on well, you see. I daresay, if her ladyship had not felt compelled to invite me, she would not have done so. I thought perhaps your aunt was acquainted with our hostess.''

Camilla shook her head. "No, indeed not."

"Curious," said Fitzwalter. A sudden look of inspiration came to his face. "Of course, it must have been Tony's doing!"

"Lord St. John?"

"Lady Claverham was in love with his father, you know. Yes, it must have been Tony."

Camilla had barely enough time to register surprise when she heard the name St. John called out. She and Fitzwalter both turned to see the viscount enter the ballroom. On one arm was Lizzy St. John, looking very pretty in an ivory-colored gown. On the other arm was a tall stately blond woman of great beauty, dressed in a stunning green gown.

"I fear green is not the dowager viscountess's best color," sniffed Fitzwalter.

"That is Lord St. John's stepmother? Why, she is very beautiful."

Fitzwalter shrugged. "Some would say so, I suppose. Lizzy looks very well. She is becoming such a pretty girl."

"Yes," commented Camilla absently. She was not looking at the viscount's sister, however, so intent was she on St. John himself. He was so very handsome in his impeccable evening clothes, she thought. However, he did look rather formidable, for on his face was the look of hauteur she knew so well. His bearing was princely and as he passed through the crowd, St. John directed rather cool nods to those of his acquaintance.

"I shall never forgive Tony for being so tall," said Fitzwalter, as they watched the St. Johns stop to greet their host and hostess and then proceed on. When Lizzy spotted Camilla and Fitzwalter, she smiled brightly. Camilla smiled in return and watched Miss St. John address a few words to her brother, who then looked in her direction.

Camilla experienced a rather electrifying sensation as she met the viscount's gaze. She smiled at him and he smiled slightly in return. "Ah, good, here they come," said Fitzwalter. "I do warn you that Tony's stepmother is something of a gorgon." He had scarcely the opportunity to express this opinion when the St. Johns appeared before them. "Lady St. John," cried Fitzwalter, "How very charming you look."

"Fitzwalter," replied the dowager coolly.

"Oh, Miss Selwyn," said Lizzy. "I am so glad to see you. If I had known you would be here, I would have been far more eager to come." Ignoring the look of disapproval her mother directed at her, she continued, "Oh, might I make the introduction, Tony? Mama, this is Miss Selwyn. Miss Selwyn, may I present Lady St. John?"

The dowager viscountess nodded condescendingly and then directed an unabashedly appraising look at Camilla, who felt uncomfortable under such scrutiny. "How do you do, Miss Selwyn? My daughter has told me of meeting you. I have heard how my stepson and Fitzwalter came to meet your family. I believe your family's estate is not so very far from Ramsgate. We do not spend much time there, as I find the country so wearisome."

Camilla smiled slightly. "I know many do think it dull, Lady St. John, but I enjoy the country."

"You do?" replied Lady St. John with an expression that implied enjoying the country quite extraordinary.

"I, too, love the country," said Lizzy. "I am never bored there." She smiled. "In town, it is a very different matter."

Amanda St. John frowned, but she ignored her daughter's remark. "I expect you find society in town so very different, Miss Selwyn."

"I confess, Lady St. John, that I, thus far, have had few opportunities to find out. We have not been here very long and know so very few people. This ball is my first venture into society."

The dowager lifted her delicate eyebrows slightly. How

extraordinary, she thought, that this little nobody would be attending Lady Claverham's ball. Amanda eyed Camilla again, trying to find some fault with her appearance. Miss Selwyn did look pretty enough in the apricot gown, her ladyship grudgingly told herself. However, Amanda was able to take comfort in the fact that Camilla was unfashionably short.

"You are most fortunate to enter society at such an event, Miss Selwyn," said Amanda. "Everyone of significance is to be found here. The Prince Regent always attends."

"My dear Lady St. John," said Fitzwalter, "take care or Miss Selwyn may swoon in anticipation!"

Amanda's expression made it clear that she did not appreciate the remark, but the others burst into laughter.

"Fitzwalter is only joking, Mama," said Lizzy. "I think it quite thrilling to see His Royal Highness."

Not in the least placated, Lady St. John looked about the room. "There is Lady Pemberton. I have not seen her in so very long. And, Lizzy, there is Lord Iverson. How handsome he looks." The dowager's face suddenly expressed surprise. "Who are those persons talking to that dreadful Mowbray? That is the most vulgar woman! Her dress is the most horrid shade of pink and that hat is quite ridiculous. And look at the young jackanapes beside her! He is the most outrageous fop! However could Lady Claverham invite such persons here? I must find out who they are immediately."

"Amanda!" cried the viscount, recognizing the Selwyns beside Mowbray.

"What is the matter?" said Amanda, glancing over at him in surprise.

St. John directed an apologetic look at Camilla, who turned toward the dowager. "I shall tell you who those 'persons' are, Lady St. John. They are my aunt and brother. Do excuse me, I think it best if I join them."

She walked away abruptly, leaving Lady St. John to stare after her in astonishment. "Oh dear, you cannot mean that they are her relations?"

"They are indeed," muttered St. John.

"Oh, Mama," cried Lizzy. "Poor Miss Selwyn. How could you say such things about her family?"

"However was I to know that such creatures were members of her family? Why, the girl looked quite presentable herself. I could not expect her aunt and brother to look like that. Indeed, if one has relations such as those, one should be accustomed to receiving slights. Why, I think it was very rude to take offense and go stalking off like that."

"Confound it, Amanda," said St. John irritably, "first you insult Miss Selwyn and then call her rude for taking offense. In the future, I suggest you discover the identities of persons before you openly ridicule them."

"Am I to find out the identities of every absurd person before I open my mouth to express an opinion? If so, I would hardly be able to say a word."

"That would be an improvement," said the viscount.

Lady St. John glared at her stepson. "Come, Lizzy, let us leave the gentlemen. I so want to speak to the Duchess of Welton. There she is with her son Iverson and dear Lady Mary Cummings." Lizzy directed a long-suffering look at her brother and Fitzwalter, and then allowed her mother to lead her off.

"That woman," said St. John.

"Yes," said Fitzwalter. "Now Miss Selwyn is going to have to speak to Mowbray. Poor girl."

The viscount said nothing, but watched Camilla join her aunt, Dick, and the obnoxious baronet. He frowned.

St. John and Fitzwalter were then greeted by two gray-haired gentlemen, one a distinguished general, who had been well acquainted with the viscount's father. His lordship and Fitzwalter talked for some time to these gentlemen, although St. John's attention frequently wandered.

When the gentlemen finally left them, the viscount looked about the crowded ballroom for Camilla, but could not find her anywhere.

"Are you looking for someone?" asked Fitzwalter, knowing very well that his friend was trying to find Miss Selwyn.

"I just wondered if Lizzy was enjoying herself."

"Oh, of course," said Fitzwalter. "Well, if you wish to

ask whether I am enjoying myself, the answer is decidedly not. Although I think General Sir Christopher Richardson a charming fellow, I did not enjoy the recitation of his many accomplishments in the Peninsular campaign. By my faith! If that were not enough to endure, here comes my nephew Reginald and two of his dreadful young friends!''

Three young men approached the viscount and Fitzwalter. They were all very grandly dressed, and the eldest of them did not appear to be more than eighteen. "Uncle Trenton.'' One of the newcomers, a stocky, amiable looking youth smiled at Fitzwalter and then bowed slightly to the viscount. "Good evening, Lord St. John.'' The young man turned again to Fitzwalter. "Dashed fine ball, eh, Uncle?''

"Indeed,'' said Fitzwalter without enthusiasm.

Reginald did not let his uncle's attitude deter him. "I believe you have met my friends, Uncle Trenton. I should like to introduce them to Lord St. John.''

"Oh, very well,'' said Fitzwalter, "if his lordship can bear it.''

Receiving no protest from the viscount, Reginald Fitzwalter introduced his friends, who seemed quite awed to meet so illustrious a personage as St. John. They remained silent, allowing Reginald to do the talking. "I met a most curious fellow not long ago.'' Fitzwalter's nephew grinned. "He said he was a friend of yours, Uncle, and of his lordship's.'' Reginald raised his eyebrows, indicating he found this statement highly suspect, and continued, "He said you stayed with him in February during a snowstorm. I thought it must be bosh. He is a loutish, countrified person with the most damnable taste in clothes. I wonder that I was civil to such a bumpkin! I asked him who his tailor was so I could make sure to avoid the fellow.''

Reginald's two friends laughed, but stopped quickly when they noticed that neither Fitzwalter nor St. John were smiling. "Are you referring to Mr. Selwyn, perchance?'' said Fitzwalter.

"You do know him?'' Reginald looked startled.

"Of course I know him. He is a very good friend of

mine and Lord St. John's. We take it very ill, hearing a cub like yourself speak disparagingly of him.''

"But he looked so . . . common.''

"Common? My dear nephew, the Selwyns are a family so decidedly uncommon that they have hitherto found London society beneath them, and are only now condescending to mix with persons such as yourself.''

"Surely you are quizzing me, Uncle.''

"I assure you, I am completely serious. Be rude to Mr. Selwyn at your peril, Reginald.''

"I am sorry, Uncle Trenton.''

"Now, do go on, my boy. It was so nice speaking with you.''

Thus dismissed, the young men hastened off, looking very much chagrined. A slight smile appeared on the viscount's face. "Weren't you doing it a bit too brown, Fitz?''

"Indeed not, we must save the Selwyns from such calumny. It will be my mission for the Season. I do not doubt that that venomous stepmother of yours will also speak ill of them at every opportunity. No, I shall not have it! The Selwyns shall be extremely successful. My first course of action will be to ask the fair Camilla to dance with me.''

St. John looked at Fitzwalter as if he had not heard him correctly. "Fitz, you do not dance. Indeed, I have never seen you dance in all the years I have known you.''

"My dear Tony, the fact that you have never seen me dance does not mean that I cannot do so. Indeed, I dance very well. I shall claim Miss Selwyn for the first waltz. Pray excuse me.''

Fitzwalter rushed off, leaving the viscount quite dumbfounded. It was a fact well known in society that the fashionable Mr. Fitzwalter disdained dancing. Indeed, those young gentlemen who danced poorly often took comfort from the fact.

It was also well known that Mr. Fitzwalter was immune to the charms of the ladies of society, rebuffing the many who attempted to win him. However, Fitzwalter's interest in Miss Camilla Selwyn seemed to belie this assumption.

St. John frowned as he watched his friend disappear into the throng. The viscount was then joined by two worthy matrons and an elderly marquess and found himself trapped in conversation for a time. As soon as he heard the first strains of a waltz, however, he excused himself hastily and hurried toward the dancers. Foremost among them was Fitzwalter, and in his arms was Camilla Selwyn. St. John watched his friend skillfully lead Miss Selwyn about the dance floor and noted that the young lady was smiling and laughing at the undoubtedly droll comments Fitzwalter was making.

A good many of those in attendance viewed Fitzwalter in some surprise and the ballroom buzzed with remarks about his unusual behavior. They wondered at the identity of the lovely young woman in the apricot dress, and knowingly decided that Fitzwalter had finally succumbed to feminine charms.

St. John found the sight of Fitzwalter and Camilla waltzing together strangely irksome, and decided that his dearest friend was far too interested in the lady. It seemed that the music lasted an intolerably long time, and when it finally ended, he headed toward Fitzwalter and Camilla.

"Tony! What did you think? Did I do well enough?"

"Quite admirably, Fitz." St. John looked over at Camilla, who regarded him questioningly. "My friend Fitzwalter does not usually dance, Miss Selwyn. Indeed, I did not realize he could dance at all."

"Why, you dance so well, Mr. Fitzwalter."

"I pray you do not call me 'Mr. Fitzwalter'. I should prefer Trenton."

"Very well . . . Trenton, but you must likewise call me by my given name."

"I should like that very much, Camilla." Fitzwalter smiled at Camilla and St. John frowned, finding the new familiarity between his friend and Camilla most aggravating. "I do hope you will dance with me again," said Fitzwalter.

"Fitz, you have monopolized Miss Selwyn's attention too much. I think you might allow another man, such as myself, the pleasure of her company."

"Oh, very well," said Fitzwalter. "I shall not object, although it strains our friendship. I shall depart." He directed an exaggerated bow toward Camilla and left them.

"He is the nicest man," said Camilla.

"Yes, he is." St. John offered his arm to her. "Would you do me the honor, Miss Selwyn?"

Taking his arm, she looked up at him with a smile. "I should be happy to do so, Lord St. John." They started off together. "How kind of Trenton to dance with me," said Camilla. "I did not know he was breaking tradition by doing so. Oh dear, was everyone watching us?"

St. John nodded. "Of course, but that is very good. A young lady certainly wants to be watched."

"I don't know if I do, my lord." She glanced about as they took their place among the dancers. "Why, I believe people are still watching me."

"Indeed they are. You are the woman who has danced with Fitzwalter."

"Oh dear," said Camilla, smiling mischievously at St. John. "I am uncertain I can bear the honor."

The viscount smiled and as the music started, he took her hand and placed his other arm about her waist. Camilla found the viscount's proximity quite disconcerting, but tried to appear calm. They began to waltz and as she had expected, St. John was an expert dancer. Whirling about in his arms was the most delightful sensation and Camilla found herself hoping the music would never stop.

"Trenton said you were responsible for our invitations to the ball, my lord," said Camilla as they danced.

St. John looked down into her brown eyes. "I was very glad to do it."

"It was so awfully kind. I am so grateful. It means so much to my aunt and to Dick."

"I hoped you would enjoy it. I am sorry about my stepmother. You must ignore her."

Camilla smiled. "I shall try."

"I do hope she did not ruin your evening."

Camilla shook her head. "Indeed not, my lord. I am having the most wonderful time. First to dance with Mr.

Fitzwalter and now with you. I shall be the most envied lady here.''

He raised his eyebrows and Camilla laughed. "I am perfectly serious. You and Trenton are very august personages and I am very fortunate.''

"It is I who is fortunate," said St. John, smiling, and they continued waltzing, both of them aware of nothing but each other. They barely noticed when the music ended and experienced severe disappointment when they realized that the others had stopped.

The viscount would have liked to dance with Miss Selwyn for the rest of the evening, but the sudden clamor of gentlemen for her attention made this impossible. The fact that Fitzwalter had danced with the young lady made nearly every man at the ball wish to do so, too. Camilla was overwhelmed by eager gentlemen asking for the honor of her company, and she found it difficult to refuse any of them. St. John, not the sort to dangle after a young lady, retreated and spent the rest of the evening watching Camilla from a distance and wondering if he would ever forgive Fitzwalter for her newfound popularity.

15

The afternoon after the ball, Anthony St. John pulled his phaeton up to his stepmother's townhouse and, handing the reins to his groom, jumped nimbly down. He was not at all eager to see the dowager, but he had promised Lizzy he would call. Amanda's butler ushered him to the library, where he found his sister perusing a thick volume.

"Oh, Tony!" Lizzy hurried to put down her book and rushed to greet her brother. "I am so happy you have come! Sit down."

"And where is your mother?" asked St. John as he sat down.

"Oh, she is in her rooms. You know Mama, the afternoon after a ball is a time to rest. She is attending a party at Lady Hatfield's tonight."

"Are you going?"

"Oh, no. And I am very glad. I do detest parties."

"But didn't you enjoy the ball? I saw you dancing with several young gentlemen."

Lizzy shook her head. "I don't know, Tony. They all seem so very foolish. They can talk of nothing but horses and hunting and who is not speaking to whom. It is all so wearisome. But did you have a wonderful time?"

The viscount shrugged. "It was tolerable."

"But you danced with Miss Selwyn."

"I danced once with her. That was all I had opportunity to do."

Lizzy nodded. "All the young men swarmed about her. She was a great success. Mama says it is because of Fitzwalter, and she is so very vexed with him."

127

The viscount made no reply, but reflected that he, too, was rather vexed with his friend.

"I would so like to call on Miss Selwyn," said Lizzy. "Could we do so?"

"Call on Miss Selwyn?"

"Yes. Could we not go now?"

"I don't know, Infant. My stepmother would not approve."

Lizzy frowned. "I know, and therefore my only opportunity to call upon her is if I would go with you. Oh, do say yes, Tony. I had so little chance to talk with her last night and I think we could be such good friends."

"Oh, very well."

Lizzy looked overjoyed and hastened to fetch her wrap and bonnet. A short time later, they arrived at the Selwyn home. Waiting in front of the townhouse were two stylish carriages, one of which was emblazoned with a ducal coat of arms. "Look, Tony, I believe that is Iverson's carriage. I should say, it is his father's, the duke's."

St. John viewed the elegant equipage with disapproval. So young Iverson was calling upon Miss Selwyn? He eyed the other carriage with disapproval, wondering which other impudent cub was paying a visit to the Selwyns. The question was quickly resolved, for just as the viscount and his sister started toward the Selwyns' door, two gentlemen appeared. One was young Lord Iverson and the other Sir Peregrine Mowbray. St. John frowned darkly at the baronet.

The two gentlemen came down the walk and both lifted their hats to Lizzy. Mowbray ignored St. John and climbed into his carriage and was off. Iverson, a lanky young man in fashionable clothes, stopped to exchange a few words with them. Lizzy addressed a few polite but distant remarks to Iverson, who then took his leave.

St. John escorted Lizzy toward the door and, once there, glanced back to see Iverson get into his carriage and drive off. "We must not tell Mama that Iverson was here," said Lizzy. "She thinks him the perfect suitor for me and would be furious to know that he is calling upon Miss Selwyn."

"And are you not at all disappointed, Lizzy?"

"Disappointed?" Lizzy smiled. "Not at all. It is Mama who thinks George ideal for me. I most certainly do not. Why, I would prefer Mowbray to him."

"Lizzy!"

"Oh, I am quizzing you, Tony," said Lizzy, bursting into laughter. "Everyone knows Peregrine Mowbray is a despicable man. Surely Miss Selwyn could not like him?"

"Most assuredly not," said St. John. "The idea is quite preposterous. Mowbray is a friend of Miss Selwyn's brother. He was probably calling upon him."

The viscount knocked on the door and the butler admitted them and showed them into the drawing room where Camilla and Lucinda were sitting.

The viscount was greatly encouraged to see that Miss Selwyn seemed undeniably happy to see him. "Oh, do come in," she said, rising from her chair and smiling brightly at him. "I am so happy you have called." Camilla looked over at her aunt. "I don't believe you have met Miss St. John, Aunt. Miss St. John, may I present Miss Lucinda Selwyn."

"How do you do?" said Lizzy, smiling at Lucinda. She remembered the older woman from the ball and thought of the brilliant pink dress she had been wearing. Now Lucinda Selwyn was attired in a rather somber gray dress and was wearing a prim cap over her graying curls.

"Miss St. John, I am so happy to meet you. I only wish my nephew Dick had not gone out, for he would have been so very honored to make your acquaintance. Indeed, I was so disappointed to have missed you when you called before. Such a great pity. I did see you last night at the ball. You looked simply lovely! I do hope you had as wonderful a time as we did."

"Oh, it was very nice," said Lizzy, seating herself on the sofa beside Lucinda.

Camilla motioned for the viscount to be sit down and he did so, taking an armchair near her.

"Do you know Lord Iverson, Miss St. John?" said Lucinda. "He was just here."

"I am acquainted with him," replied Lizzy.

"He is such a charming young man," continued Lu-

cinda. "And the heir to a dukedom as well. And Sir
Peregrine Mowbray was here. I do so like that gentleman.
And Mr. Nigel Foxworthy and Sir John Rutherford."

Rather embarrassed by Lucinda's enumeration of the
callers, Camilla felt it necessary to explain. She looked at
John and Lizzy. "We have never before had so many
visitors."

"That is because you were a triumph last night, Miss
Selwyn," said Lizzy. "I'm certain everyone is talking
about it. You will be the most sought-after lady in town."

"I doubt that," said Camilla modestly. "And I do not
think I wish to be the most sought-after lady in town in
any case."

"You don't?" Lizzy smiled. "I thought I was the only
one who thought that way. My mother thinks I'm quite
odd because of it, but I do not see why it is so exceedingly
fine to have so many dull gentlemen dangling after one."

"My dear Miss St. John," cried Aunt Lucinda, "surely
not all the gentlemen are dull."

"Oh, no. My brother is not dull, or not usually, and
Fitzwalter is never dull."

"Lizzy, you are so very hard on my sex," said St.
John, smiling indulgently at his sister.

"I do not think I am so very hard. Miss Selwyn, Lord
Iverson was only just here—I'll wager I can tell you
precisely what you discussed."

Camilla smiled. "Very well, Miss St. John, what was
the topic of our conversation?"

"A bay horse named Calliope."

Camilla laughed. "I believe there was some mention of
Calliope."

"Well, I enjoy talking of horses," said Lucinda in
defense of Lord Iverson.

"But surely not incessantly, ma'am," said Lizzy
earnestly.

St. John exchanged an amused glance with Camilla.
"That reminds me of a roan stallion I once had."

"Tony!" cried Lizzy.

The viscount laughed.

"Well, I never thought the gentlemen I have met to be

so dull," said Lucinda. "Of course, I do know that there are many who do not think what one says is at all interesting, but how can one be interesting all the time? No, indeed, one must be glad that some conversation is quite stultifying for that gives one's brain an opportunity to rest."

Camilla glanced over at St. John, wondering if he was glad of the restful properties of her aunt's conversation. When, some time later, the viscount and his sister left them, Camilla suppressed a sigh as she and Lucinda once again sat down in the drawing room. The visit had seemed so short, she thought, and she had so hated to bid farewell to St. John and his sister. She was, Camilla realized, becoming dangerously fond of St. John. The memory of dancing with him at the ball came to her and she remembered his strong arm encircling her waist and the touch of his gloved hand on hers.

"Another gentleman?"

Her aunt's words brought Camilla out of her reverie and she looked over to see the butler Baxter. "Mr. Wilton-Lynes, ma'am."

"Oh, Aunt," said Camilla, "do we have to receive him?"

"We must be polite," said Lucinda, quite eager to see yet another prospective suitor. Camilla sighed and continued to think of St. John as the next guest entered.

16

After returning Lizzy to his stepmother's townhouse, St. John drove his stylish phaeton to Fitzwalter's residence. Although still a little put out with his friend, the viscount decided to pay a call.

St. John was admitted by Fitzwalter's manservant, a tall Indian dressed in picturesque native costume. While the viscount was accustomed to the man's exotic appearance, many thought Fitzwalter's servant most unconventional. "Good day, Akshay."

The Indian bowed. "Good day, my lord. I shall tell the master you are here." He led the viscount to the parlor and then, bowing again, retreated.

St. John looked about the room, and as usual was faintly amused at his friend's rather eccentric tastes. On the walls were painted Egyptian columns and all around there were enormous palms in brass pots. The furniture appeared to be more suitable to ancient Thebes than London and all about were peculiar artifacts from Africa and the Orient. The viscount eyed a stool in the shape of an elephant's foot and smiled.

"Tony, I had not expected you!"

St. John looked over at his friend and, noting he was attired in his Chinese silk dressing gown, the viscount nodded. "So I see. Don't tell me you were still in bed at this hour."

"My dear Tony, I was simply exhausted from the ball."

"It was probably the dancing."

"I believe it was," said Fitzwalter. "Now do sit down."
They were both seated and he continued, "Oh, I so en-

joyed last evening. Camilla is a charming dancing partner and such a lovely girl.'' Observing his friend's reaction, he suppressed a smile. "She was the success of the evening. Indeed, Camilla will be the most sought-after woman in town.''

Remembering seeing Iverson and Mowbray leaving the Selwyn house, St. John frowned.

Fitzwalter continued. "The ball was so amusing. Did you enjoy it?''

"It was like any other ball,'' said the viscount, affecting indifference.

Fitzwalter started to disagree, but was interrupted by the appearance of his servant. "Yes, Akshay?''

"Someone to see you, Mr. Fitzwalter.'' The Indian smiled in amusement. "It is Mr. Selwyn.''

"Our dear friend Dick! How fortuitous. Do show him in.'' The Indian bowed and left them and Fitzwalter looked over at the viscount. "I do not think Akshay approves of Mr. Selwyn's tailor.''

"Fitzwalter!'' Dick Selwyn entered the room. Seeing St. John, he smiled. "Why, St. John, you are here, too. What luck.''

"Indeed, my dear Selwyn,'' said Fitzwalter, rising from his chair and trying to hide the pain the sight of Dick caused him. Camilla's brother was dressed in his usual flamboyant style. His extravagantly cut striped coat and lavender waistcoat offended Fitzwalter's aesthetic sensibilities.

Dick shook Fitzwalter's hand vigorously and then directed a gaze at that gentleman's attire. "Bang-up dressing gown, Fitzwalter. I must get one just like it.''

St. John almost laughed at his friend's expression.

"Sit down, I pray you, Selwyn,'' said Fitzwalter politely.

Dick flipped the tails of his coat up and sat down on the Egyptian sofa. He glanced around him. "It is all very Chinese, isn't it, Fitzwalter?''

"Excessively Chinese,'' replied St. John, smiling over at his friend.

"I do like it,'' said Dick.

"I am relieved to hear it,'' said Fitzwalter.

"Interesting fellow, that servant of yours. Dashed odd hat he is wearing."

"He is an Indian and his turban is quite usual."

"Well, I hope they never become the fashion, for I fancy I would look deuced silly in one," said Dick.

St. John smiled, reflecting that Dick looked deuced silly in his present attire.

"And so, my dear Selwyn, did you enjoy the ball?" said Fitzwalter.

"I have not had so much fun since the Sibbley Dale fair."

Fitzwalter raised his eyebrows. "Then it appears you had a wonderful time."

"I did indeed. There were so many pretty ladies. I scarcely knew which to dance with next. If I may say so, some seemed quite taken with me."

St. John eyed Dick, wondering how Camilla Selwyn could have such a brother. Young Selwyn continued, "Of course, my sister was the true success of the evening. The gentlemen simply flocked about her. Oh, Cam had many suitors back at Selwyn Manor, but none to compare with these gentlemen. The way Lord Iverson looked at her, I should not be surprised if she were a duchess someday." Dick grinned. "My sister a duchess! That would be grand."

Fitzwalter glanced over at St. John, who was regarding Dick sourly. "Indeed it would," said Fitzwalter.

"It was a glorious evening for the Selwyns to be sure." Dick continued to talk about the ball. When that topic was exhausted, young Selwyn turned the discussion to fashion. "I say, Fitzwalter, I was wondering what you thought of my coat. My man Pierre thought the gold and lavender stripes very distinctive and the cut most exceptional."

"I fear, my dear Selwyn, that your man Pierre is clearly not a judge of coats."

"You mean you do not like it?"

"To be frank, no."

"But why?"

"Because, Selwyn, one must avoid frivolity in dress and that coat is extremely frivolous. Fashion is a serious affair."

"But this coat has caused a sensation. When I walked in the park with Sir Peregrine Mowbray, everyone looked in my direction."

"I do not doubt it. My dear sir, one does not want heads to turn as one passes by. Indeed, a well dressed gentleman never attracts attention. Be advised by me in this and change your tailor."

Dick seemed quite distressed by this remark. "I pray you are not offended. I gave precisely the same advice to the Prince Regent."

"You did?" replied Dick, somewhat heartened.

"Certainly, and Prinny was quick to take it, with most gratifying results. If you wish, Selwyn, I shall be happy to introduce you to my tailor and give you whatever assistance I might."

"That would be so good of you," said Dick eagerly.

"Then we will go this very afternoon. You will accompany us, of course, Tony?"

"I should like nothing better," said St. John ironically.

"Good. Then if you gentlemen will excuse me, I shall dress. I shall return shortly."

Once Fitzwalter had gone, the viscount turned to Dick. "Selwyn, there is something I want to tell you. You said that many turned to watch you when you walked with Mowbray in the park. I fear that it was your company and not your attire that was of interest."

"What do you mean?" said Dick.

"I mean that Sir Peregrine is a disreputable man. I am well acquainted with him and can tell you as a friend that it is wise to sever your connection with him."

"But he is the best of fellows. Why, I met him the first day I arrived in town. It is he who has shown me about. I am very much in his debt for doing so."

"You are better off without such a friend," said St. John sternly. "If you continue to hang about with Mowbray, you will have reason to regret it. There is no man in London more disliked, and with good reason."

Dick frowned. "I must ask you to say nothing further about Mowbray, sir. I do not enjoy hearing my friends maligned."

"I tell you this for your own good and also for the sake of your sister. The man is not to be trusted."

"I am no schoolboy and am well able to choose my own friends, St. John."

"Very well, I shall say no more about it," said the viscount. The two of them sat in silence until Fitzwalter returned and then they all set off for the tailor's.

17

The following morning, St. John paid an obligatory call on his late father's old friend General Sir Christopher Richardson. Since the elderly general was very long-winded, the viscount did not return home until early afternoon. His butler met him at the door. "Miss St. John is here, my lord."

"When did she arrive?"

"Nearly an hour ago. She is in the library, my lord." The butler paused. "With Mr. MacNeil."

"I see." A frown crossed his lordship's face. In the short time the solicitor had been employed, MacNeil had shown himself to be a diligent and clear-sighted young man. He had already made a number of astute observations about the viscount's financial affairs, and it had not taken St. John long to realize MacNeil was a man of uncommon ability.

In addition to his merits as a sagacious solicitor, MacNeil was an undeniably likeable man. Although showing, at all times, the proper deference to his lordship's rank, MacNeil exhibited none of the fawning obsequiousness that the viscount so disliked. Unlike St. John's former solicitors, MacNeil expressed his opinions openly and had no difficulty getting to the point of a matter.

Indeed, the viscount found his new solicitor admirable in many ways, thinking that had circumstances of birth and fortune been different, MacNeil was the sort of man he might have called friend. However, St. John's newfound respect for MacNeil did not prevent him from feeling rather irritated at the sight that greeted his eyes upon entering the library.

The solicitor was seated at his lordship's desk, his elbows propped on the desktop and his head resting on his hands. He was listening intently to Lizzy, who was sitting in an armchair on the other side of the desk, talking excitedly. They did not notice St. John's arrival, and, as Lizzy finished her remarks, MacNeil made a comment and they both burst into laughter.

"Lizzy." The sound of St. John's voice made MacNeil and Lizzy turn toward him in surprise.

"Tony!"

"My lord." The solicitor jumped to his feet.

Noting her brother's glowering look, Lizzy rose hastily. "Mr. MacNeil and I were having the most interesting conversation, Tony, about the new reform bill."

The viscount directed a skeptical look at MacNeil.

"Do not be cross with Mr. MacNeil. I fear I interrupted his work. It is my fault."

"I did get through most of these papers, my lord," said MacNeil. "I have written several notes, regarding some of your recent acquisitions."

"It looks very complicated," said Lizzy, smiling at her brother. "There are so many properties, it seems. I'll wager you have never even heard of the Sorcerer's Stones?"

St. John looked blankly at her.

Lizzy smiled. "I thought as much. It is at a place called Woodley Grange, one of your properties. Mr. MacNeil told me about it. Oh, do not think he is revealing your secrets to me. I saw the drawing on the desk." She turned to retrieve a paper from the desktop. "It looks like a very interesting place, don't you think?"

St. John glanced down at the paper and saw a faded drawing of a circle of rocks. It appeared to be some sort of ancient monument. "What the devil is this, MacNeil?"

"That is a stone circle, my lord, apparently of ancient and mysterious origin. I have listed Woodley Grange among your most unprofitable lands. The income from it has been far too small to warrant keeping it. I suggest you sell it, my lord, along with several other small holdings in the area.''

"Oh, no, Tony," cried Lizzy. "You could not part with such an intriguing place! How I should love to see it."

St. John handed the drawing back to his sister and was about to say that he had no interest whatsoever in such things, when the butler interrupted them. "Your pardon, my lord. Two ladies are here to see you, the Misses Selwyn."

The viscount brightened at this information and instructed his butler to bring them in at once. Directing a glance at her brother as the Selwyns walked into the library, Lizzy smiled knowingly. There was no mistaking St. John's keen interest in Miss Camilla Selwyn. Lizzy looked at Camilla, noting the way the attractive Miss Selwyn smiled at the viscount, and she realized that her brother's feelings for Miss Selwyn were clearly reciprocated.

"Ladies," said the viscount, nodding toward them.

"Lord St. John," said Camilla, "and Miss St. John." She smiled at MacNeil. "Good afternoon, Charles." Then turning to the viscount, she continued, "Oh dear, I expect my aunt and I have interrupted your business. Perhaps we have come at a bad time."

"Oh, no," said Lizzy, thinking their arrival most fortuitous. "We were just discussing a very odd thing." Still holding the drawing of the stone circle in her hand, she held it up. "The Sorcerer's Stones. It is very mysterious, don't you think?"

"My word," said Aunt Lucinda, taking up the paper and eyeing it. "It is very like that dreadful Stonehenge."

Charles laughed. "A good deal smaller, Miss Selwyn."

"I should hope so," murmured the viscount.

"Well, I do not like such heathen things," said Lucinda, passing the drawing to Camilla. "They are quite barbarous."

"Come now, Aunt," returned Camilla. "They are so very fascinating. One wonders how they came to be there and what sort of people put them there."

"Exactly," said Lizzy. "They are certainly enigmatical. I do love thinking about them."

"I assure you, Miss St. John," said Lucinda, "I think it ill advised to speculate on relics left by uncivilized pagans."

Camilla laughed and looked at St. John. "And what do you think, my lord?"

"I think these Sorcerer's Stones are a dashed nuisance. MacNeil informs me that they are on a property that should be sold."

"Is that not terrible that my brother wishes to sell such a remarkable property, Miss Selwyn?" said Lizzy, directing the question to Camilla.

Camilla nodded. "Horrible."

St. John smiled. "And so I am to keep a worthless piece of land simply because it is home to a few rocks?"

"Precisely," said Lizzy. They all laughed and she continued, "Could you not at least see the property before you sell it?"

The viscount shrugged and looked at MacNeil. "It is not far, my lord," said the solicitor. "It is just west of London."

"Why, we might visit it this afternoon," said Lizzy excitedly. "Oh, it would be such fun. We could have a picnic. Tony, you could have your cook prepare some refreshments. Oh, wouldn't you ladies so love to come?"

Lucinda, despite her apparent aversion to megalithic monuments, thought an excursion in the company of the St. Johns a splendid idea. "I'm sure it would be quite delightful, Miss St. John. How I would enjoy an outing to the country. The day is very fine."

"What do you think, Miss Selwyn?" Lizzy directed an eager look at Camilla.

"It does sound wonderful." Camilla glanced over at St. John, wondering what he thought of the idea. His handsome face bore no trace of emotion, effectively concealing his feelings about the matter.

"You could come, could you not, Mr. MacNeil?" said Lizzy, casting a hopeful glance at the solicitor. "I know my brother would want your opinion of the property."

"I could, Miss St. John." MacNeil looked over at the viscount. "If his lordship would wish me to do so."

St. John was not a man to be cajoled into anything, even

at the urging of his beloved sister. Although the viscount did not think it altogether wise to go dashing off at a moment's notice with three ladies and his solicitor, the prospect of taking a ride into the country with Camilla Selwyn was decidedly appealing. "Very well. We shall all go and see these stones for ourselves."

Lizzy clapped her hands, and then hurried to place a kiss on her brother's cheek. Camilla looked over at St. John and smiled, and the viscount had the distinct impression that he had made a very good decision.

The journey from London was entirely pleasant and all the company enjoyed it immensely. The viscount found that he was having such a wonderful time seated in the spacious traveling carriage across from Camilla Selwyn that he did not even mind that Charles MacNeil was perhaps a bit unmindful of his subordinate status. The amiable solicitor was an excellent conversationalist and he often had them laughing at his humorous stories.

The time passed so swiftly that the five passengers of the coach were all very much surprised to find they had arrived in the village near the viscount's property. After pausing briefly to ask directions, the travelers continued on.

A short time later, the carriage turned into a narrow lane and proceeded along a bumpy stretch of road through a thickly wooded area. Finally emerging from the trees, the equipage burst into the bright sunlight and Camilla had her first view of a country house set back in a grove of trees some distance away. It was not a grand residence, being smaller and in an even more lamentable state of disrepair than Selwyn Manor.

St. John stared at the house, having the strangest impression that he had seen it before and yet knowing that it was quite impossible. He wondered at the age of the house, noting that its prominent feature was a gothic tower built of stone. Although there was a sadness about the aged building, the viscount was very much drawn to it.

"Why, it is hardly better than a ruin," said Lucinda. "I shall tell my brother Jarvis that this is what will become of

Selwyn Manor if he does not devote more resources to its repair.''

The carriage pulled to a stop in front of the ancient house. The groom jumped down and opened the door and the travelers emerged from the vehicle.

"Is it not charming, Tony?" said Lizzy. Not waiting for a reply, she turned to MacNeil. "Do you know the age of the house, Mr. MacNeil?"

"I believe one document said it was built about 1390," said Charles. "I fear it has become uninhabited for many years."

"That is apparent," said Lucinda distastefully. She gestured toward the tangled mass of vines and weeds that covered the grounds. "I daresay I cannot bear to think what has become of the gardens."

"But it is perfect," said Lizzy enthusiastically. "Look at the wildflowers. You do like it, don't you, Tony?"

The viscount nodded. "I do like it, Infant, although I cannot say why. It is rather dreary."

"Oh, I don't think it is in the least bit dreary," said Lizzy. She turned to Camilla. "What do you think, Miss Selwyn?"

Camilla smiled. "I think it quite enchanting. Indeed, it is the sort of place one might expect to find a princess who has been asleep for a hundred years."

Lizzy laughed, but Lucinda frowned. "I daresay, the groundskeepers have been asleep far longer."

The others laughed and they all walked toward the old house. Arriving at the door, they found a tarnished door knocker in the shape of a wolf's head. "Oh, look," said Lizzy, smiling. "I do like this. It is so inviting. Let us go inside. It would be such an adventure."

Lucinda shook her head. "It would not surprise me if such a place were haunted."

Camilla laughed. "Oh, Aunt, the poor house is not in the least frightening."

"All of us have not your courage, Miss Selwyn," said the viscount, casting an ironical glance at her. "MacNeil, you have the key, I believe?"

"Yes, my lord." Charles MacNeil placed an enormous key into the lock and opened the door.

Although not at all enthusiastic about doing so, Lucinda accompanied the others inside. She was somewhat relieved to find the place well lit with sunlight streaming in through its many windows. The house was empty save for a few pieces of furniture hidden under dusty holland covers. Its gray stone walls were bare.

The five of them wandered about, looking in the various rooms. Of most interest was a very large chamber with an enormous fireplace in the center. While Lizzy, MacNeil, and Lucinda walked over to the window and looked out at the picturesque view, Camilla stood before the great hearth, thoughtfully considering it.

The viscount came up behind her. "Do you find something particularly fascinating about the fireplace, Miss Selwyn?"

Camilla smiled. "I am only thinking of all the fires kindled here in so many years and of all the inhabitants of this house. At Selwyn Manor I would so often look into the fire and think of all the others who had done the same. It is sad that no one lives here, that the embers of this fire have been cold so many years."

St. John nodded. "Well, perhaps if I do sell it, someone will wish to make it a home once again."

"Oh, I do hope so, my lord," she replied, gazing up at him.

Looking down at Camilla Selwyn's upturned face, the viscount had a sudden urge to kiss her very inviting lips. However, he quickly came to his senses at the sound of his sister's voice.

"Tony, let us go and see the tower. Mr. MacNeil says it is through here."

They made their way through a narrow corridor until they found a door. MacNeil pulled it open to reveal a winding staircase. He looked over at the viscount. "Shall we go up, my lord?"

"Oh, I would so like to," said Lizzy.

"Well, I shall stay here," said Lucinda, peering into the doorway. "I do not like the look of that overmuch."

The others were less faint-hearted, and they proceeded up a great many steps. At the top was a small room with narrow windows looking out in different directions. "How charming," said Lizzy. "One can see the entire countryside. There is the village." She then directed a remark to MacNeil and the two of them stood at one of the windows, pointing out various items of interest to each other.

St. John and Camilla positioned themselves on the other side, viewing the scenic surroundings. "How I would have loved to have had a place like this tower when I was a boy," said the viscount.

"My lord," said Camilla, her eyes widening in mock astonishment, "you cannot mean that you were once a boy!"

He smiled. "I was indeed. And an unruly one. I was the bane of many a tutor's existence."

A dimpled smile appeared on Camilla's face. "I expect you were, indeed."

Once again the viscount had a rather maddening urge to take Camilla Selwyn into his arms, but he restrained himself with admirable self-control.

"I wish you would come down," called Lucinda Selwyn, her voice echoing through the tower. "Are you all right?"

"I fear my poor aunt is getting worried," said Camilla. "We had best return to her."

"Oh, very well," said Lizzy, not at all eager to leave. "I fancy we must do so."

MacNeil started down first, followed closely by Miss St. John. Camilla took one last look out the window and then joined St. John, who was waiting for her at the stairs.

Just as they turned to go, a tiny mouse ran out and went scurrying across the floor. The creature so startled Camilla that she jumped and nearly lost her footing. The viscount caught her quickly in his arms. "Are you all right, Miss Selwyn?"

"Oh, yes, of course," said Camilla. For a moment he held her there. Their eyes met briefly and both experienced an undeniable spark of intense excitement.

"Is something wrong?" Lizzy called to them from down below.

"No," said St. John, releasing Camilla. "We are just starting down." They exchanged another glance and then proceeded down the winding staircase.

The food provided by St. John's cook was excellent, and eating it out of doors in the lovely bucolic setting made the meal especially delicious. The five adventurers sat upon the ground, conversing about the house and the notable view from the tower. Hearing it so highly praised, Lucinda rather regretted not climbing up herself.

After they finished eating, they continued to sit there, enjoying the fine weather. "I am so glad we came," said Lizzy, smiling at her brother. "Now that you have seen this place, I am sure you will not wish to part with it."

"But you haven't even seen the stones, Infant," returned the viscount. "Indeed, have you forgotten that that is the true purpose of our coming?"

"I had not forgotten," said Lizzy. "I do wish to see the Sorcerer's Stones. Where are we to find them?"

St. John looked over at MacNeil. "I hope you have some idea, MacNeil."

"I do, my lord. The directions were quite clear. Follow the path leading north of the house for a mile. There is a very large oak tree and the path veers eastward. One is supposed to be able to see the stones from there."

"Then we must go at once," said Lizzy.

"I fear I shall stay here," said Lucinda. "I daresay I could not walk a mile after such a repast as this. You young people go on."

"Then I shall stay with you, Aunt," said Camilla. Turning to the others, she continued, "Why don't you go ahead?"

"But, Camilla," said Charles MacNeil, "I know you are eager to see the monument. I shall be happy to stay with your aunt."

"How very kind of you, Charles," said Lucinda. "I would enjoy your company. Camilla, you go with his lordship and Miss St. John."

"Oh, I don't know," said Camilla uncertainly.

"Stuff and nonsense. I am glad of an opportunity to talk with dear Charles."

"Truly, I am happy to stay, Camilla," said MacNeil.

"Very well." Camilla rose from the ground. "Are you certain you don't mind my leaving you, Aunt Lucinda?"

"Don't be a goose, Camilla. Whyever would I mind, when I have a handsome gentleman to keep me company?"

Lizzy seemed suddenly less eager to go on the excursion, and, after her brother helped her to her feet, she hesitated. "I think I should prefer to stay, Tony. I am rather tired after climbing all those stairs."

The viscount regarded her in some surprise. "But, Lizzy, I thought you wanted to see these stones of yours so very badly."

"Oh, I shall see them another time, Tony. Why don't you and Miss Selwyn go? You can tell us all about them."

"Perhaps we should all stay," said Camilla, wanting more than anything to accompany St. John, but wondering at the wisdom of such a move. To go off with a gentleman unchaperoned, especially when one was undoubtedly in love with him, seemed rather foolhardy.

"Did you want to see the monument, Miss Selwyn?" The viscount looked at Camilla.

"Why, yes."

"Then we will go. Certainly someone should see the confounded things since we have come this far to do so. I am growing weary of discussing who will stay and who will go. Come, Miss Selwyn, we will return shortly." Camilla nodded and, taking the viscount's arm, she started down the path with him.

A worldly man, St. John was not the sort to be excited at the prospect of seeing a few old stones. And yet, Camilla Selwyn's enthusiasm was contagious. As they walked along, Camilla speculated about the mysterious monument and soon the viscount found that he, too, was looking forward to viewing the Sorcerer's Stones.

Before long, Camilla and St. John arrived at the place where the path veered sharply eastward and they stopped. "I don't see it," said the viscount, looking around. "MacNeil said the stones were visible from here."

"Perhaps those trees obscure the view, my lord," said Camilla, pointing toward a grove of young maples.

"Perhaps. Shall we go and see, Miss Selwyn?"

"Indeed, yes, Lord St. John."

They left the path and walked across a stretch of grassy pastureland toward the trees. "My lord, look! There it is!" Camilla stopped suddenly as the ancient megaliths came into view, and she gazed at them with a sense of wonder. Seven of the stones were still standing, arranged in a great circle. The others lay scattered about the ground as if idly tossed there by giants.

St. John eyed the monument, surprised at the size of the stones. There were perhaps fifteen of them, each at least eight feet long and each weighing many tons. "However could such stones have been moved here?"

"There is but one explanation, my lord," said Camilla. When St. John looked over at her for enlightenment, she smiled mischievously. "Sorcery."

"Of course," replied the viscount, smiling in return. "It is the only logical explanation. Were I more clever, I might have guessed it from the clue provided by the name of the place." Camilla laughed and St. John continued, "Now shall we venture on and see it at close hand, or are we too much in danger from wizards?"

"I am willing to take the risk, my lord," said Camilla, her eyes twinkling with amusement.

He offered her his arm and they continued on. Reaching the ancient stones, they spent much time wandering about them, viewing the monument from various angles. Finally, they both sat down on one of the fallen slabs of gray sandstone. "This is a magical place." She smiled over at him. "I do wish your sister had come with us."

The viscount gazed into her eyes. "I find myself very glad that she did not do so, Miss Selwyn." St. John reached over and, taking her hand, brought it to his lips. Camilla found herself trembling at his touch. Her enormous brown eyes regarded him questioningly as he lowered her hand and then leaned toward her.

"Don't move! I pray you!"

Both St. John and Camilla started, and, turning toward

the voice, found a stout, red-faced gentleman brandishing a strange looking net at them. "Don't move!" he repeated in a loud stage whisper. "It is a Nymphalis antiopa!"

"Good God, are you mad!" St. John leaped up from his seat on the stone and faced the intruder, an expression of fury on his face. "How dare you, sir!"

The stout man did not seem in any way daunted by his lordship's anger. "Gone! It is gone! A Nymphalis antiopa!"

Camilla was, by this time, convinced that this most unwelcome stranger had, indeed, lost his senses. "Whatever are you talking about, sir?" she said.

"The butterfly, of course!" He regarded her as if she were the greatest goosecap, and then he looked wistfully at the fluttering object that was darting away. "I do not have one, you see. If only you had not moved."

St. John glowered at the man and cursed inwardly. Of all times for the fellow to show up, he thought. "Oh, well," continued the stranger, "perhaps it is not your fault. You must forgive me. I do forget myself when in pursuit of my quarry. Yes, I do hope you will forgive me."

The viscount looked as though he had no intention of doing so, but Camilla smiled charitably. "Perhaps you will find another one."

"Alas, madam, I fear that is not so very likely. They are a rare and elusive species."

Camilla found herself smiling in spite of herself, for the stout man was certainly a comical gentleman. A man of perhaps fifty years, he was dressed like a country squire save for an unlikely looking felt hat and a strange canvas pack carried over his shoulder. He wore spectacles on his round, ruddy face and had a tendency to squint.

"I suggest you search elsewhere for your damned butterflies," muttered the viscount irritably.

"Lord St. John!" cried Camilla. "I know the gentleman meant no harm."

"Did you say Lord St. John?" cried the stout man.

Camilla nodded and regretted her mention of the viscount's name. His lordship regarded the older man ill humoredly and waited for the inevitable allusion to his esteemed father.

"Then you must be Helena Chandler's son. Indeed, you are very like her."

The reference to his mother caught the viscount off guard. "You knew my mother?"

"Very well, sir. My name is Percival Chandler and I am your mother's cousin. My father was your grandfather's younger brother. What good fortune to meet you. I would never have expected to find you here."

"This is my property," said St. John coolly. He eyed his newfound relative with disapproval, thinking his avoidance of his maternal relations quite prudent.

"Of course! How silly of me to have forgotten. Your grandfather bought this property. He was so very fond of the Sorcerer's Stones and the old grange. I do think he intended to restore it and reside there, and he would have done so if his mills had not kept him so occupied.

"When I was a boy, your mother would often come to visit us, and she always wanted to see the Sorcerer's Stones. Yes, Helena was so very fond of this place."

The viscount looked thoughtfully at the stones, envisioning his mother as a young girl. So this had been his grandfather's property and his mother had loved it? Perhaps that was why he felt such an affinity for it.

"But I cannot say how delighted I am to finally meet you, my dear cousin." He grinned and then tipped his hat to Camilla. "And this young lady?"

"This is Miss Selwyn," said the viscount.

"Delighted, Miss Selwyn," said Percival Chandler. "Now, you must both come and meet my family. My home is nearby and my dear wife would not forgive me if I did not bring you to meet her."

"We are expected back," said the viscount.

Chandler appeared crestfallen. He looked at Camilla. "I implore you, Miss Selwyn, to use your influence to persuade my cousin to come."

Camilla glanced over at St. John. She was rather interested in meeting these relations of his and hoped he would change his mind. "Do you not think there would be time for a short visit, my lord?"

He smiled at her. "Yes, you are right." The viscount turned to Chandler. "We will be happy to meet your wife."

This reply seemed to overjoy the older gentleman, who happily led them away. When the home of Percival Chandler came into view, Camilla found it hard to contain her surprise. She had expected a modest cottage, but, instead, found a stately country home. Of recent vintage, the house was built in the highly favored neoclassical style, and Camilla found it quite lovely.

As they neared the main entrance of the house, a little girl of perhaps seven or eight years of age came out of the residence and ran toward them. "Papa! Did you find a Nymphalis antiopa?"

"I did not, but I found something far better—a cousin! Come, Clarissa, greet our guests properly."

Clarissa, a diminutive, dark-haired lass dressed in a simple muslin frock, eyed the visitors with interest. She curtsied politely. "Clarissa is my youngest," said Chandler. "My dear, this is Miss Selwyn and Lord St. John. Lord St. John is our cousin."

"Our cousin?" Clarissa stared at St. John with wide eyes.

"Are you a genuine lord, sir?"

"Genuine enough," replied his lordship, smiling at the youngster.

"Clarissa, do not pester your cousin with silly questions. Hurry and tell your mama we are coming." Clarissa nodded obediently and ran off. "My wife will be so excited to see you," continued Percival Chandler, escorting them inside. He then led them to his spacious and tastefully decorated drawing room. There they found Mrs. Chandler, a pleasant woman of middle years, who greeted them graciously and bade them be seated. Little Clarissa Chandler stood by her mother and watched them with keen interest.

"You must fetch your brothers and sisters, my dear,"

said Chandler to his daughter. "Go on, miss. I fancy they will be very glad to meet our company."

The little girl left them, but it was not long before she returned, accompanied by a group of young ladies and gentlemen. "Ah, here they are," said Percival Chandler, beaming at his progeny with paternal pride.

St. John eyed the Chandler brood with raised eyebrows, counting them quickly. There were nine of them, all dark-haired and handsome.

"Come, children," said Chandler. "Do not be shy. Our guests wish to meet you." He rose and stood beside the tallest of his offspring. "This is Robert, and then Harold, and Lavinia, Peter, George, Harriet, Alexander, Emily and, of course, Clarissa."

As each young Chandler's name was mentioned, the boy or girl made a polite bow or curtsy. "A pity the others are not here," murmured Percival.

"The others?" said his lordship in surprise.

"Oh, there are only three more, sir. My son Phillip is the eldest. He lives in London and oversees the textile business. My two eldest girls, Nan and Charlotte, are married, but, I am glad to say, live not far away."

Mrs. Chandler sat serenely throughout these introductions. "Would you have tea, Miss Selwyn and Lord St. John?"

"I fear we must return to Woodley Grange," said the viscount, surprised at his reluctance to do so. "We must start back for London."

"Start back for town? But it is so late in the day, Cousin. Why don't you stay here with us?"

"That is so kind," said the viscount, "but quite impossible."

Realizing that St. John seemed resolved, Chandler nodded. "Very well. But you must see my collection before you go."

"But my dear," ventured Mrs. Chandler, "Lord St. John did say he must be going."

"Oh, I shall not detain them long, dearest," replied Chandler. "Do follow me. I promise it will not be but a moment."

All of them followed Percival Chandler down the corridor and into a wainscotted room. "This is my collection," he said, gesturing toward row upon row of glass-topped cases. Inside each case was an assortment of butterflies.

Camilla, who preferred her butterflies perched upon flowers in the garden, was nonetheless impressed by the size of the collection. "They are beautiful, Mr. Chandler," she said.

"Thank you, Miss Selwyn," replied Chandler, casting the same proud look at the glass cases that he had earlier bestowed upon his children.

"Did you find them all here?" asked the viscount, eyeing the butterflies with some interest.

"My dear sir, of course not," cried Chandler, amused at the question. "Why, they are from the four corners of the earth." He turned to one of his daughters. "Harriet, point out the South American butterflies to your cousin." Harriet, a girl who appeared to be about ten years old, did so quickly, naming several of them.

"How very clever of your daughter to know such complicated names," said Camilla.

Chandler grinned proudly. "All my children know almost as much about butterflies as I do, Miss Selwyn. It is a family passion."

Camilla directed a glance at the viscount, who lifted a dark eyebrow and smiled. Some time later, St. John and Camilla were able to take their leave of his lordship's new cousins, promising the Chandlers to return another day.

Although the viscount protested that it wasn't necessary, Percival Chandler insisted on having one of his servants drive them back to Woodley Grange in a trap. The viscount would have preferred to have walked back alone with Camilla. He had not forgotten how the untimely appearance of his mother's cousin had interrupted them. However, as it was growing late, St. John accepted the ride with good grace, thinking it best to return to Woodley Grange as soon as possible. It was very likely that Lizzy and the others were wondering where they were.

Arriving back at Woodley Grange, Camilla and the viscount hurried to the back of the house to join Lizzy,

Lucinda, and MacNeil. Camilla smiled as she caught sight of her aunt. Lucinda was fast asleep. Beside her sat Lizzy and MacNeil, so engrossed in conversation that they did not notice the approach of Camilla and St. John. "I know we are late," said St. John.

"Late?" Lizzy looked at him in some surprise. "You are back! Is it late, Tony? I had no idea."

MacNeil rose to his feet. "Did you see the stones then, my lord?"

"We did," replied the viscount.

"They were quite wonderful!" said Camilla.

At that moment, Aunt Lucinda awakened. "What? Are you back so soon, Camilla?"

Camilla and the viscount exchanged an amused look. "We are back, Aunt. It is a pity all of you did not see the Sorcerer's Stones."

"Oh, yes," said Lizzy. "I would have liked to see them. I fear it is too late now."

"It is, indeed," said St. John. We must get back to town. But I do not doubt that you will have many opportunities to see the Sorcerer's Stones, Lizzy."

Lizzy broke into a smile. "Does that mean you will not sell Woodley Grange? Oh, I do hope so!"

"Yes, I shall keep it. Indeed, I believe I shall spend more time here."

"Time here, my lord?" said MacNeil, very much surprised.

"What better place to find a Nymphalis antiopa?" St. John looked at Camilla and they both burst into laughter, leaving Lizzy, Lucinda, and MacNeil to exchange puzzled looks.

18

Lady St. John frowned as her daughter entered the dining room. "Oh, Mama," said Lizzy, noting her mother's expression, "I can see you are still vexed with me about yesterday."

"Indeed I am, miss, and I am even more vexed with your brother. It was quite irresponsible of him, taking you off like that without even leaving me a note. What was I to think when you had not returned by five o'clock?"

"It was my idea to go, Mama," said Lizzy, sitting down at the table. "It was not Tony's fault."

Amanda St. John shook her head, indicating she did not agree. "And I did not approve of your unsuitable companions."

"Hardly unsuitable, Mama."

"You may think those Selwyn women and Anthony's solicitor fit company, but I do not. I do not like the Selwyns and I wish you would have nothing further to do with them."

"But they are very nice, and they are completely respectable."

"Respectable? That is what your brother tells me, but I did not think it so respectable the way the Selwyn girl flirted with all the men at the Claverhams' ball. I saw how she lured away some of your suitors, Elizabeth."

Lizzy burst into laughter. "Really, Mama, do not be absurd."

"You mean you did not mind her stealing Iverson away from you?"

"Miss Selwyn did not steal him away, but, in truth, she is welcome to him."

"Elizabeth! Iverson would be a brilliant match. Indeed, the duchess is very much in favor of it."

"But I am not."

"Elizabeth, you try my patience. I cannot imagine who would suit you better than Iverson. There are, however, others on my list, and I am hopeful you will choose one of them."

"Your list, Mama?"

The dowager viscountess nodded. "My list of eligible suitors. I believe, at last count, there were eleven gentlemen."

Lizzy smiled. "It is unfortunate you do not have eleven daughters, Mama."

Lady St. John did not look amused. "I do not think a young lady should jest about such things, Elizabeth. Eleven daughters, indeed!"

"Oh, I am sorry, Mama. Do tell me who is on your list."

Lady St. John appeared in a better humor as she began to discuss the prospective suitors for her daughter's hand. "First, there is the Marquess of Lindhaven. He has a most illustrious ancestory, and, of course, his fortune is enormous. Then, there is the Viscount Perriville. He will be an earl one day and has a tidy income. Admittedly, he is a bit of a slow top, but that does not signify. There is also Lord Abbington. His uncle is the Duke of Wexbridge, you know . . ."

Lady St. John continued to name the suitors, and Lizzy found herself growing more depressed by the minute. Although she was only slightly acquainted with the gentlemen, the idea of being married to any of them was not very appealing. Indeed, marriage to some of them seemed positively appalling.

Despite the fact that Lizzy knew she must marry someday, she had always thought it an event far off in the future. Now, as the prospect loomed directly in front of her, Lizzy was filled with dismay. If only she could meet a gentleman she liked, she reflected. A wistful smile came to her face as she thought of Charles MacNeil. If that gentleman had appeared on her mother's list of suitors, she would have had no difficulty deciding among them.

Lizzy's daydream about the young solicitor was interrupted by her mother, who asked in irritation, "Elizabeth, are you listening to me?"

"What, Mama?" Lizzy was momentarily startled, but she attempted to make a recovery. "Oh, you said he had a large fortune, did you not?"

Her ladyship smiled. "I see you were listening. Yes, the earl has a substantial fortune. He has considerable holdings in Cornwall. And of course, his family is so very distinguished." Lady St. John continued to enumerate the advantages of the various suitors, and Lizzy thought again of Charles MacNeil.

After concluding her recitation, Lady St. John advised her daughter to think carefully about all the suitors. When Lizzy assured her she would do so, her ladyship appeared satisfied and she turned her attention to breakfast.

Following the meal, the dowager announced she was going to see the milliner and suggested that Lizzy accompany her. Not eager to do so, Lizzy begged to be excused and was surprised when her mother did not insist upon her going. After her mother had left, Lizzy went to the library, where she sat, thoughtfully considering her suitors and MacNeil.

A short time later, she rose and paced across the room. If only mother would understand, she reflected. Suddenly feeling the need to talk to someone, Lizzy had the urge to visit Camilla Selwyn. Although knowing her mother would not approve, she decided to risk Amanda's displeasure. Lizzy went to her room and changed her clothes. Then, after informing one of the servants that she was going out, she left the house.

Camilla Selwyn was arranging flowers in a vase when the butler entered the parlor. "There is a Miss St. John here to see you, miss," said the servant.

Camilla regarded him in surprise. "Miss St. John? Is she alone?"

"Yes," said the servant, looking as if he disapproved of the fact. "She is quite alone, miss."

"Well, do send her in, Baxter."

Camilla glanced down at the wolfhound Rufus, who was lying at her feet. "It seems we have company, Rufus." The big dog rose and looked expectantly at the door. When Lizzy entered the room, the wolfhound wagged his tail eagerly and hurried over to her.

"Rufus!" said Lizzy, patting the dog. "What a fine fellow you are." Rufus barked, as if in acknowledgment of the compliment, and Lizzy laughed.

"Come, Rufus," said Camilla, "I think you had best sit down and get out of Miss St. John's way." The wolfhound obediently sat down and grinned at Lizzy.

"Do come in, Miss St. John. It is good to see you again."

"Could you not call me Lizzy?"

"Indeed, I should be happy to. And you must call me Camilla. Please do sit down."

Once ensconced on the sofa, Lizzy smiled. "And where is your aunt?"

"She is still in bed. I fear she is tired from yesterday's excursion."

"It was exciting, was it not? I had such a marvelous time."

"And so did I," said Camilla.

"We must go again soon. I am so eager to meet the Chandlers."

"You would have liked them."

"I know Tony did. He so enjoyed meeting them." Lizzy paused. "Mr. MacNeil is such a nice man." Camilla regarded the young woman shrewdly as Lizzy continued, "He is so unlike other gentlemen I know. He is so interesting and intelligent. I know my brother thinks he is very clever."

"Lizzy," said Camilla, "you are fond of him, aren't you?"

Lizzy looked down for a moment and then nodded. "I am."

"He is a wonderful man, Lizzy, but surely you are

aware of the difference in your stations. I know very well how your brother would feel about your interest in Charles."

"But it is so unfair."

"I know," said Camilla sympathetically.

"What am I to do, Camilla? Mama wants me to marry one of her list of suitors."

"And are they all so terrible?"

"I have not the slightest interest in or affection for any of them." Lizzy sighed. "If only Charles MacNeil were truly your Sir Charles."

"But, alas, he is not, Lizzy."

"Yes, I know." Lizzy looked sad, but seemed to put these thoughts aside. "At least I am glad that you will not have such problems." She laughed at Camilla's expression. "I refer to you and my brother, of course."

Camilla reddened. "I don't know what you mean."

Lizzy smiled. "I do not mean to cause you embarrassment, but I am so happy that my brother has found you."

"Lizzy . . . really!"

Lizzy laughed. "I think you are perfect for him. You know, Camilla, I had lost hope that my brother would ever form a true attachment for anyone. Indeed, although like most gentlemen he has had his light skirts—" Lizzy stopped. "Oh, dear, a lady should not mention such things. Indeed, Mama would be quite shocked to hear me talk this way. In any case, he has never truly cared for anyone until now. You are fond of him, are you not?"

Camilla paused. "I confess I am."

"I knew it. How I shall love to call you sister."

"My dear Lizzy, you are being premature, I assure you."

Lizzy smiled knowingly. "Very well, I shall say nothing more about it." She switched her topic once again to the previous day's journey to Woodley Grange. Although Camilla tried to listen to Lizzy's words, she found herself thinking of what she had said about St. John. Could it be true? Did the viscount feel the same way that she did? Suspecting it was so, but not daring to believe it, Camilla continued to reflect about St. John while his sister chatted on.

So intent was Camilla on her thoughts that she looked up in surprise at the sound of the butler's voice. "I beg your pardon, Miss Camilla, but Mr. MacNeil is here."

Camilla and Lizzy exchanged a glance. "I don't know. . ."

"It is all right, Camilla. Surely there is no harm in Mr. MacNeil's joining us."

"Very well. Baxter, show the gentleman in."

If Camilla had any doubts whether Charles reciprocated Lizzy's feelings, they quickly vanished when that gentleman entered the room. Seeing Lizzy, the solicitor's face lit up, and it was clearly apparent that he was very pleased to see that young lady.

"Good morning, Charles," said Camilla.

"Camilla." He looked over at Lizzy. "Miss St. John, and I must not forget Rufus." The wolfhound wagged his tail in greeting.

"Mr. MacNeil," said Lizzy, smiling up at him.

"Sit down, Charles," said Camilla, motioning him toward a seat away from Lizzy. "I must say, I am surprised to see you. I thought you would be imprisoned at the offices of Sir Lawrence Neville."

"I had an appointment nearby which finished far earlier than I had expected. I thought I would stop by to see you. I did not know I would have the good fortune to see Miss St. John here. Actually, I was anxious to show off my new carriage."

"Charles, you have a carriage!" said Camilla in some surprise.

The solicitor grinned. "It is not a very grand carriage, to be sure. In fact, I must confess it is not quite new."

"We must see this not quite new vehicle, Lizzy," said Camilla, rising from her chair and going to the window. Lizzy and Charles followed and the wolfhound Rufus tagged along. Camilla viewed the carriage and found it to be a very presentable phaeton pulled by pair of good looking bay horses. "Why, Charles, it is very nice."

"Indeed," said Lizzy, "I think it handsome."

"I fear Dick would find it quite shabby," said Charles, smiling at the ladies.

"Dick," said Camilla, turning toward Lizzy. "I fear my brother is very extravagant. But let us sit down again." Camilla did not fail to note with disapproval that Charles hastened to sit beside Lizzy on the sofa.

"And so, ladies," said Charles, "have you recovered from our adventure at Woodley Grange?"

"I had the most wonderful time," said Lizzy. "How glad I am that my brother is not selling it. I do hope you will not try to advise him otherwise, Mr. MacNeil. I know you think it unprofitable."

"There are things far more important than profit, Miss St. John." He exchanged a glance with Lizzy that made Camilla decidedly uncomfortable. "I think his lordship wise to keep Woodley Grange. He seemed very much taken with it."

"Indeed so," said Lizzy. "Why, one might have thought a spell had been cast on him." She directed a meaningful look at Camilla. "Perhaps it had."

The butler reentered the room at that moment. "Excuse me, miss, but there is a problem in the kitchen requiring your presence."

"Oh, dear. I fear I must go and see what is the matter. I shall be back shortly." Camilla noted that neither Lizzy nor MacNeil seemed distressed at her leaving. She left the drawing room and followed the servant to the kitchen.

Returning some fifteen minutes later, Camilla frowned to see Lizzy and MacNeil talking earnestly together. "That is settled," said Camilla. "Indeed, I do not know why Baxter could not have handled the matter."

Charles looked up at her, his face flushed. "Oh, I hope it was nothing serious."

"Oh, no."

Lizzy seemed momentarily discomposed. "Camilla," she said finally, "Mr. MacNeil has suggested we might take a ride in his carriage."

"Oh, I do not think so, Charles."

"Oh, Camilla, do say yes."

Camilla hesitated, knowing very well it was not a good idea. However, Lizzy directed such an imploring look at her that Camilla, against her better judgment, nodded.

Lizzy seemed very happy, and the three of them left the house and went out to Charles's carriage. "Would you ladies like to sit in back?"

"Certainly not," said Lizzy. "There is room for all of us in front."

Before Camilla could protest, MacNeil was helping Lizzy up into the driver's seat. He then assisted her up beside Lizzy. That this put Lizzy in close proximity to MacNeil, did not please Camilla overmuch, but there was nothing she could do about it.

They started off with Charles at the reins. Lizzy looked over at him. "You are a very competent whip, Mr. MacNeil."

The solicitor grinned. "I daresay that while I cannot hold a candle to your brother, I have driven many a wagon in my time." He glanced over at Camilla. "Do you remember, Camilla, how I would drive the hay wagon for old Reynolds?"

"I do, Charles, and I especially recollect one time when you turned rather too sharply and hit the corner of the barn, tearing a big hole in it. And then, Lizzy, he had the audacity to suggest to my uncle that it was the perfect place for a window."

They all laughed. "It was only a slight mishap, Miss St. John," said Charles. "Of course, I did much better driving Sir Jarvis's carriage. When I was a lad, several of the men took sick and I had to attend to the driving. Does your uncle still have that antique equipage, Camilla?"

"Did you think he would part with it, Charles? Uncle Jarvis does not think it old."

Charles grinned. "It was old in Cromwell's time."

Lizzy laughed. "How I would love to meet Sir Jarvis."

"I think you would like him," said Charles. "He is a loveable curmudgeon. I am much indebted to him." Directing his attention to his horses, Charles turned down a fashionable street lined with residences.

Camilla had started to enjoy herself and had forgotten her misgivings over Charles and Lizzy. As they continued on, the three of them laughed and talked, oblivious to the other vehicles and passersby watching their progress.

As Charles's carriage approached two well-dressed matrons who were walking on the sidewalk, one of the ladies regarded it with interest. "Good heavens," she said, clutching her companion's arm, "I do believe that is Elizabeth St. John in that vehicle."

The other woman stared at the oncoming phaeton. "Why, yes. And that is the Selwyn girl, who created such a sensation at the Claverhams' ball. But who is that red-haired man?"

As the carriage passed by, the first matron registered surprise. "Why, that is the young man employed by Sir Lawrence Neville. He recently consulted with my husband on some legal matters. His name is MacDuff or some such thing."

Both ladies turned and watched the carriage travel down the street. "He seemed rather familiar with the young ladies," said the second woman.

The other nodded. "I wonder if Amanda St. John knows of this?" They exchanged a glance and knew that if Lady St. John did not know of it, that would soon be remedied.

19

Since returning from Woodley Grange the previous day, Lord St. John had scarcely thought of anything but Camilla. Eager to see her again, the viscount prepared to pay her a call that afternoon.

However, just as St. John was about to leave his house, a messenger arrived with a note from the Prince Regent. Reading the note, the viscount frowned. The Prince was requesting his lordship accompany him to Brighton that very day.

St. John was surprised and irritated by the request, which was, in effect, a royal summons. One could not refuse such an invitation, he realized, no matter how much the viscount wished he could do so.

Although once friendly with His Royal Highness, St. John had, for some time, been out of favor. Why he was being restored to the Prince's good graces was a mystery to him.

Despite the honor of it, the viscount was not at all happy at being included in the royal retinue. In addition to knowing that it would be a dreadful bore, St. John did not like having his plans to see Camilla disrupted.

Knowing there was no escape, the viscount scowled. Then, after writing a hurried note to Camilla, he called to his servants to prepare for the journey.

It was a long, dismal three days before St. John returned to London. Not a courtier by nature, the viscount had found it difficult to constantly humor the Prince. His Royal Highness had not been in the best of tempers, making him a disagreeable companion. Toward the end of the stay in

Brighton, St. John had ceased trying to be pleasant. His cool civility did not please the Prince, and the viscount had the distinct impression that His Royal Highness would exclude him from any future parties of gentlemen.

As the viscount entered his townhouse on his return, he found his good humor restored. At last he was free of onerous royal duties, and he could see Camilla Selwyn again.

St. John had not been at home more than an hour when his butler presented him with a calling card, informing his lordship that a gentleman wished to see him. Not in the mood for callers, St. John eyed the card with disfavor. Then reading the name embossed there, "Phillip Chandler," a smile crossed the viscount's face.

He remembered the visit to his Chandler relations. This must be the absent oldest son, he thought. Although he once would have been very irritated at having one of his maternal relatives appear at his doorstep, St. John found himself quite willing and almost eager to see the young Chandler. Indeed, his sojourn at Woodley Grange had caused him to reconsider his avoidance of his mother's family. Why had he been so proud and unwilling to accept them? He realized now that he had been very wrong. "Send him in, Weeks."

Phillip Chandler entered the room a short time later, looking a trifle ill at ease. St. John noticed the resemblance to the rest of the Chandler children immediately. He was tall, dark-haired, and rather handsome, and he was dressed in a fashionable unostentatious manner.

The viscount greeted him. "So you are my cousin Percival's eldest son. I am happy to meet you." St. John extended his hand to the young man.

Phillip Chandler appeared surprised at the warmth of his reception. "How do you do, Lord St. John?" he said, shaking the viscount's hand and regarding him curiously.

"Do sit down." St. John motioned him toward a chair and they both sat down.

"I hope I am not intruding, my lord, but my father

wrote to me saying I must be certain to call. It is very kind of you to receive me."

"Nonsense, we are cousins after all." Noting the young man's somewhat skeptical expression, St. John smiled slightly. "I very much enjoyed meeting your family."

"I know that they were very honored by your visit."

"I hope to call upon them again. Indeed, I have decided to restore Woodley Grange."

"Have you, my lord? That is good news."

The two gentlemen continued their conversation and the viscount further surprised young Phillip Chandler by asking about his work with the textile firm. The young man had been told that St. John disdained his connection with trade, but the viscount seemed quite interested in the business that had been started by his grandfather.

After some time, the butler reentered the room. "Lady St. John and Miss St. John are here, my lord."

"Then I shall be going," said Phillip hastily.

"No, do stay. I would like you to meet my sister."

Young Chandler, who had been reluctant to call upon St John, thinking he would snub him, found it quite remarkable that his lordly cousin now wished him to meet his sister.

The moment that his stepmother and Lizzy entered the room, the viscount realized that something was very much the matter. Amanda looked even more ill-humored than usual, and Lizzy appeared very much upset. Noting the presence of Phillip Chandler, Amanda seemed annoyed at finding that her stepson was not alone.

"Amanda, Lizzy." He walked over and greeted his sister with a kiss on the cheek. To his surprise, Lizzy made no reply, but looked most unhappy.

St. John turned toward young Chandler. "I should like to present Phillip Chandler. He is the son of Percival Chandler, my mother's cousin. Phillip, this is my stepmother, Lady St. John, and my sister, Elizabeth."

Lady St. John did not seem altogether pleased to make the young man's acquaintance. She nodded stiffly.

Lizzy was more congenial. "Oh, Tony has told me all about meeting your family. They sounded so very charming. I regret I did not see them."

"Well, Miss St. John, since his lordship has informed me of his intention to restore Woodley Grange, I am sure you will have many opportunities to do so."

Amanda directed a disapproving look at her stepson at this intelligence, and then she eyed Phillip imperiously. Feeling rather intimidated by Lady St. John, Phillip hastened to take his leave. Once he had gone, Amanda frowned at St. John. "You are suddenly very friendly with your mother's family."

"I do regret not having met them sooner. Phillip appears to be a most capable young man. Despite his youth, he has a position of great responsibility with the textile firm started by my grandfather."

"How very admirable," said Lady St. John scornfully. "I hope your newfound delight in your trade connections will not make you accepting of your sister's shameful conduct."

"What are you talking about, Amanda?"

"I am talking about your sister's undue familiarity with your solicitor. But perhaps you think the idea of Elizabeth's wishing to marry such a man not in the least alarming."

"What the devil?" St. John looked at Lizzy. "You and MacNeil?"

"Of course," cried Amanda. "It should not surprise you. You brought him into your house. I blame you that your sister has formed such an unfortunate attachment to a man who is, I have discovered, the son of a servant. I do not doubt that you encouraged it. Indeed, you have always been envious of your sister's Mountifort connections. I daresay you wish to drag her down to the level of your Chandlers!"

St. John's face grew dark with fury. "I will hear no more of your nonsensical talk, Amanda." He turned to his sister. "Lizzy, explain to me what this is about!"

"Oh, Tony." Lizzy burst into tears.

The viscount put a comforting arm around her shoulders. "Come, Infant, tell me what happened." Lizzy was too upset to reply, and buried her head against her brother's chest.

"I shall tell you what happened," said Lady St. John angrily. "Lady Gorley and Lady Wilmington saw your sister riding about town with that Selwyn girl and your solicitor. They appeared to be on the most shocking terms of familiarity."

"You accept the word of society's worst gossips?"

Her ladyship eyed him indignantly. "Your sister will not deny it. Indeed, she admitted that she is in love with the fellow!"

The viscount looked down at his sister, who had by now regained her composure. "I do love him. Tony." Looking at her brother's shocked expression, Lizzy's self-control crumbled and she sobbed again.

"You see," said Lady St. John, "and it is your fault. It was you who introduced her to that Selwyn girl. Indeed, what can one expect from someone who treats the son of a servant as if he were an equal? I do not doubt that she was behind this unfortunate situation."

"Do not be absurd," said the viscount testily.

"Am I so absurd? If this Miss Selwyn did not want to encourage them, why did she allow my daughter to parade about town with her and this man?"

The viscount looked from his stepmother to his sister, who was still crying pitifully. "Amanda, take Lizzy home."

"What are you going to do?"

"I shall get to the heart of this matter, I assure you."

"But what do you mean to—" began Amanda.

The viscount cut her off angrily. "Take Lizzy home," he commanded. And without another word, St. John turned and stormed out of the room.

St. John drove his phaeton recklessly toward the Selwyn

home. He was very much upset by his stepmother's words,
and he cursed himself for his stupidity. The viscount had
been aware of Lizzy's interest in the solicitor, and he
should have realized the danger. He was suddenly irritated
with Camilla. Why had she not tried to put a stop to it? If
what Amanda had said was true, Camilla must share some
responsibility in this unfortunate matter.

Arriving at Camilla's door, the viscount surprised the
butler by his glowering expression and abrupt manner.
Baxter hastily showed him into the parlor, and then the
servant went off to inform Camilla of his lordship's
presence.

Camilla, alone in the house, was, at first, delighted to
hear that the viscount was there. However, she did not fail
to note the butler's uneasy look. "Is something the matter,
Baxter?"

"It is only that his lordship looks somewhat . . ."

"Somewhat what?"

"Annoyed, miss. I left him in the parlor."

"I shall see him immediately," said Camilla, wondering at the butler's remark. However, having thought of
little else but St. John for the past three days, she was
most anxious to see him. Camilla hurried to the parlor,
and, entering it, she smiled brightly.

"Lord St. John."

"Miss Selwyn."

Seeing from his expression that something was wrong,
Camilla regarded him with concern. "What is the matter,
my lord? I can see that you are upset."

The viscount frowned. "I have just been informed, Miss
Selwyn, that my sister has been seen riding about town
with you and MacNeil."

"Oh dear, I can see why you are displeased. But, Lord
St. John, it was only one short ride and really quite
harmless. A few days ago, Lizzy called upon me and
Charles happened by—"

"Happened by? How convenient that he happens by
when my sister calls."

"Surely you cannot think it was by design?"

"And why not? I know MacNeil. He is a clever and ambitious young man. Thanks to you, Miss Selwyn, he has ideas above his station, and I do not think him beyond insinuating himself into my sister's affections."

Camilla's reaction turned from dismay to anger. "Truly, you cannot think—"

"I can indeed. How it must please MacNeil to have my sister dangling after him. I do not doubt that he is audacious enough to think that he might marry Lizzy!"

"That is ridiculous! Charles is an honorable man."

"Oh, yes, you think him so very honorable. To you he is a shining knight on a white horse. No doubt, you think it perfectly acceptable for my sister to marry a man with neither title nor fortune."

"Perhaps it would not be as bad as having her marry someone of noble birth who would make her miserable. There are qualities far more important in a man than rank and fortune."

St. John regarded her incredulously. "By God, you do not find the idea of my sister and MacNeil outrageous! Indeed, you approve!"

"I did not say that."

"It sounded very much like that is what you said."

Camilla regarded him in frustration. "You are too angry to be reasonable, my lord."

The viscount shook his head. "My stepmother was right. I should never have allowed Lizzy to become friends with you. Your influence upon her has been quite regrettable. I think it best that she sever all ties with you." St. John's eyes met hers. "And I think it is best that I do so as well. Would that I had never had the misfortune to find shelter at Selwyn Manor."

Camilla regarded him angrily. "Indeed, I wish you had been buried in a snowbank instead!"

The viscount directed a furious look at her, and then turned abruptly and stalked off. Camilla sat down on the sofa, astonished at what had just occurred. She had so anticipated St. John's return, knowing she was so much in love with him. A feeling of disbelief came over Camilla as she realized that she might never see the viscount again. Certainly, whatever feelings he had had for her were now gone, she reflected. Camilla sighed, and, as she sat there in the empty parlor, she fought back tears.

20

Late that evening, the Viscount St. John sat in his drawing room staring morosely into the fire. Pouring himself a large glass of brandy, his lordship reflected on the unhappy events of the day.

Thinking again of Lizzy and MacNeil, St. John frowned. He then turned his reflections to Camilla. The viscount had been somewhat surprised by the intensity of his feelings for that lady. Although St. John had had a number of affairs, none of them had ever been more than mere dalliance for him. However, his regard for Camilla had seemed to be of a much more serious nature.

"Damn it," muttered the viscount, downing his glass of brandy.

A servant entered the room. "What is it?" said St. John irritably. "I said I didn't want to be disturbed."

The man spoke somewhat fearfully. "I am very sorry, m'lord, but Mr. Fitzwalter is here and he insists upon seeing you."

"Oh, very well. Send him in."

The servant gratefully departed and returned a moment later, followed by Fitzwalter. That gentleman was dressed in his evening finery and seemed in remarkably high spirits.

"Tony, what is this about your not wanting to receive anyone? I can understand your not wanting to see certain persons, but your old friend Fitzwalter? You cut me to the quick."

The viscount shook his head. "I am sorry. Fitz, but I fear I am poor company this evening. I am in the devil of a mood."

His dapper friend smiled at him and sat down languidly

on the sofa. "My dear Tony, it is not unusual for one to be blue-deviled after spending three days with Prinny. Of course, I was a trifle offended that I was not invited. I fear it is the fault of the remark I made about one of the royal waistcoats."

St. John shook his head. "It has nothing to do with that, Fitz, although, I daresay, it was a miserable three days."

"Well, in your absence, I have not enjoyed myself. This evening, for example, I have just suffered a most excruciating dinner party at my brother Ponsonby's."

A faint smile appeared on his lordship's countenance. "Come, Fitz. it could not have been that bad."

"Indeed, it was, Tony. My sister-in-law insisted on having my niece Annabelle provide the entertainment for the company. Egad, one does not know true suffering until one has heard Annabelle sing. But, come, tell me what has you so blue-deviled."

The viscount stood up and, after pacing the length of the room, he turned back toward his friend. "It's Lizzy."

"Lizzy? Oh dear. Whatever is the matter?"

"She has fallen in love with a most unacceptable fellow."

"I daresay you would find any fellow who wins your sister's heart unacceptable."

"This is a serious matter, Fitz. The man I am talking about is Charles MacNeil."

"The solicitor? The one who is Camilla's friend?"

"And the son of her uncle's former butler."

"I do recall his name being mentioned. 'Pon my honor, he does sound like a bold fellow. Or perhaps foolhardy is a better word."

"Foolhardy?"

"Indeed, one would have to be foolhardy to incur your wrath, my lord St. John. But, however did this MacNeil capture Lizzy's affection? They do not exactly travel in the same circles."

St. John frowned. "They met but a few times, first at Miss Selwyn's and then here."

"Here?"

"I hired him as my solicitor."

Fitzwalter appeared astonished. "You did? But I thought you considered him an upstart."

"It does not signify why I hired him. I very much regret it. Lizzy and he last met at Miss Selwyn's a few days ago. I thought you would have heard about it by now. I do not doubt it is all over town."

"My dear Tony, it is scarcely all over town if I have not heard about it. Whatever happened?"

"Lizzy was seen riding in a carriage with MacNeil and Miss Selwyn. My stepmother was quickly informed of the matter."

"But this is hardly that serious. Lizzy was in no way compromised, since Miss Selwyn was there."

"Damn it, Fitz, that is not the point. Lizzy thinks that she is in love with the man. I cannot forgive Miss Selwyn for her part in this."

"Good heavens, Tony. You talk as if Camilla was involved in some plot. That is perfectly ridiculous."

"She might have put a stop to it. Surely, Miss Selwyn could have prevented them running about town in that damned carriage. Why, when I spoke to her about it, she acted as if the idea of MacNeil and my sister was not so preposterous at all. I would almost believe she would encourage them."

"Stuff and nonsense, old friend. Camilla would not do any such thing."

St. John shook his head. "I fear, Fitz, that you are allowing your affection for Miss Selwyn to cloud your judgment."

His friend raised his eyebrows. "My affection? Whatever do you mean by that, Tony?"

The viscount shrugged. "It is obvious that you hold Miss Selwyn in the highest esteem. Come now, Fitz, I have known for some time your feelings for Miss Selwyn— Camilla as you have the effrontery to call her. You're in love with her."

Fitzwalter grinned. "I fear you can be the most corkbrained fellow, Anthony St. John. Oh, I am quite fond of Camilla, but I do not cherish any romantic fancies toward her." Fitzwalter stopped and paused. "Unlike a certain friend of mine."

The viscount scowled. "What the deuce do you mean by that?"

"Oh, come, Tony, you may have jumped to the wrong conclusion about my feelings for Miss Selwyn, but I am quite certain that I am right about yours." He grinned. "I am a much more perceptive fellow, don't you know? You are in love with Miss Selwyn, Tony!"

The viscount met his friend's smiling gaze and then looked away. "Damn it, Fitz, take that silly grin off your face."

Fitzwalter laughed. "I am sorry, old boy. But, I must say, I quite approve. Camilla Selwyn is a dashed fine lady, and she would make you an excellent wife. I think it is time you married."

"And I think it is none of your business!" This exclamation brought a smile to Fitzwalter's face. St. John continued, "Even if I did have . . . certain feelings for Miss Selwyn, this matter has come between us."

"Be reasonable, Tony. You know very well that Camilla would not wish to hurt you or Lizzy."

St. John frowned again. "I do not want to discuss it any more, Fitz. Indeed, we have spoken enough of Miss Selwyn."

Fitzwalter regarded his friend for a moment, and then nodded. "All right, Tony. If that is what you want. Now do quit glowering at me." He took out his snuff box and delicately inhaled a pinch. "You need some diversion, Tony. Why don't we go somewhere? I should like to try my luck at hazard."

"I don't think so, Fitz."

"Very well, but what about tomorrow evening? Do say you will go. We can dine at Watier's and then go to one of the more lively gaming establishments on Pall Mall."

St. John nodded, but without enthusiasm. Finding it best to retire, Fitzwalter took his leave and departed.

* * *

The next morning the viscount called at his stepmother's house. He was anxious to talk with his sister, and he was happy to see that Lady St. John was not at home. He found Lizzy in the library, sitting glumly in the corner with a book.

She looked up at him as he entered. "I do hope you are not here to lecture me, Tony. I have had enough of that from Mama."

His lordship smiled. "That was not my intention, Infant."

Lizzy closed her book and, rising from her chair, hurried to her brother. She threw her arms around him. "Oh, Tony, it is all so dreadful!"

"I know. Come let us sit down. We must talk." After they were seated, he continued. "I am sorry you have been hurt, Lizzy. I blame MacNeil and Miss Selwyn."

"Miss Selwyn? But, Tony, she had nothing to do with it. Indeed, when I told her how I felt about Mr. MacNeil, she tried to discourage me. She told me you would not like it. And Camilla did not want me to go riding in Mr. MacNeil's carriage. That was my doing."

Lizzy's words made the viscount regret his confrontation with Camilla. How could he have been such a fool as to blame her? She must think him insufferable. His sister continued, "No, Camilla is not at fault, nor is Charles, that is, Mr. MacNeil."

"I hold him very much responsible. You are only a young girl. You are bound to have such infatuations."

Lizzy regarded him indignantly. "I am not a silly schoolgirl, Tony, and this is no childish infatuation. I love him."

"But you scarcely know him."

"Sometimes one does not have to know a person for very long. I believe I realized the first time I met Charles that he was not like other men." Lizzy paused and gazed intently at her brother. "I do not understand why I am so wrong to have affection for him. He is a very good man, and he is so very intelligent! Mr. MacNeil has quite impressed Sir Lawrence Neville, and you know Sir Lawrence is highly respected. Indeed, with Sir Lawrence's patronage and his own ability, Mr. MacNeil has a brilliant future ahead of him! He may even become a member of Parliament someday!''

The viscount shook his head. "I don't care if he becomes prime minister. MacNeil is not going to marry you!''

Lizzy frowned. "How can you be so unreasonable, Tony? I would think you, of all persons, would understand . . .'' She stopped in midsentence.

"Yes? What were you going to say?''

Lizzy hesitated, but then she plunged rapidly ahead. "I would think because of your mother . . . Some people would have considered her unsuitable for Papa. After all, her father was in trade.''

"I am quite aware of my mother's lineage, Lizzy,'' said the viscount ill-humoredly.

"But then, how can you be so unsympathetic, Tony? I know how much you loved your mother and how it hurts you to hear the dreadful things Mama and other people say about her family. And you did like the Chandlers. Why, just yesterday I met Mr. Chandler at your house! Surely, it is wrong to judge persons solely on the circumstances of their birth.''

St. John regarded her closely for a moment. "Perhaps it would be better if such things did not matter, if a man could be judged on his character and ability. But that is not the case, Lizzy. My mother was never accepted in society. I was always ashamed of her family. As a boy, my enemies never ceased to remind me of my grandfather, the 'textile king.' '' A wry smile crossed his face. "I got into many scrapes because of it.''

"And Mama constantly reminded you of how superior the Mountiforts were,'' said Lizzy with a slight smile.

"So you must understand that you could never marry a man like MacNeil. It would be very difficult for you.''

"I do not care a fig for society's opinion.''

"And what of your mother and the Mountiforts?''

Lizzy nodded. "Oh, the Mountiforts! I think they have always disapproved of me. They are such prosy old fossils!"

St. John smiled in spite of himself and Lizzy regarded him hopefully. He quickly dashed her hopes. "I am sorry, Lizzy, but you must give up the idea of marrying Mac-Neil. I shall never condone such a match. You will understand one day. Now, I shall leave you." The viscount leaned over and kissed her cheek. Lizzy made no reply, but watched sadly as he left the room.

21

St. John sat beside his friend as Fitzwalter's stylish carriage made its way through the dark streets. Glancing out the window, he wondered why he had agreed to accompany Fitzwalter that night. He was hardly in the mood for an evening of gaming.

Since leaving Lizzy that morning, the viscount had spent his time worrying about his sister and thinking about Camilla Selwyn. Many times that afternoon he had almost set out to call on Camilla, but his pride had prevented him. That evening he continued to think about her, hardly mindful of his friend's company.

"I daresay, I feel lucky tonight," said Fitzwalter jubilantly, shaking the viscount out of his reverie.

"What?"

"I said that I feel lucky tonight."

"As I recall, Fitz, you said that two weeks ago at the faro table at Crockford's."

"Tony!" cried Fitzwalter. "How cruel of you to mention that! But I must be lucky tonight or my tailor will be a pauper."

The viscount smiled slightly. "I do wish you luck for your tailor's sake."

"Thank you. I would wish you luck, but I know it is unnecessary. You are always lucky at hazard." Fitzwalter sighed. "Indeed, my dear Tony, you are lucky at everything."

St. John frowned. "Not everything, Fitz."

Fitzwalter looked questioningly at his friend, but said

nothing. The carriage came suddenly to a stop. "We are here at Prestwick's already, Tony."

"So it seems," replied the viscount with a notable lack of enthusiasm.

The two gentlemen got out of the carriage and made their way into the gambling establishment. Although decidedly less respectable than such well known clubs as White's and Brookes', Prestwick's was an exceedingly popular place. More commonly called "Lucifer's Lair," it was frequented by the most daring gamesters of the day.

There were many incidences of fortunes being lost and won at Prestwick's, for the play was fast and the stakes were high. The company was always rowdy and few in attendence cared that the wine was inferior and that the decor was appallingly tawdry.

Once inside, Fitzwalter eagerly surveyed the frenzied activity. "Everyone is here. 'Pon my word, Tony, we shall have a memorable night of it!"

St. John looked bored. He scanned the crowded room, noting the same familiar faces. He directed his gaze to a large round hazard table and was surprised to see Dick Selwyn. Seated at Dick's side and looking quite happy, was Sir Peregrine Mowbray. A large and boisterous crowd surrounded them, shouting noisily and placing wagers on the play.

Dick tried to appear nonchalant as he shook the dice in the cup, but, in truth, he was tremendously nervous. He had already lost a large sum of money and much was riding on his next toss. Having recklessly accepted all bets placed against him, Dick stood to lose more than a thousand pounds on the one throw. He held his breath and flung the dice from the cup. "Eleven," shouted the groom porter, raking in the dice with his stick. "Caster loses."

There was a roar of approval from the crowd and Dick tried hard to fight the queasy feeling in his stomach. "Bad luck, old boy," said Sir Peregrine with a grin.

Dick scarcely heard him. He was trying to calculate how much he had lost so far, but his brain was so befuddled by wine that he could not do so. He knew, however, that it was a very large sum and that if he did not win some of it back soon, he might lose everything. Dick tried to console himself by reasoning that the evening was still young and fortunes in hazard could turn quickly. Although far from reassured, he turned his attention to the game and placed a modest wager against the next player.

St. John frowned as he watched Dick and Sir Peregrine. So Mowbray had led the boy to this gambling hell, thought the viscount disapprovingly.

Fitzwalter had been watching another table, and looking at his friend, noted that St. John's attention was directed elsewhere. Following the viscount's gaze, Fitzwalter shook his head. "Dick Selwyn here, of all places! The cub will be eaten alive."

St. John nodded. "I do not doubt that Mowbray intends to emerge a far richer man tonight."

"Damn him," muttered Fitzwalter. "Come, let us take a closer look."

They soon joined the clamorous onlookers that were jammed around the hazard table. The state of Dick's fortunes was made immediately clear by a slightly inebriated gentleman of Fitzwalter's acquaintance.

"Fitzwalter!" said the gentleman, grinning broadly. "This fellow Selwyn is having the worst luck I have ever seen. Why, I reckon he's lost nearly twenty thousand pounds, and most of it to Mowbray."

"The devil you say!" Fitzwalter exchanged a glance with St. John. The informative gentleman turned his attention once again to the play and shouted a bet.

St. John looked over at Dick Selwyn and noted how pale and shaken he looked. Dick was continuing to play, doubtlessly hoping his luck would turn. The viscount walked to young Selwyn's side and placed a hand on his shoulder. "Don't you think you've played enough for one evening, Selwyn?"

Dick looked up in surprise. "St. John?"

Mowbray directed an irritated look at the viscount. "So you are interrupting us again? We are engaged in a game here, St. John."

"I see that, Mowbray," returned St. John. "I was but

hoping to get a place at the table. I thought I might take Selwyn's.''

''I doubt Selwyn wants to leave,'' said Mowbray. ''His luck will soon be changing.''

''You would do me a service letting me play, Dick.''

Dick Selwyn seemed dazed. ''If you wish to play . . .'' he began uncertainly.

St. John assisted the young man to his feet before he could finish his sentence. ''That is good of you, Dick. Fitz, see to our good friend Selwyn.''

Fitzwalter took Dick's arm and St. John sat down at the table. ''Gentlemen,'' he said, ''I think I'm ready.''

Mowbray scowled. St. John was known and feared in gaming circles as a formidable opponent. The viscount had an almost uncanny knack for figuring odds and accepting and placing bets accordingly. No one had ever known St. John to lose substantially, and the other players viewed his arrival in their midst as ill-omened.

Mowbray frowned and took up the dice cup. It took him several tosses to obtain a match point and once he had done so, the other players shouted their wagers. He glanced over at St. John, who was directing a cool, appraising look at him. ''Five hundred,'' said the viscount. Mowbray nodded and threw the dice.

''Nine! Caster loses!''

Mowbray muttered an expletive and St. John smiled slightly. It appeared, thought the viscount, that he may enjoy the evening after all.

The play continued on through the night and as time went on, all interest was diverted from the other games taking place in Lucifer's Lair. The observers crowded about, eager to witness the contest between St. John and Mowbray. That the two were enemies was well known to everyone in society and this fact made the game even more exciting.

Mowbray's luck had changed immediately when the viscount had joined the game. Sir Peregrine's increasing anger at St. John's good fortune made him foolhardy and he raised his bets substantially.

After having deposited the exhausted Dick Selwyn on a

chair in the corner of the room, Fitzwalter watched Mowbray's face gleefully. Fitzwalter had the additional satisfaction of betting against Sir Peregrine himself and winning time and again.

The game continued until the light of dawn filtered through the windows of Lucifer's Lair. The crowd had thinned by then and those remaining were bleary-eyed and yawning. Sir Peregrine Mowbray looked as if he hadn't slept in weeks. His eyes had a wild look about them and his usually neatly arranged hair was in disarray. Mowbray's once smartly tied cravat now hung loosely around his neck.

In contrast, the Viscount St. John still looked the elegant Corinthian. He seemed unfazed by the long evening's play. St. John looked over at Sir Peregrine. "Well, Mowbray, do you accept my bet?"

Sir Peregrine frowned darkly. He had long ago lost all he had won before and a good sum more, most of it to St. John. Already he was plunged dangerously in debt and he knew very well that should he lose this wager, it would be disastrous.

"Curse you to hell, St. John," said Mowbray. "I accept." He then tossed the dice and waited for them to roll to a stop. "Damn!" The baronet pounded his fist against the table.

St. John raised an eyebrow. "My dear Mowbray, do not despair. Your luck may yet change. Let us continue."

Sir Peregrine threw the dice cup down and stood up. "I shall not give you the pleasure of bleeding me dry, St. John. I have had enough!" He then stalked off, pushing his way through the sparse group of onlookers.

St. John looked at the two remaining players at the table. "Do you wish to continue, gentlemen?"

"Indeed not," said one, happy at the opportunity to quit.

The other man shook his head. "No, I've had enough, St. John."

"Very well," said the viscount. "It was beginning to grow very tedious."

Fitzwalter clapped his friend on the back exuberantly.

"You were brilliant, Tony! I shall never forget how Mowbray looked! It was not so very different from when you thrashed him at Eton."

The viscount allowed himself a smile. "It was just as satisfying, Fitz, and far easier on one's hands."

Fitzwalter laughed delightedly and others in attendance came up to congratulate St. John on his remarkable luck. After the room had cleared, the viscount walked over to the corner where Dick Selwyn was sleeping soundly in a chair. He shook him awake and the young man started.

"Selwyn, wake up. It's over."

"What?" said Dick groggily.

"It's over. It's time to go home," said Fitzwalter.

Dick looked around the room, realizing where he was. "Aye, it's over. It's over for me." He got wearily to his feet. "How can I ever tell Camilla about this? My entire fortune is gone."

Fitzwalter patted him sympathetically on the shoulder. "Hard luck, old man. But you may be glad to know that Mowbray lost all he won from you and more."

Dick regarded him in surprise.

"Yes, it's true," said Fitzwalter. "St. John won it all."

Dick looked at the viscount. "How very lucky for you, St. John."

St. John nodded. "I hope you now realize that Mowbray is not your friend. It was his intention to get your fortune from the very first."

Fitzwalter voiced his agreement. "I know you thought him a great fellow, but what St. John says is correct."

"You are right, I see that now," said Dick sadly. "And I am the greatest fool imaginable. My uncle was right. He told me I would regret coming here. I only hope they all can forgive me."

"Look, Selwyn," said St. John. "I think Mowbray took unfair advantage of you, and it is only right that I restore to you what you have lost."

Dick eyed him in astonishment. "You cannot mean that. It is more than twenty thousand pounds."

"I won considerably more than that, Dick, and besides, I took enough pleasure at besting Mowbray."

Dick grabbed the viscount's hand and shook it vigorously. "I am overcome, St. John. I cannot express my gratitude. If only there was a way I could repay you."

"You would best repay me by staying away from such persons as Peregrine Mowbray and such places as this."

"Indeed, I will, sir. I have learned I am no gamester and in future will confine my wagers to the horse races at the village fair."

St. John smiled. "Come on then, let's all go home." The three of them left Prestwick's and walked into the early morning sun.

22

Camilla Selwyn sat in the parlor, trying to write a letter to her uncle. Finding it impossible to concentrate, she put her pen down. The Viscount St. John was too much in her thoughts.

She looked pensive for a time, and then sighing, Camilla took up her quill pen again. Her uncle would be expecting her letter and she must endeavor to complete it. Camilla frowned. It was becoming increasingly difficult to write to Uncle Jarvis, since it meant avoiding mentioning her brother Dick's behavior.

The thought of her brother further depressed Camilla. She worried about him more and more each day. Dick was continuing to spend money at an alarming rate, and Camilla knew that he had fallen in with very unsuitable companions, foremost among them Sir Peregrine Mowbray.

Getting up from the desk, Camilla walked over to the window and stared down at the street below her. Uncle Jarvis had been right in thinking that London would be disastrous for Dick. Frowning again, Camilla reflected that coming to town had proved disastrous for herself as well.

Camilla sighed, thinking again of the viscount. She could not blame St. John for becoming upset about Lizzy and Charles. After all, to someone who did not know Charles very well, the young solicitor might very well appear to be a scheming fortunehunter.

Camilla's dreary reflections were interrupted when Aunt Lucinda rushed into the parlor. "Oh, Camilla, thank goodness you are here!"

Camilla regarded her aunt in alarm. Lucinda's face was

flushed and she looked extremely agitated. "Aunt Lucinda, whatever is the matter?" asked Camilla, eyeing her aunt with concern.

"Oh, Camilla!" moaned Aunt Lucinda piteously. "It is too dreadful! Oh, what shall my brother say!" and she suddenly collapsed on the sofa in a fit of the vapors.

"Aunt!" Camilla rushed to Lucinda's side, and then she quickly rang for the servant. When a maid appeared, Camilla instructed her to fetch some smelling salts. The girl quickly reappeared with them, and Camilla placed the smelling salts under her aunt's nose.

Lucinda sputtered, and then she sat up abruptly. "Oh, Camilla, it is so very horrid! Oh, dear, what shall we do?"

"But whatever has happened?" Camilla patted her aunt reassuringly on the arm. "Please calm yourself, Aunt, and tell me what calamity has befallen to put you in such a state."

Lucinda took a deep breath and then spoke. "I fear we are ruined!"

"Ruined? Whatever can you mean, Aunt?"

"It's Dick! The boy has lost every farthing of his fortune! My dear girl! What shall we do?"

Camilla stared at her aunt in astonishment. "He's lost his fortune? Who told you this?"

Lucinda sighed tragically. "I heard it from Lady Buckthorne, but I daresay it is all over town by now. It seems that Dick lost everything at the gaming tables last evening. He is ruined! Ruined!"

"Aunt, you must calm yourself! It has to be a mistake. Why, Dick has been sleeping upstairs all day long. Surely, if this had happened, he could not do so."

"But, my dear, you know your brother has always been such a sound sleeper."

Camilla directed a frustrated look at her aunt. "I shall go talk to Dick and find out the truth of the matter right now."

Lucinda nodded in uncharacteristic meekness and Camilla, casting one last worried glance at her aunt, left the room and then raced up the stairway. She stopped in front of her brother's room and knocked. When there was no answer, Camilla pounded loudly on the door. "Dick!"

Camilla heard a moan from the room and quickly flung open the door. There she found her brother still lying in bed, looking quite pale. "Dick!" she cried and rushed toward him. Dick Selwyn winced and, opening his eyes, he regarded her with an annoyance.

"Good lord, Cam. What the devil is the matter?"

"I have just heard some rather disturbing news about you."

Dick moaned and pulled the bedclothes up to his chin. "Egad, Cam, can't this wait? It's dashed early."

"Early? It's past two o'clock."

"Yes, but I didn't get in till after dawn and I have the most frightful headache."

Camilla stared sternly down at him. "A headache may be the least of your troubles, Dick."

Her brother looked up at her and then reluctantly sat up in bed. "Oh, all right, Cam. What is it?"

"Aunt Lucinda heard that you lost your entire fortune at the gaming tables last night. Is it true?"

Dick appeared startled. "Aunt Lucinda heard about it?"

Camilla's heart sank. "Then it is true?"

Her brother nodded, looking quite shamefaced, and Camilla sat down heavily on the bed. "Oh, Dick! How could you do such a thing?"

"Oh, don't worry, Cam," said her brother quickly. "I got all my money back."

Camilla regarded him with a puzzled expression. "But I thought you just said you lost everything . . ."

"I did. Oh, lord, I have never spent such a miserable evening, Cam! We were at this dreadful place, playing hazard, and Mowbray was winning every throw."

"Mowbray?"

Dick frowned. "You and St. John were right about him."

"St. John?"

"Yes, St. John warned me that Mowbray was a bad one, but I would not listen to him. Good lord, what a fool I've been! I thought Mowbray was a great fellow, and it turned out that he was just waiting for the opportunity to snatch my fortune away. How he and his friends must have laughed at me, the ridiculous, gullible bumpkin!''

Camilla urged him on, a trifle impatiently. "But what happened then, Dick? You said Mowbray was winning?''

"Yes, he was having the devil's own luck, while I . . .'' Dick shook his head. "I was losing everything. Toward the end, every throw of the dice became sheer agony for me. And then, it was over. I had nothing left.''

"But, then how . . . ?''

"Yes, I shall get to that, Cam. Anyway, Lord St. John and Fitzwalter came over to watch the play and then St. John took my place at the table. I was in quite a state, as you can well imagine.'' Dick paused. "And then I fell asleep.''

"You fell asleep!''

"I had had quite a bit of wine,'' he said sheepishly. "The next thing I knew it was dawn, and St. John was waking me. The game had just ended. and St. John had won more than twenty thousand from Mowbray.

"And you know what he did, Cam? He gave me my money back! I could scarcely believe it. What a dashed fine fellow he is!''

Camilla appeared stunned by Dick's story. Her brother continued, "By God, I never want to see a pair of dice again!'' Dick looked over at her. "I am sorry, Cam, to worry you and Aunt Lucinda so. I have been a great idiot and I hope you can forgive me.''

Dick's face took on such a look of boyish contrition that Camilla smiled in spite of herself. "Oh, of course, I forgive you, Dick. It appears that but for some unfortunate gossip, no harm has been done, thanks to St. John. But I do hope you learned your lesson.''

"Indeed, I did, Cam.'' Dick paused and looked thoughtful. "If St. John hadn't been there and intervened, I would have lost everything. I realize now how foolish I've been, acting the man about town. Oh, I must admit I've had some great larks, but to tell you the truth, I'm a bit homesick for the country and old Selwyn Manor. I even find myself missing that old lickpenny of an uncle.''

Camilla smiled. "I am sure he would be glad to hear it. He really does care about you, you know."

Dick nodded. "I fear I have not always been the best of nephews."

"Indeed," said Camilla, "you can be quite incorrigible, Dick. But then, I daresay Uncle Jarvis can also be somewhat difficult."

Dick grinned. "Lord, can he be difficult! But, he was right about my going to town. I behaved like a true jackanapes!"

"I shall not dispute it, Dick," replied Camilla mischievously, and he laughed.

Dick put a hand through his unruly hair. "I think I shall get up after all. It is time I tried to make amends with Uncle. Indeed, I shall go and see him today."

"Today?" Camilla looked surprised.

"Yes, I really feel that I must, Cam. You do understand?"

"Of course. I am very glad that you wish to make things right with Uncle Jarvis. But don't you want Lucinda and me to go with you?"

"I think it would be best if I went alone. I shall take the carriage, but I will not be gone for very long. Perhaps I may even be able to persuade Uncle Jarvis to return to town with me."

Camilla smiled. "That would be an astounding feat, indeed!" She stood up. "I shall leave you to get ready then." He smiled in return, and she left the room to go inform her aunt of the fortunate news. As she started down the stairs, she thought of St. John. Why had he done such a thing, she asked herself? Very much puzzled, she continued on down the stairs.

23

Early the following day, Camilla took Rufus for a walk. As usual, the wolfhound was overjoyed to be outside, and Camilla had some difficulty keeping up with him. They walked to the park, and entering it, Camilla thought of how she had met St. John there the day after she had arrived in London. She smiled, remembering how embarrassed she had been.

Camilla walked for some time and then, knowing that her aunt expected her back, she turned her steps homeward. As Camilla neared the gates of the park, the wolfhound let out an excited bark and strained at his leash. Camilla was surprised to see St. John up ahead, mounted on a fine chestnut horse.

Camilla regarded him in some embarrassment, wondering how he would react at seeing her again.

Espying Camilla, the viscount tipped his hat and then he started toward her. Pulling his horse up alongside her, he dismounted. "Miss Selwyn."

"Lord St. John," she replied, her brown eyes meeting his. Rufus barked and the viscount stroked his head absently. Camilla looked away in some confusion, unsure of what to say to him. "My lord," she said finally, "I heard what you did for my brother. We are all so very grateful to you."

He smiled slightly. "I was glad to have the opportunity to teach Mowbray a lesson."

"That horrible man. But surely, you had no obligation to return Dick's money to him. Truly, it was a most generous thing for you to do, my lord, especially . . ."

Camilla's voice trailed off. "That is, since I know how you feel about me."

St. John fastened his eyes upon hers. "Are you so certain you know how I feel about you, Miss Selwyn?" She regarded him questioningly, and the viscount continued, "I must apologize to you, Miss Selwyn, for the things I said. I lost my temper. I fear I was just too upset about Lizzy and her attachment for MacNeil."

"I understand, my lord. I know how worried you are about Lizzy."

St. John smiled and started to reply, but before he could speak, they were interrupted by a loud shout. "I say, St. John!"

They turned to see two riders approaching. One of them was a rabbit-faced fellow of middle years who bore a silly grin. His companion was a young man of about eighteen, who, although more somber in expression, showed a distinct family resemblance to the older gentleman.

"Fitzwalter," said the viscount, looking up at them without enthusiasm. He turned to Camilla. "Miss Selwyn, may I present Baron Fitzwalter and his son Reginald? The baron is Fitzwalter's brother. Gentlemen, this is Miss Selwyn."

"Selwyn?" The baron grinned amiably. "How very good to meet you, ma'am. My brother Trenton told me how he stayed with your family. I hope he was a better houseguest there than he is at Ponsonby Hall."

Camilla smiled. "He was quite charming."

"Indeed, everyone thinks he is charming. I daresay, everyone thinks so except his family." The baron burst into laughter.

"Really, Father," said the younger Fitzwalter.

Lord Fitzwalter ignored his son and looked down at Rufus. "Egad, that is a large beast! Is that your dog, St. John?"

"It is Miss Selwyn's dog."

"Is it indeed?" said the baron, eyeing the wolfhound with interest. Looking down from his horse, he inspected Rufus closely. "Fine looking hound. I'll wager he could bring down a stag easily enough. What sport you must

have with him! Yes, a fine looking dog, that one. Puts me
in mind of a lurcher I had once. Now that was a remarkable hound. There was not a rabbit safe from him. Why, I
remember one hunt some years ago when I took old Achil-
les . . .''

St. John suppressed a groan, knowing that his friend's
brother was about to launch into one of his interminable
hunting stories. The viscount had always thought Ponsonby
Fitzwalter the biggest bore imaginable and, indeed, only
tolerated him for the sake of his friend. How frustrating it
was to stand there listening to Lord Fitzwalter when he
wanted so much to be alone with Camilla.

The baron droned on for a time, and Rufus, who seemed
to be growing impatient, whined. Lord Fitzwalter smiled
at Camilla. ''I fear we are detaining you, miss. It appears
your noble hound wishes to be off.''

Camilla nodded. ''I am expected back. I fear I should
be going.''

''And what of you, St. John?'' said the baron. ''I
should like to see that horse of yours at his paces. From
the look of him, he has the bloodlines of Jupiter's Thun-
der. Aren't you going to give him a bit of exercise?''

The viscount frowned, but then nodded. He turned to
Camilla. ''Good day, Miss Selwyn. I hope to see you
again soon.''

Camilla smiled and then she and Rufus hurried off.

That afternoon Camilla sat on the drawing room sofa
with a book. However, instead of looking down at the
pages, she was gazing thoughtfully into space.

''Excuse me, miss.''

''What?'' Camilla looked up in surprise to find the
butler standing in the doorway. ''There is a gentleman to
see you. Mr. MacNeil.''

''Do show him in, Baxter.''

MacNeil appeared moments later. ''Camilla, I was hoping you might be alone. I must talk to you.''

''Is something the matter, Charles? Do sit down.''

The big man sat down in an armchair. ''There is no one

else I might talk with about this matter." He paused awkwardly. "I don't know quite how to start."

"It is about Lizzy, is it not?" When Charles's face showed surprise, Camila continued, "Lizzy told me how she feels about you, and I suspected that you have similar feelings for her."

He nodded. "Oh. Cam, I am so in love with her."

"My poor Charles," said Camilla sympathetically.

"Who would have thought me so empty-headed to have fallen in love with a girl like Elizabeth St. John?"

"One is not always sensible about falling in love."

"No, I suppose not," said Charles, smiling ruefully. "I have certainly made a muddle of it. Now, I have hurt Elizabeth and created problems for her with her family." Charles shook his head. "I received a letter from Elizabeth in which she informs me she has told her mother and brother of the affection we have for each other. Can you imagine what the viscount must have thought?" Camilla, although knowing very well his lordship's opinion of the matter, made no reply. "Yes, I have been a great fool," added Charles glumly.

"But what will you do?"

"What can I do? There surely can be no future for a man like me and Elizabeth. I know that well enough. No, I must forget her." He smiled again. "That will not be very easy, I assure you."

Camilla reached over and took his hand. "I am so sorry, Charles."

"And I am also sorry. I do not doubt this has been awkward for you since it was here that I met Elizabeth."

"Oh, you must not worry about me," began Camilla, but before she could continue, the butler reentered the room. "Miss Camilla, a messenger has brought a letter from Selwyn Manor."

Camilla took the letter. "It is not my uncle's hand," she said, looking down at it, and then hurriedly breaking the seal. "Do excuse me, Charles." She began to read the letter and a worried expression came to her face.

"What is it, Cam? Is something wrong?"

Camilla nodded. "My uncle. He is very ill. The letter is

from our housekeeper. She asks that we return to Selwyn Manor immediately.''

"Then you must go at once."

"Yes, we will have to hire a post chaise. Dick has taken the carriage. He left yesterday to return home."

"My dear Camilla, Sir Lawrence has put a closed carriage at my disposal. I shall take you myself."

"But surely you are too busy. You must have appointments."

"Oh, hang my appointments. It is time I got away from town. Sir Lawrence will understand. Do let me accompany you, Cam."

"If you are certain . . ."

"Of course, I'm certain."

"Then I would so appreciate it, Charles. You would be a great comfort."

"Well then, I shall hurry back and make ready. I shall return as soon as possible. There is still enough time this day to make a good start on the journey."

"Oh, yes, Charles. Thank you. I shall tell my aunt. I do hope she will not be too upset. She will be so grateful you are coming with us."

Charles nodded and took his leave and Camilla hurried off to inform her aunt of the unfortunate news.

24

Lucinda Selwyn stood looking over her maid's shoulder, scrutinizing her servant's efforts to make ready for the journey to Selwyn Manor. The maid would have been far happier if her mistress had allowed her to work alone, for Lucinda's constant questions and suggestions were most annoying. However, the servant did her best, suffering Lucinda's frequent criticisms in silence. Lucinda Selwyn was not usually such a difficult mistress, but that day she seemed nervous and impatient. She was genuinely worried about her brother Jarvis. They had never gotten along, and yet the idea that Jarvis might one day be seriously ill had not occurred to her, and she found the prospect most unsettling.

Camilla entered the room. "Aunt Lucinda, I have finished packing. Is there anything I might do to help you?"

"No, my dear. We are nearly ready. Why don't you go down and wait for Charles?"

"Very well, Aunt." Camilla went downstairs and stood rather nervously in the drawing room. She worried about her uncle and was glad that Charles was accompanying them to Selwyn Manor.

At that moment the butler appeared. "Miss St. John is here to see you, Miss Camilla ."

Camilla looked surprised. "Baxter, show the lady here at once."

Lizzy looked very much agitated as she entered the room. "Oh, Camilla, I am so unhappy."

"Lizzy, do sit down," said Camilla, leading her to the sofa. As soon as she was seated, Lizzy burst into tears.

195

Camilla placed a comforting arm around the young woman's shoulders. "What has happened?"

"Oh, Camilla, I can scarcely bear to talk of it." Lizzy dabbed at her eyes with her handkerchief and then continued. "You know how much I love Charles."

"Of course."

"I would have given up everything to be with him. But, Camilla, he would not have me!" Lizzy burst once more into tears.

"Do tell me what you mean."

"Oh, Cam," said Lizzy, speaking with some difficulty. "I wanted to elope with Charles."

"Lizzy!" Camilla looked shocked. "Surely, you would not do such a thing."

"I would, indeed," cried Lizzy. "I very much intended to do so. I wrote to Charles, telling him we must flee to Gretna Green, that it was our only chance for happiness. I did not expect this!" Lizzy produced a paper from her reticule and handed it to Camilla. "It is his reply."

Camilla took the paper, unfolded it, and read the words inscribed in Charles' neat hand. "My dearest Elizabeth," it began. "You cannot know how difficult it is for me to pen these words to you. I do love you, and I shall always do so, and, although there is nothing that would give me greater joy than spiriting you away and making you my wife, alas, I cannot. I was mad to forget the difference in our stations, to think even for a moment that I could dare to love you. No, my darling, we cannot deny the vast gulf between us. Were we to marry without your family's knowledge and consent, I would be branded a dishonorable villain and you would be ostracized and pitied. I could not live with this. My dearest Elizabeth, we must try and accept what fate has decreed. I only pray that, in time, you will find another more worthy of your affections. Charles."

"Oh, Lizzy, I am sorry. But Charles is right. It would have been folly to elope." Camilla handed the letter back to her.

"Would it have been?" said Lizzy, taking the letter and glancing down at it. "I don't understand why. Would I be more unhappy than I am now? Will I ever find anyone like Charles again? The answer is no to both questions. We might have been happy, despite everything. I need neither fortune nor society. All I need is Charles. If he felt the same way, he would have come for me.''

"That is not true. He loves you. His letter has said so.''

"His letter!'' Lizzy tossed it on the floor. "If he truly loved me, he would have married me. It is obvious he worries far more about society's conventions than he does about me.''

Camilla regarded the other young woman in frustration, knowing that it was clearly impossible to reason with her at this time. "I am so sorry,'' she said gently.

Lizzy wiped a tear from her eye and would have said more, had Lucinda not arrived in the drawing room. "I am packed, Camilla. Oh, Miss St. John, I did not know you were here.'' Noting Lizzy's tear-stained face, she regarded her with concern.

"Oh, Miss Selwyn, are you going somewhere?'' said Lizzy, attempting to act as if nothing was wrong.

Lucinda nodded. "My brother Jarvis is ill. We are going to Selwyn Manor.''

"Oh, dear. Forgive me. I mustn't intrude upon you.'' She rose from her chair. "I do hope Sir Jarvis is better.'' Lizzy looked at Camilla. "Do call on me when you return.''

"Of course.'' Camilla embraced Lizzy, and then the unhappy young lady left them.

"Whatever is the matter with Miss St. John?'' asked Lucinda.

"Do sit down, Aunt, and I shall explain it to you.'' She then related the cause of Lizzy's tears. Lucinda shook her head sympathetically. After asking her aunt to say nothing about the matter to Charles, Camilla noted that his letter still lay on the floor. She sighed, and picked it up and put it into her reticule for safekeeping. Then, sitting down beside her aunt, Camilla waited for Charles to arrive.

Later that afternoon, St. John arrived at his stepmother's townhouse. Hoping to see Lizzy, the viscount was surprised to find both his sister and Amanda out. "Do you expect them back soon?" he asked the butler.

"I expect her ladyship back in an hour. I do not know about Miss St. John, m'lord."

"You mean she is not with her mother?"

The servant nodded. "Miss St. John left the house shortly after her ladyship."

"Alone?"

"Indeed so, m'lord."

The viscount frowned. "And did she say where she was going?"

"No, m'lord. However, she did receive a letter just before she left."

"A letter?"

"Aye, m'lord. A messenger brought it 'round."

"And do you know whom the letter was from?"

"A Mr. MacNeil, m'lord. It has been some two hours since Miss St. John left. Perhaps she will return shortly, m'lord."

"Then I shall wait in Miss St. John's sitting room." The viscount then proceeded up the stairs to his sister's rooms. How dare MacNeil write her, he thought. He paced uneasily across Lizzy's sitting room and wondered where she had gone. Would she have dared to go to MacNeil? Lizzy was so enamoured of the man that she had lost all her usual good sense.

St. John walked to a window and looked out at the street below. Then, turning, his eye fell upon a leather volume sitting on his sister's writing desk. The viscount recognized it as Lizzy's diary. He had often joked with her about the secrets it doubtlessly contained. St. John reached down and touched the embossed leather cover of the book. "No," he said aloud, "I will not read her diary."

He walked back to the window, but returned shortly to the diary and guiltily opened it, turning to the last entries. As he read Lizzy's words, his expression turned to a look of astonishment. "I have now only to await Charles's word and we will be off to Gretna Green to be wed. I know Tony and Mama will never forgive me, but it is what I must do."

St. John put the diary down and called for a servant. The man who had admitted him hurried up the stairs. "Where is Miss St. John's maid? I must see her!"

The servant hurried to fetch Lizzy's maid. "Did Miss St. John have you pack her bags?" said St. John, addressing the woman.

The confused maidservant shook her head. "Pack, m'lord? No, indeed not."

"See if she has taken any of her things."

The maid exchanged a look with the other servant, and then she hurried to Lizzy's wardrobe. "No, m'lord. All is in order."

St. John appeared relieved. Surely, Lizzy would not have run off without taking any of her clothes. Upon further reflection, the viscount frowned. There was the possibility that she would leave without taking anything. MacNeil was no pauper and could afford to buy her new, albeit, more modest things.

The viscount said nothing more to the two servants, but headed quickly from the room and out of the house, where he mounted his awaiting horse and hurried off in search of MacNeil and Lizzy.

It did not take long to locate someone who knew where Charles MacNeil lived, and St. John was soon at MacNeil's residence, a prosperous looking dwelling in a respectable, although not fashionable section of the city.

In response to St. John's furious pounding, an elderly servant opened the door and regarded the viscount disapprovingly. "I want to see MacNeil."

"Mr. MacNeil is not in, sir."

"Then where is he?"

"Might I have your name, sir?"

"By God, it does not signify what my name is. Tell me where I might find your master, or, I warn you, you will regret it."

Cowed by St. John's words, the elderly servant replied, "Mr. MacNeil will be gone for some days, perhaps a fortnight. He is going to the north, sir."

"The north? Where exactly, man?"

"In truth, I do not know, sir," said the servant, alarmed

at St. John's expression. "He was very much in a hurry, sir, and did not say exactly."

"In a hurry?" St. John scowled at the man. So it was true? Lizzy had flown off with MacNeil! "Was he taking the North Road?"

"I know not, sir," said the man, now quite frightened. "I think it likely." St. John's face had taken on a look of such terrible fury that the servant feared for his safety.

"Damn him," said the viscount, turning away from the door as the relieved servant slammed it shut. St. John mounted his horse and galloped off, determined to catch Lizzy and MacNeil well before they reached the Scottish border.

25

The Stag's Head Inn was a busy establishment on one of the main coaching routes north of London. Its position ensured it good business and, oftentimes, the innkeeper and his staff were hard-pressed to find enough room for the numerous travelers who found their way there.

When Charles MacNeil, Camilla, and Aunt Lucinda arrived, tired and hungry, at the Stag's Head, they were very glad to find that although crowded, the inn had space enough for them. It had not been the pleasantest of journeys. Camilla and Lucinda were preoccupied with Jarvis's condition, and Charles was not at all his usual cheery self.

After the innkeeper informed them that there would be a wait for their supper, Lucinda announced she would rest in her room for a time, leaving Camilla and Charles to sit in the inn's public room. They sat without speaking for a time, and then Charles broke the silence. "I fear I have not been the best of traveling companions, Camilla."

"I think all of us are a trifle dispirited," she replied. "My poor aunt was quite upset to hear of my uncle's illness. I am so very grateful to you, Charles, for taking us. How kind of you to find time to leave your duties."

Charles smiled slightly. "You know that I am very glad to leave London for a time."

"My poor Charles," said Camilla. She hesitated for a moment. "I saw Lizzy today just before you arrived."

"You saw Elizabeth?"

Camilla nodded. "She told me about her letter to you. How could she think for a moment that you and she should elope?"

201

"How indeed?" said Charles. He looked over at Camilla. "I nearly did."

"You what?"

"I nearly eloped with her. God in heaven, I love that girl, Cam."

"I cannot believe that you actually thought to do anything so rash."

Charles smiled. "I came very close. I do have some money, you know. Sir Lawrence has been very generous to me and I have made some very profitable investments." He nodded thoughtfully. "I even thought we might go to America."

Camilla's eyes grew wide for a moment. "And what changed your mind?"

"The cold light of reason, my dear princess. How could I wrench Elizabeth away from her family and everyone she knows, to journey into what would be, at best, a most unsettled state. She deserves better."

Camilla made no reply, suddenly wondering if Charles had been right. Indeed, Lizzy and Charles might have gone off to start a new life together, and perhaps they might have been gloriously happy. Now, they would never have the opportunity to make an attempt at happiness. The thought, along with her own problems, depressed her.

"Don't look so sad, Camilla. It is all for the best. I know that now." A humorless laugh escaped him. "The idea that I even thought of marrying Elizabeth St. John, grandniece of a duke and daughter of a viscount! It was absurd. Of course, I must blame you for it."

"Blame me?"

Charles laughed. "You always treated me like a gentleman even as a boy." He reached out and took her hand, squeezing it affectionately. "I can thank you and your uncle for believing in me. I shall be grateful for the rest of my life for that."

"Oh, Charles," said Camilla, "you need thank no one but your own abilities for what you have done." She pressed his hand in return. "I think I had best see how my aunt is faring. I know the supper will be here shortly."

She rose from the rough-hewn bench on which she was

sitting. Charles rose, too, and she kissed him quickly on the cheek before leaving him. After calling for a pint of ale, Charles returned to his seat and waited.

The Viscount St. John arrived at the Stag's Head Inn in a dangerous mood. He had not spared his horse for a moment, and the animal was nearly spent. He was very sure that he was on the right track, having questioned numerous persons along the way, until he found a man who had, indeed, remembered a red-haired man in a carriage accompanied by a pretty young woman.

St. John knew the road well, having often journeyed over it to his estate Ramsgate. He also knew the Stag's Head and had figured that it was a likely stopping off point after a day's journey from town. Entering the inn, the viscount frowned and noted the large crowd of people inside. He looked from face to face, expecting to find his sister and MacNeil among the noisy wayfarers. At first, he saw no sign of either of them, and then his eye alighted on MacNeil, sitting alone, his mug of ale before him.

The angry viscount rushed over to Charles. "There you are, you scoundrel!" he cried.

"Lord St. John!" Charles regarded his lordship in astonishment, and rose to his feet.

"Where is my sister?"

"Your sister?" A flicker of realization came suddenly to Charles. "You cannot think she is here with me?"

"I do indeed, you blackguard!" Then, without further warning, St. John threw his fist back and directed a violent blow to Charles's midsection. The unexpected punch caught Charles off guard and knocked him off his feet. He landed heavily on the floor.

"Charles! St. John!" Camilla Selwyn stood at the entrance to the public room, an expression of horror on her face. The other customers at the inn had ceased all conversation, and all eyes were fixed upon the viscount and the prone form of Charles MacNeil. Camilla ran to Charles and knelt down beside him. "Charles, are you all right?"

Sitting up, Charles nodded. "Aye, I think so."

Camilla looked angrily up at the viscount. "Explain yourself, my lord!"

"What are you doing here?" demanded St. John.

"What am I doing here? Good heavens! What are *you* doing here?" Camilla's brown eyes flashed with anger as she helped a rather shaky Charles to his feet.

"Then Lizzy is not here?"

"Of course not," said Camilla.

St. John looked from Camilla to Charles. "And you are with MacNeil?"

"Yes, and I do not see how that concerns you, my lord."

"Then he is an even worse blackguard than I had thought. Damn you, MacNeil," cried St. John, throwing another punch at Charles, hitting him in the jaw and once again knocking him down.

"St. John!" Camilla shouted. "Have you taken leave of your senses?" She once again stooped down beside the dazed Charles.

"Whatever is going on here!" Aunt Lucinda made her way through the gawking crowd and stood beside Camilla. "Explain yourself, Lord St. John!"

The viscount regarded Lucinda in some surprise. "You are here, Miss Selwyn?" He looked down at Camilla and Charles. "I thought MacNeil and your niece . . ."

"You thought what about Charles and me?" Camilla rose to her feet and faced St. John.

"That you had run off together."

"That we had run off together?" A look of incredulity came to Camilla's face. "I must inform you, my lord, that Mr. MacNeil is escorting my aunt and me to Selwyn Manor, where my uncle is lying ill. My brother had already left yesterday."

Charles had, by this time, risen once again to his feet, and he was rubbing his chin. "And so you now think I have run off with Miss Selwyn instead of your sister? Do you think I change my affections so easily, my lord?"

"I would not doubt it of a man like you, MacNeil."

At these words, Charles bristled, and Camilla hastened

to come between them. "Whyever did you think you would find Lizzy here?"

"I had good reason to believe she intended to elope with this person. Thank God she showed better judgment than I credited her with."

"You may thank Charles," said Camilla indignantly. "It is he who stopped Lizzy from such a plan."

St. John regarded Camilla in disbelief. "You expect me to believe that? Why, this fellow has schemed to marry Lizzy since the first day he met her."

"That is enough, my lord," shouted MacNeil. He clenched his fists ominously.

"Stop it, both of you!" cried Camilla. "It is true, St. John. Look, I have the letter!"

"What letter is that?" said Charles.

"The one that you wrote to Lizzy." She hurriedly opened her reticule and extracted the letter.

"I wrote that to Elizabeth," cried MacNeil.

"Charles, allow his lordship to see it, I beg you." Charles made no further protest, and Camilla handed the missive to St. John. Camilla watched his face as he read Charles's words. "You see? Charles could not hurt Lizzy!"

St. John reread the letter, and then he looked at Charles. "It seems I owe you an apology, MacNeil. Perhaps I have misjudged you."

"And so you have, my lord," replied Charles. "Yes, I have the audacity to love your sister, but I know well she is beyond my reach. I shall never see her again, and that, combined with your blows, seems ample punishment enough for my presumption. Now, if you will excuse us, we will have our supper."

"Of course," said St. John, feeling suddenly very foolish. He quickly turned away and made his way back through the crowd.

Camilla ate little of her boiled mutton, and she found it difficult to concentrate on the conversation. Charles and Lucinda talked steadily, and Lucinda commiserated with him over life's unhappy fortunes.

When Camilla and Lucinda finally withdrew to their

evening's accommodations, Camilla was restless. "I don't think I shall be able to sleep at all, Aunt."

Lucinda regarded her niece sympathetically. "It has been a very difficult day for all of us." She gazed critically about her. "And this room is quite dreadful. I daresay, that bed is hardly inviting. However, we must both try to get some rest. We have a long journey in the morning."

"I think I should like some air."

"Some air? My dear girl, it is very late."

"Oh, I shall only be a short while. You go to bed, Aunt."

"Camilla, you cannot think to go out of doors at such a time alone."

"Truly, Aunt, I shall not be gone long. Now, do go to bed. I shall try not to disturb you when I return." Camilla did not allow her aunt any further opportunity for reply, but hurried out of the room.

Lucinda frowned and wondered at her niece's state of mind. Camilla had always been such a strong, steady young woman that it was surprising to see her so obviously discomposed. Lucinda pondered this for a few moments and then she started to prepare for bed.

Camilla hurried from the inn, glad to be out of its stifling closeness and into the cool darkness. There was no one about, and the only noise came from the still occupied public room of the inn. Camilla strode briskly away from the sound of the laughter and men's voices, and then she stood for some time, reflecting about St. John. How shocked she had been to find him there in a rage, venting his wrath upon poor Charles. A sigh escaped Camilla, and she wondered how she could love such a man. Common sense told Camilla she should be happy at the idea of never seeing St. John again, but her heart informed her clearly that that was not the case.

Camilla started back toward the inn. She was so deep in thought that she did not notice the presence of a man standing near the door to the inn. "Miss Selwyn?" Camilla started at the unexpected sound. "It is I, St. John. I am sorry to have frightened you."

"St. John!" cried Camilla. "What are you doing here? I thought you went back to London."

The viscount shook his head, and Camilla studied him questioningly. St. John appeared weary in the faint light and very much dispirited. "It was too late," he said. "I had no choice but to stay here. The innkeeper is readying my room." He regarded her closely. "You should not be wandering about at such an hour, Miss Selwyn. You will catch a chill."

Camilla crossed her arms in front of her, aware of the coldness of the night air for the first time. "I needed to walk a little before retiring. I am going in now."

"That is a good idea. It is exceedingly damp this evening," said St. John lamely. He paused for a moment, as if unsure what to say, but then continued, "Miss Selwyn, I am sorry about what happened. I do not doubt that you are still angry with me."

"I know you were very much agitated, thinking Lizzy had flown off with Charles, but to resort to violence was quite unnecessary."

"You are right, of course. I shall not expect you to forgive me."

The contriteness of his tone made her smile. "You are an intemperate man, Lord St. John, but let us say no more about the matter. It is late, and we are both tired. I do not doubt that my aunt is wondering where I am. Good evening, my lord."

The viscount seemed reluctant to let her go. "Miss Selwyn, I . . . that is . . . good evening."

They stood looking at each other for an awkward moment, and then Camilla went inside and hurried up to her room. There, thinking of Anthony St. John, she silently made ready for bed.

26

A short time after Camilla retired, the innkeeper at the Stag's Head ushered St. John into a modest private room. He was relieved when the viscount did not exhibit any signs of displeasure at seeing his night's lodgings. The innkeeper had seen enough of his guest's temper to know that St. John should be placated at all costs. After asking if his lordship required anything else, the innkeeper bowed subserviently and hurried away.

St. John took off his now dusty boots and his elegant coat, and lay down on the bed. As he had expected, it was impossible to sleep. He kept thinking of Camilla, picturing her lovely face and wishing that she were there beside him. Turning over in the uncomfortable bed, he tried to force her from his mind. It was, he soon realized, useless to try. Reflecting on their brief meeting, St. John was filled with a maddening longing for her that was unlike anything he had ever felt before. Why, he asked himself, hadn't he taken her into his arms there in the darkness and declared his true feelings?

"Damn MacNeil," muttered St. John aloud. How much better it would have been if the fellow had never renewed his old acquaintance with Camilla. If only Lizzy had never met him.

The viscount frowned as his thoughts turned to his sister and MacNeil. He had misjudged the man, he conceded. The solicitor had not been so villainous as to agree to an elopement. Certainly, a man of fewer scruples would have done so.

No, it seemed that MacNeil truly cared for Lizzy. St.

John frowned again. It was a pity MacNeil was not a man of respectable birth. Lizzy and he did seem otherwise well matched.

St. John continued with his reflections long into the night, until finally he fell into an uneasy sleep. Shortly before dawn a loud pounding at his door jolted him awake. "Wake up! Fire!"

St. John rushed to the door and flung it open. There stood Charles MacNeil in shirt and trousers, his red hair disheveled. "Good God! St. John!"

"MacNeil, what the devil?"

"The inn is on fire! Get out at once!"

St. John smelled the smoke. "Where is Camilla?"

"On the upper floor. Don't worry. I saw her going out with her aunt. I must rouse the others here."

"What can I do?"

"Help me awaken the rest of the people on this floor, and then get out quickly!" The solicitor continued on, pounding on doors and shouting to the startled faces that peered out into the corridor.

The viscount hurriedly put on his boots and then, grabbing his coat, he ran into the hallway. The smoke grew thicker as he continued on, knocking on any closed doors and shouting to all he saw to make haste and leave the building. Satisfied that everyone had been alerted on that floor, St. John hurried out of the inn.

A great crowd of people, some of them in nightshirts and dressing gowns, stood watching as flames shot up from the burning building. By this time everyone in the village had come hurrying out to see the fire or assist in getting it under control. A group of men pulled an ancient pump into place and a row of volunteers worked feverishly, passing buckets to fill the pump's tanks. Soon they were directing a stream of water at the inn.

Concerned only with finding Camilla, the viscount barely noted the firemen's efforts. He looked wildly about and then, finally spotting Lucinda attired in her nightclothes, he ran to her.

"Miss Selwyn," he cried, grasping her by the arm. "Where is Camilla?"

"St. John, praise God you are here! I am beside myself with worry about Camilla!"

"What do you mean? MacNeil said she got out."

"Just as we were going down the stairs, we heard a child's cry and Camilla ran back. Oh, why did I let her go?"

"Then you didn't see her come out?"

"No!" Lucinda wrung her hands in consternation. "Oh, St. John, I thought she had gone out another door, but I did not see her in back. I fear she may be trapped inside!"

Horror and astonishment registered on the viscount's face and then, without further hesitation, he ran back toward the burning inn. Ignoring the warning cries of the men fighting the fire, St. John rushed inside. The heat was by now intense and the smoke was suffocatingly thick. Placing his handkerchief over his face, the viscount groped his way to the stairs and shouted Camilla's name.

At first there was only the roar of the fire, but then he heard Camilla's voice. "I'm here! St. John!"

Seeing Camilla Selwyn appear at the top of the stairs, a little boy in her arms, St. John was filled with tremendous relief. He raced up to meet her. "Give me the child," he said, taking the boy from her. Then, grasping Camilla's hand firmly, the viscount started down.

It did not take long to get outside and once there, both St. John and Camilla gasped for breath. The child St. John carried cried piteously, and the viscount awkwardly tried to comfort him.

A pale young woman in a dressing gown and nightcap rushed toward them. "You have my boy!" she cried, taking the youngster from St. John and hugging the child tearfully. "However can I thank you, sir?"

"It is this lady you must thank, ma'am," returned his lordship, looking over at Camilla. "She saved the lad." The woman thanked Camilla profusely and left them.

After she had gone, St. John took Camilla's hands in his. "Are you all right?"

She nodded and looked up at him. "Yes, I am fine."

He shook his head. "I was mad with worry. I don't

know what I would have done if anything had happened to you. Oh, Camilla, I am so in love with you!''

"Oh, St. John!" cried Camilla, throwing her arms about the viscount's neck.

The viscount embraced Camilla tightly. ''My dearest Camilla,'' he said and then kissed her long and passionately. Camilla responded eagerly, thrilled to find St. John's strong arms about her and his lips on her own.

For a time, the viscount and Camilla seemed oblivious to the noise and confusion about them, but Lucinda Selwyn's voice brought them quickly back to reality. ''Camilla! What happened? You were not hurt?''

Still in St. John's arms, Camilla looked over to find her aunt standing before them. ''Yes, Aunt, I am unharmed. There was a little boy hiding under a bed, and it took the longest time to get him out.''

''I thank Providence you are safe, Camilla,'' said Lucinda, eyeing the viscount and her niece with interest. ''More than safe, it would appear.''

''Oh,'' said Camilla, pulling away from the viscount and blushing deeply.

''But now I do not know where Charles is,'' said Lucinda. ''I was so worried about you that I did not have time to think of him. I do not see him anywhere.''

St. John and Camilla both scanned the crowd. ''When I last saw him he was waking all the guests,'' said the viscount. ''Surely he must be about somewhere. Do not fear, I shall find him.'' After firmly requesting that the ladies retreat to a safer location, St. John started to look for Charles. He walked about shouting the solicitor's name and asking bystanders if they had seen a red-haired gentleman. When the viscount could not find MacNeil or anyone who had seen him, he began to grow uneasy.

Finally, a corpulent man in a night shirt addressed him. ''I did see a red-haired man not long ago. He was rushing about in his shirtsleeves helping as best he could.''

''Where did he go?'' asked St. John, very much encouraged by this intelligence.

The corpulent man looked around. ''That woman there,'' he said, pointing to a distraught-looking matron, ''began

wailing that her mother was still in the building. The
red-haired gentleman ran back in. That was just moments
ago. Aye, he is a brave one, he is.''

St. John frowned as he stared at the burning inn. It was
now completely ablaze and it appeared certain that anyone
inside would be doomed. A feeling of dread came to the
viscount as he continued to watch the flames.

"Poor fellow," continued the corpulent man. "I'd not
wager on his chances."

The remark irritated St. John, but before he could reply,
there was a loud shout behind him. "Look there! "There's
someone at that window. There in back!"

"Good God!" St. John looked up to see MacNeil at one
of the windows of the inn. Leaning out, the solicitor
shouted down at the crowd and threw what appeared to be
a blanket to the ground.

"I've got a woman here I must lower down," cried
Charles. "Some of you men take up the blanket! You'll
have to catch her!"

St. John and a number of the other men ran to the spot
beneath MacNeil and taking up the blanket, held it taut.
MacNeil lifted an elderly woman out the window and
began to lower her down using bedclothes tied about her
waist. When he got her halfway to the ground, he released
his grip and the woman fell the rest of the way. Luckily,
the awaiting men caught her neatly.

St. John looked up. "MacNeil, get out! Come on, man!
You'll have to jump!"

MacNeil looked down at him and, recognizing the viscount, he grinned. "Aye, and you'd best not drop me, St.
John."

The men pulled the blanket taut once again and looked
expectantly upward as the solicitor hurried out the window. Grasping the sill and lowering himself as far as
possible, Charles let go and fell into the blanket below
him.

The men assisted MacNeil to his feet and he appeared a
trifle shaky, but apparently unhurt. His face was grimy
with soot, giving him a comical appearance as he smiled.
"I seem to be well enough."

Camilla and Lucinda had hurried over to join the crowd watching Charles. Now that he was safely on the ground, Camilla rushed to embrace her old friend. The assembled crowd roared its approval and many offered Charles hearty congratulations, proclaiming him a hero for his rescue of the elderly woman. MacNeil modestly protested his actions were hardly heroic, and seemingly uncomfortable with the acclaim, announced he must go help the men at the pump. St. John smiled over at Camilla and then hastened off with Charles to offer his assistance.

Although the men fought valiantly against the fire, it was soon apparent that nothing could be done to save the inn. Finally abandoning the building, the firefighters moved the pump near the stables where they concentrated on keeping the blaze from spreading to nearby buildings. Fortunately, the wind cooperated nicely, blowing in the direction opposite the other structures. This favorable condition and the fact that there had been no loss of life, human or animal, gave the onlookers much cause to be grateful.

As the inn continued to burn, the crowd dispersed a little. Several helpful villagers invited travelers into their homes, providing them with food and clothing if necessary. Since St. John and Charles were still engaged in helping to fight the fire, Camilla was reluctant to leave the site. However, after reminding her niece that they were both still dressed in their nightclothes, Lucinda persuaded Camilla to accept the generosity of a kind local lady who invited them to her nearby house.

After donning some borrowed clothes and having tea, Camilla and Lucinda thanked their benefactress and returned to the fire scene. There they found St. John and Charles finally leaving their posts at the pump.

The two men walked toward the ladies and Camilla smiled at the picture they presented. Both were filthy and obviously exhausted. St. John's exquisite coat was black and his pantaloons a complete disgrace. Certainly, thought Camilla, Mr. Fitzwalter would swoon at the sight his usually elegant friend now presented. Yet despite their sorry appearances, both St. John and Charles seemed to be in excellent humor.

"You poor gentlemen," cried Lucinda, "how you have labored!"

Charles grinned. "I do admit my arms feel as if they are about to fall off."

"I shouldn't wonder at that," said St. John, glancing over at the solicitor. "By heaven, MacNeil, the way you handled that pump lever would have killed a lesser man."

"I only did what I could," said Charles. He looked at Camilla. "His lordship quite astonished me. Never thought a man of his cut could work." The solicitor grinned at St. John. "I certainly misjudged you, my lord."

Camilla, delighted at this newfound amiability between St. John and Charles, smiled at the viscount. He smiled at her in return and then faced MacNeil. "It is I who has misjudged you, MacNeil," he said, his face growing serious. "It has taken an ordeal such as this to show a slow top like myself how wrong I have been." Charles regarded St. John curiously and the viscount continued. "A lady whom I esteem highly," said St. John, directing a fond look at Camilla, "once told me that there are qualities in a man far more important than rank and fortune. You, MacNeil, are a man of strength, courage, and intelligence. Only the most chowder-headed fellow would not see that such characteristics are far more important than the circumstances of a man's birth. You are a good man, MacNeil. Will you take my hand?"

"Gladly, my lord," said the solicitor, extending his hand.

The viscount shook it warmly. "I do not doubt you will make Lizzy a good husband." Charles regarded St. John incredulously and the viscount laughed. "You heard me correctly, MacNeil. I am removing my objections to your marrying my sister. If Lizzy will have you, I shall be glad to call you brother-in-law."

"But, my lord," said Charles, "what about Elizabeth's mother?"

"You will doubtlessly make my stepmother and her Mountifort relations most unhappy." St. John grinned.

"However, that will please me immensely. Now, after you have rested sufficiently and found some way to look presentable, I suggest you return to London. You may take my horse. I am certain poor Lizzy is miserable and I depend upon you to change that."

Charles appeared overcome. "My lord, I do not know what to say."

"Say nothing and for God's sake, cease calling me 'my lord'."

"Very well . . . St. John." Charles looked at Camilla and Lucinda, and he suddenly remembered that he was escorting them to Selwyn Manor. "But I was taking the ladies to Sir Jarvis."

"Do not worry. I shall escort the ladies to Selwyn Manor." The viscount smiled at Camilla. "That is, if it is acceptable to you."

"It is, indeed," replied Camilla, gazing affectionately up into St. John's blue eyes.

A most perceptive man, MacNeil did not fail to note the way Camilla and the viscount were regarding each other. He smiled. "Well then," said Charles "if I am to return to town, I had best clean myself up and see to your horse."

"I shall take you to Mrs. Claybrook's house," said Lucinda. "I know she would be happy to assist you. She is the kindest woman. Indeed, she loaned us these dresses. Of course, I daresay, they are not quite the thing, but they will do. We must see to the carriage, too. How lucky that almost all the boxes were left there last night. Indeed, we are all so very fortunate." After these remarks, Lucinda took the solicitor's arm and led him forcefully away, leaving St. John and Camilla standing there together.

"Your aunt is right," said the viscount. "I am the most fortunate of men."

Camilla smiled up at him. "Oh, I love you so much. And you have made Charles so happy. I know he and Lizzy will do well together. You are remarkable, you know."

"Since it took me so long to come to my senses about MacNeil, I suspect I am remarkably dull-witted."

"You are nothing of the kind! You are the most wonderful man!'' Camilla's eyes took on a mischievous look as she eyed his dirty clothes and soot-smudged face. "Of course, I will say, you are scarcely the cleanest."

St. John laughed and, enfolding her in his arms, he kissed her soundly.

27

The sight of Selwyn Manor made St. John think of the first time he had come there. He smiled at Camilla, who was sitting beside him, and he remembered the snowy day when he and Fitzwalter had found themselves stranded in what had seemed the most out of the way spot in the kingdom.

How different Selwyn Manor appeared now, reflected St. John, looking out the carriage window and noting the lush green of the lawn and trees. In the bright spring weather, the ancient run-down house had a picturesque quality, and the viscount wondered how he had never before noted its quaint charm. He reached over and took Camilla's hand, suspecting that from now on the world would appear so much lovelier than it had before.

Camilla pressed the viscount's hand. "We are here. I do hope we may find uncle improved."

"I pray God we will find him so," said Lucinda as the carriage pulled to a stop in front of the manor house. One of the Selwyn servants rushed out to open the carriage door, and the ladies and St. John hurried to leave the vehicle and make their way to the door. They were greeted by the Selwyn's butler, who appeared very happy to see them. "Miss Selwyn! Miss Camilla! Welcome home." He regarded St. John in some surprise, remembering well the last time he had seen that difficult gentleman.

"Jackson." cried Lucinda, "how is Sir Jarvis? We have not come too late?"

"Nay, ma'am. The master be much improved."

"Heaven be praised!" said Lucinda.

"Is he out of danger, Jackson?" asked Camilla, very much relieved.

The butler nodded. "It would appear so, miss. Very sick he was too, miss, and sore worried we all were. In my mind, it was Master Dick what turned him around."

"Master Dick?" Lucinda looked quite astonished.

"Aye, ma'am. Why, the physician was here this morning and said Sir Jarvis be so much better as it would appear a miracle. A miracle be what he said, ma'am."

"We must go to him at once," said Lucinda.

"The master be in his room and Master Dick as well."

The ladies and St. John made their way quickly to Sir Jarvis's room and as they neared it, they were quite surprised to hear hearty laughter.

The three of them stopped at the open door. There was Dick seated beside his uncle's bedside. The two men were playing chess and looked in the best of humors.

"Jarvis!" Lucinda rushed into the room. "Thank God, you are better."

"Lucinda?"

"Oh, my dear Jarvis, I was so worried that I would not be in time."

"In time? I assure you, Lucinda, I had no intention of dying before you and my niece arrived." Jarvis spoke in his usual gruff way and Camilla smiled. Seeing him on such amicable terms with her brother had worried Camilla for a moment, making her wonder if her uncle's illness had impaired his mental faculties.

"Uncle!" Camilla went to Jarvis's bedside and kissed him.

"My dear niece." Sir Jarvis looked over at St. John, who was standing in the doorway. "Lord St. John, I did not expect to see you, sir, but you are most welcome. After what Dick has told me, I see I owe you a great deal."

"Indeed so," said Dick, rising from his chair and going to shake the viscount's hand. "Were it not for St. John, I would be penniless." He looked back at his uncle. "When I go next to London, I shall be a far wiser man and heed my uncle's words. Indeed, I must go soon and settle my affairs. I daresay, I shall first rid myself of poor Randall's house. I'll have no use for such a place."

Sir Jarvis allowed a smile to cross his dour countenance. "The lad has admitted his mistakes like a man. It seems he's learned much from his stay in town." The baronet looked over at St. John. "I am in your debt, St. John."

"Indeed, Sir Jarvis, I shall be in your debt if you will give me your permission to marry your niece."

Sir Jarvis looked amazed. He turned to his niece. "Camilla, you wish to marry this man?"

"With all my heart."

Sir Jarvis frowned at the viscount. "My niece's happiness means very much to me."

"You have my word, Sir Jarvis, that I shall do everything in my power to make Camilla a good husband." He exchanged a glance with Camilla, and he continued, "I assure you, sir, I can well afford to take care of your niece."

"Dash it, man, I was not concerned with your fortune," muttered Sir Jarvis.

"Have I heard correctly?" cried Lucinda, directing a shocked look at her brother.

Sir Jarvis scowled. "Be quiet, woman," he said testily. Then turning back to St. John, he continued, "No, I do not care overmuch about your fortune, Lord St. John," continued the baronet. "I know very well you are as rich as Croesus. Dick has told me as much. But Camilla deserves a man who will love her and treat her well."

St. John extended his hand to Camilla, who came to his side and looked up at him affectionately. "I love Camilla, sir, and by my honor, I will do all I can to make her happy."

"Then I approve most heartily," said Sir Jarvis. Camilla kissed her uncle joyfully and Dick hurried to shake the viscount's hand once again.

Lucinda then launched into a long explanation of the extraordinary events that had taken place since Dick had left town. So intent were Sir Jarvis and Dick on Lucinda's story that they did not notice St. John and Camilla silently slip from the room. Hand in hand, they hurried from the house and out into the bright sunshine of the garden. There amid the tangled perennial beds, so woefully neglected in Lucinda's absence, the viscount took his lady into his arms. "And so, my darling Camilla, it appears that all will be well."

Camilla buried her head against his chest. "It is all so perfect. My uncle and Dick reconciled. And Charles and Lizzy! I know they will be happy."

"Let us hope they can overcome the problems of unsuitable family connections," said St. John, speaking with unexpected severity.

Camilla looked up at him in surprise. "But, St. John, I thought you had accepted Charles, despite his family."

The viscount's dark eyebrows arched slightly. "I was not thinking of Charles's family." A mischievous smile appeared on his face. "It was the Mountiforts I had in mind." Camilla burst into laughter, but was quickly silenced by the viscount's kiss.

About the Author

Margaret Summerville grew up in the Chicago area and holds degrees in journalism
and library science. Employed as a librarian,
she is single and lives in Morris, Illinois,
with her Welsh corgi, Morgan. She is also
the author of three other Signet Regencies,
Scandal's Daughter, *The Duke's Disap-
pearance*, and *Highland Lady*.

SIGNET Regency Romances You'll Enjoy